BREAKING POINT

TURNING POINT SERIES : BOOK TWO

N.R. WALKER

COPYRIGHT

The author acknowledges the trademarked status and trademark owners of the following wordmarks mentioned in this work of fiction:

iPad: Apple, Inc.

Kleenex: Kimberly-Clark Corporation

Mission: Impossible: Paramount Pictures

Percocet: Endo Pharmaceuticals

Ruger: Sturm, Ruger

Tylenol: McNeil Consumer Healthcare

Vicodin: Abbott Laboratories

BLURB

A fight for what's right becomes a fight for his life.

As guilt plagues him, Matthew Elliott's world begins to spiral out of control. The harder he holds on, the more it slips through his fingers, and he's helpless to stop it.

Entering into the underground cage-fighting scene, he starts out fighting for what's right. The deeper he gets, the more guilt consumes him—the more pain he takes for his penance—and he's soon fighting for more than justice.

He's fighting for love.

He's fighting for his life.

DEDICATION

For my readers.
You inspire me more than you'll know...

BREAKING POINT

N.R. Walker

CHAPTER ONE

IT WAS a usual Friday night at the bar. Except it wasn't.

My partners, Mitch, Kurt, and Tony, were there with me. My boyfriend, Kira, was there too, along with my boss, Berkman, and most of the guys from my division. There were celebratory drinks, a tab on the bar, and congratulations all round.

I should have been happy. And part of me was. But part of me wasn't. The smile on my face and laughs with the boys didn't quite sit right, but the more I had to drink, the easier it got.

"Here it is!" someone called out. "Turn it up!"

The attention in the bar was drawn to the TV as the bartender turned up the volume.

"...in this breaking story, after almost eleven years, Detective Matthew Elliott has announced his resignation from the LAPD..."

There were cheers and applause from around the bar, a few claps on my shoulder. Kira squeezed my thigh under the table. I smiled and lifted my beer in a salute before taking another swig.

I hated press conferences. I had a healthy distaste for the media and the paparazzi, and I hated having to put my life on display for the public. Yet there I stood in front of a dozen cameras and even more reporters about to give the biggest announcement of my career.

It was ironic that the biggest would be my last.

I was on screen announcing to the good people, and the not-so-good people, of LA that I was no longer a detective. I was no longer a part of the Fab Four. I was no longer a cop.

The questions started and I heard myself reel off the well-rehearsed answers on the TV. I'd given dozens of press conferences over my time with the LAPD Narcotics Division, and I'd never dreamed I'd be standing there announcing to the world that I was walking away from all I'd ever known.

Yet there I was, doing exactly that.

The questions on screen continued.

"Can you tell us why? Why are you retiring, Detective Elliott?" one reporter asked.

"Does this have anything to do with being outed as a gay cop last year?"

"Where does this leave the Fab Four? Do you have a replacement?"

"Are you planning a career in politics?"

I laughed at that, on screen and at the table in the bar. Mitch, who was sitting across from me, laughed as well. "No plans for running for Governor? Come on," Mitch joked. "You'd make a good politician."

I finished the last mouthful of my beer and pointed my empty bottle at him. Instead of telling him to get fucked, I said, "My turn to buy. 'Nother beer?"

"Hell yes, if you're payin'," he slurred.

I turned to Kira and leaned in toward him and asked,

"Drink, baby?" He shook his head at me. I must be drunk if I'd called him 'baby' in front of the boys. Fuck.

"Nah, I'm fine," he said. "Someone has to make sure you guys get home okay."

"'M sorry," I said, trying to apologize. "S'been a big day."

Kira smiled sadly. "I know it has."

I nodded and stood up off my stool. I swayed as I made my way to the bar. I was drunk. It had been an emotional day, after an emotionally charged few weeks since I'd announced that I was leaving.

It hadn't been easy. It had been one of the hardest decisions I'd ever made, but it was the right decision. My partners at work, Mitch, Kurt and Tony, were surprisingly okay with it. My boss had warned me against it but ultimately agreed it was the right thing. But Kira... Kira didn't like the idea at all.

He didn't understand why I was leaving the department. No matter what reason I gave him, he didn't believe me. He knew I loved my job; it was a part of who I was, he'd said.

And it had been a bone of contention between us since.

It wasn't that he wasn't being supportive. He just didn't understand. I told him it was a decision I'd toyed with over the last twelve months, since he was abducted and tortured, beaten, held hostage because of me. And that wasn't a lie. It just wasn't the whole truth.

The whole truth was something I couldn't tell him.

Kira knew there was something else to it. Of course he did. We'd been living together for almost twelve months. He *knew* me. And I'd never lied to him before. I'd never had to. And he knew I wasn't telling him something.

He'd get quiet whenever I talked about leaving, waiting

for me to explain the truth, but I never did. The night I told him I'd handed in my resignation was our first real fight. He yelled and I yelled back, and he threw a glass into the sink and I slammed some doors.

We hadn't spoken for two days afterwards.

It had damn near killed me.

A hard thump on my arm and a large hand on my shoulder snapped me out of my memories. My boss, my ex-boss, Berkman stood beside me and threw some twenties on the bar. "Whatever this man wants," he told the bartender.

I ordered some shots of bourbon under the watchful eye of the man who'd been like a father to me. I looked at him and gave him the best confident smile I could fake.

"You sure about this?" he asked quietly.

I nodded. "Yeah..."

Berkman's jaw bulged and he exhaled through his nose. "But?"

I looked back to where Kira was sitting with Mitch and the others. "I've never lied to him," I said, suddenly feeling every drink I'd had.

Berkman nodded. "It won't be easy."

"Mmm," I agreed, swaying where I stood. I didn't want to talk about it. Not here, anyway. Not that Berkman would have said anything. "Need another drink," I mumbled, picking up a fresh shot of liquor. I threw back the bourbon, and when I put the glass back down, the bar wasn't as close as I thought. Berkman put his hands on me, I realized, to steady me. Fuck, I was drunk.

"I'll carry these to the table," Berkman said, indicating to the drinks on the bar. Then he pointed me in the direction where Kira and Mitch were sitting. "You go that way."

The bar was loud and busy, and as I crossed the floor, I bumped into familiar faces with pats on the back and rounds of good luck and best wishes. Berkman beat me back to the table with my drinks, and when I finally got there, everyone was smiling at me.

I slid my arm around Kira's shoulder, and he maneuvered me onto my stool and handed me a drink. I held up the single shot, and Mitch, Kurt, Tony, and Berkman all raised theirs. Kira held up his soda, and they all bumped their glasses against mine.

"To Matt," Berkman declared. "To the future and wherever it may take you. We wish you well."

"Cheers!"

"To Matt!"

I downed my shot and sucked back the afterburn. "Fuck. I'm gonna be sick tomorrow."

"And you don't have to be in the office by eight!" Kurt cried. He looked as drunk as I felt. "You get to sleep in!"

I laughed. "No more all-nighters, no more double shifts. I am done with that shit."

Mitch shook his head at me. "You really doin' it," he slurred. "You really won't be there tomorrow?"

I shook my head. "Nope."

"Fuck," Mitch mumbled. He pointed his finger at me. "If I get some rookie punk as a partner, I'm gonna kick your ass."

I laughed at him. "Like to see ya try."

He shook his head at me. "You really gonna do that fighting thing?"

I grinned and raised my hands to protect my chin. "Yep."

"You're fucking crazy," Mitch said, shaking his head.

"Yeah, maybe that's why he left," Kurt said with a sly grin. "Hey, Berkman," he called out to the boss. "Did Elliot fail his psych?"

The older man snorted. "You *all* failed psych."

Everyone laughed, and even Kira smiled and shook his head at us.

"So when do you start?" Tony asked. I was pretty sure I'd told them all this already. "This new career of yours."

"Monday," I answered. "I plan on being very sick tomorrow and possibly still sick on Sunday, but I'm signed up for the first official session on Monday."

"You know," Mitch said thoughtfully, "if you want to pay good money to get beaten up, you could've just paid me."

"Fucking boxing," Kurt said, shaking his head.

"It's not boxing," I corrected for the twentieth time. "It's MMA."

"Mixed martial arts, what-the-fuck-ever," he said, rolling his eyes. "It's punishment, that's what it is."

"Frankie." Tony called Kira by his nickname. Most of the guys still did. "Frankie, talk some sense into this boy."

"I've tried," Kira said quietly, turning his glass of soda on the table. "I thought you guys might've had more luck. He won't listen to me."

I sighed. "We're not going through this again. It's a done deal," I told them. "Cheer up, boys. It's my farewell." I changed the topic. "Whose turn is it to buy me a drink?"

It was all an act.

We each had our part.

Everyone at that table had a role to play. Except Kira.

And that was what tore at me. That was what made this so damn hard.

I'd been part of covert ops before. I'd done my time undercover. That was until our little group of the famous Fab Four had our faces plastered on every screen, newspaper, and Internet news and celebrity site. Any chances of us doing undercover work again were pretty much over.

Unless one of us wasn't a cop anymore.

If one of us left the police force, left the spotlight, left everything we'd ever known, then maybe one of us could get some inside information on a drug ring we'd been watching for months.

It would have to be public. It would have to be completely watertight, and it would have to be, for all intents and purposes, very real.

No one would know.

No one would know I was going undercover, except Mitch, Kurt, Tony, and Berkman.

Not even Kira.

For his own safety, he could have no part in this.

Kira knew my decision to leave my job hadn't been easy for me, he just didn't understand why. I'd told him I'd had enough. The last twelve months since his abduction and beating had been hard—not just for him, not just for me, but for everyone. I told him I realized, while I loved my job, I loved him more, and I would never risk his safety again.

And as much as that was true, I couldn't tell him the whole truth.

He disputed the whole idea, and God, we argued. But at the end of the day, I had a job to do.

I didn't know what this would mean for us. I didn't know where it would lead or how long it would take. Months, a year... there was no way of knowing.

I loved him, and I knew he loved me. I just hoped it would be enough.

I looked at him and squeezed his thigh. I'd had far too much to drink, and I really needed to go home. Even drunk, a part of me didn't want the night to end. Because I knew, when I woke up in the morning, not only was I going to be hungover, I was also going to be *just* Matt Elliot. Not a cop, not a detective. And I didn't know what it was like to not have that security, that camaraderie. My brothers.

That was what it felt like.

It felt like I was losing my brothers.

"Love you guys," I told them.

"Oh, fuck," Mitch said, standing up. "He's up to the 'I love yous.' That's Matthew Elliott code for 'I'm drunk.' It's time to get him home."

"Don't be like that," I said, shaking my head. I knew I was drunk. I knew my words were slurred and I was not staying upright very well, but I knew what tonight meant.

"You's are my family, my brothers," I told them, suddenly choking up on emotion. "I'm gonna miss ya's." I looked at Mitch. "You the most, you son of a bitch."

He smiled and said something I think was supposed to be funny, but when he hugged me, he hugged me hard. He whispered in my ear, "I'll miss you too."

Kira was standing beside me now, and Mitch handed me over to him. "Get him home," he said. Mitch looked a little teary-eyed, and he smiled sadly. "Jesus Christ, Elliott. Never would've thought I'd be sorry to see the back of ya."

I had more claps on the back, another round of applause from the cops who were still there, and they dragged my sorry ass out the door. I hugged Tony and Kurt, and even Berkman, who handed me back to Kira. Apparently to keep me upright. I told them all I loved them again, then I told them leaving the police department wasn't as hard as it was to say goodbye to them.

"It's not really goodbye," Kurt said kindly. "You'll see us all the time. We'll do barbeques and poker or something."

"Yeah, dinner with me and Anna next weekend,

remember?" Mitch said. "Jesus, don't forget that or she'll kill me."

Tony hugged me. "Yeah, and you'll see us laughing as we write you up for parking tickets, traffic violations, jaywalking..."

They all laughed, but I frowned. "'S not funny."

"Yes it is," they said in unison, and with another round of laughter and goodbyes, they bundled me into Kira's car. They stood on the sidewalk as we pulled out onto the street, and it was weird. As drunk as I was, I knew the look on their faces would stay with me.

My head fell back on the headrest, and I exhaled loudly. "Gonna miss them."

Kira was quiet for a long while, and I turned my head to look at him. He glanced at me, then back to the road as he drove. "Then why are you leaving?"

I sighed, and the last shot of bourbon swirled through my brain. "You know why. I've told you why." I was drunk and was sick of having this conversation with him, and my words probably sounded harsher than I meant them to.

He shook his head. "Whatever."

Whatever. He fucking said 'whatever' to me. Well, fuck that shit. Deciding I needed fresh air right the fuck now, I tried to open the window, but the little button wouldn't work. "What the fuck is wrong with your window?"

"Nothing," he answered calmly. "It was locked." Then he pressed a button and all of a sudden my window went down.

I sighed. "Whatever."

The rest of the car trip home was quiet, and when we pulled up in the driveway, he opened my door and offered to help me out of the car. "I can get out myself," I snapped, then almost fell out of the car. I lined up the front door and stumbled toward it. "I don't need your help," I told him, so he left me, walked up the front steps, and opened the door. And those front steps looked a mile high. "Babe?" I felt myself sway and stagger. Kira stopped and turned back to face me. "I need your help."

He tried not to smile as he came back down the stairs toward me. "Thought you said you didn't need me."

"I do need you."

He grabbed me as I misstepped. "I can see that."

"Sorry I'm drunk," I told him.

"It's okay."

"Sorry 'bout before."

He helped me up the stairs. "It's okay, Matt."

"Sorry, babe," I apologized again. "Sorry I love you."

He hauled me inside and shut the front door behind us. He stopped walking and held me up so he could look in my eyes. "Don't apologize for that," he said.

I put my hand to the side of his face. "I'm drunk."

"I know."

"I'm sorry."

"I know."

He slung his arm around me and led me to our room. I just wanted to lie down, but he kept me upright and pulled my shirt off.

"Love you.".

"I know."

I swayed and Kira steadied me. "I'm really drunk."

"I know." He undid my jeans and pushed them over my hips.

"Too drunk for sex, babe."

He laughed. "I know."

I fell onto the bed and Kira pulled my boots off, then my

jeans. The room started to spin, and not even closing my eyes made it stop. I groaned. "Love you."

I felt his lips at my temple. "I know."

GOOD LORD, the thumping pain in my head was phenomenal. It matched the nausea. I hadn't been asleep for anywhere near long enough, and yet something was telling me to wake up.

"Matt?"

"Mm-hmm."

"Matt, wake up."

"No," my voice croaked.

"I got you something," Kira said from somewhere close by.

I dared to open one eye, and the early morning light pierced my brain. "Ugh."

Kira chuckled and tapped my leg. "Sit up. I got you something."

I groaned again as I rolled over, and a wave of nausea crashed through me as I gingerly sat up. "Fuck."

Kira was sitting on our bed. He was holding a small box. "I got you a present."

"What for?"

"Your first day of civilian life," he said cheerfully. He held out the box. "Open it."

I didn't mean to sound ungrateful, but my head felt like it had been kicked in. "Kira, babe. I feel like shit."

"Open it."

I took the gift and pulled at the wrapping, more concerned with the pain in my head than what was in the box. Until I opened it.

It was a pair of MMA training gloves. Black, fingerless, and padded. They weren't anything spectacular; they weren't anything profound.

But what they meant was.

Kira had been against me wanting to cage-fight since day one, yet there he was giving me a symbol of acceptance. "I don't want to fight with you about this anymore. If it's what you want..."

I looked from the fighting gloves to him. "Kira..." I struggled to find the right words. "Thank you."

His smile faded. "It's what you really want?"

I nodded. "It is."

Kira got off the bed, and it was then I noticed he was dressed in his running gear. "Then get up. Training starts today. You're running five miles before breakfast."

CHAPTER TWO

I RAN UNTIL I VOMITED. Then Kira made me run some more.

I was in the best shape I'd ever been. In the last twelve months since the Tomic incident, Kira had turned a lot of negative energy into positive through exercise. And of course, I did it with him, and it showed.

He found peace running or cycling or swimming laps. He said the more energy he burned, the clearer his head was. He still worked at the gym but had taken on teaching self-defense classes, including kickboxing, boxing, and some Mauy Thai boxing, which was where I spent a lot of my time.

I'd always loved my sparring sessions. And the more kickboxing Kira taught me, the more I wanted to learn. The more boxing and Mauy Thai he taught me, the more I loved it.

I was pretty fucking ripped. I was one hundred and eighty-five pounds of lean muscle. I was fit; I was the poster guy for health. Living with a fitness instructor and maintaining the same fitness programs as him meant I was in prime physical condition.

Which was probably why I felt every ounce of the alcohol I'd drunk last night.

I was suffering. It felt like my head was being hammered from the inside and my stomach was lurching with every step. Kira, on the other hand, was doing it easily. I stopped running and was leaning over with my hands on my knees, trying not to dry heave. Kira, who'd barely worked up a sweat, laughed at me and patted my back.

"Want a shot of bourbon?"

"I hate you."

He laughed at me again. "Wanna go home?"

"God, yes."

"Well, too bad. Keep running."

"I hate you."

"Nearly all the people I train tell me that at some point," he said with a smile. "It means I'm doing something right."

"I'm not just someone you train," I whined. "I'm your boyfriend. You're supposed to take it easy on me."

He leaned over and whispered in my ear. "If you be a good boy and finish this run, when we get home, I'll put you in the shower and take it *real easy* on you."

I groaned as I stood upright. "Do you offer all your students sexual rewards?"

"Only the cute ones," he said with a grin. "Now get your ass moving, or I won't go easy on you at all."

I started to jog again. "You know, I'm half-tempted to *not* get my ass moving just so you'll *not* go easy on me."

He laughed as he ran beside me. "Yeah, I should have known better... How about, if you finish this run without stopping, I'll finish you off in the shower, then let you go back to sleep."

It almost killed me, but I did it.

Kira shook his head at me and pushed me down the hall toward the bathroom. "Now at least I know your motivation. Get your sorry ass into the shower."

"You love my sorry ass," I said, stripping my shirt off as I went.

The water over my skin was heavenly. I washed my hair, brushed my teeth, and scrubbed the stench of the night before from my body. By the time Kira joined me, I was feeling remotely human.

He stood under the stream of water, lifting his head back, letting the water run over his hair. I turned him around so his back was to me, poured some shampoo onto my hand, and lathered up his hair, massaging his head with my fingers.

His head lolled back and he groaned. "Mmm, that's good."

Then I ran my soapy hands down his shoulders, down his back to his perfectly rounded ass. "Mmm, it sure is."

He chuckled and turned around to wash the shampoo out of his hair, and I continued to skim my hands over his chest, his abs, down to his half-hardened cock. He groaned at my touch, then his head fell forward. "Oh," he said, like he'd just remembered something. "Mom wants us over for dinner tomorrow night. Is that okay?"

My hand froze, still cupping his balls. "Is it okay that we go there for dinner? Or is it okay you mention your mother when I have my hand on your balls?" I asked with a chuckle. "Because dinner is fine..."

He laughed. "I just remembered."

"You know what I just remembered?" I asked.

He smiled. "What's that?"

"You said you'd finish me off in the shower..."

His dark eyes shined, and he licked his perfect lips. He turned us around so I was under the stream, then he oh-so-slowly fell to his knees.

Between cold tiles, warm water, and a hot mouth, my senses were in overload. Kira knew how to bring me to climax so quickly. He knew my body, what I liked, what I responded to. His lips, his tongue, his hands cupped me and fingers probed me, and he sucked me until I came hard down his throat.

And when my legs gave out, he turned off the water and towel-dried me. He took my hand and led me to bed, where he laid me on my stomach and knelt between my legs.

I loved having him inside me. I fucking craved it.

I lifted my hips for him, and when he was sheathed and slicked, he pressed against me. Into me. Slowly he filled me; slowly he fucked me. He nipped his teeth at my shoulder and he dug his fingers into my hips. He whispered in my ear, and he kissed down the back of my neck. Then he thrust a little harder, his fingers dug a little deeper, his groans became grunts, and he came.

Without moving off me, Kira lifted his hips and pulled out of me. He discarded the condom, wrapped his arms around me, and rolled us over so we were on our sides, then nuzzled his nose into the back of my neck. "Feel better?"

"Mmm," I hummed my answer. "You?"

"Much."

I smiled. These last few weeks had been a little strained between us—with my decision to leave my job—but now that it was done, things seemed to be back to good.

"I'm better now," I told him, snuggling into his arms.

He kissed my shoulder. "Want another shower?"

"No. I like the smell of you on me," I told him sleepily. I wiggled my ass. "And the feel of where you've been."

I could feel his lips smile on my skin. "You're not sore?"

"Mm-mm. Not at all." I tightened his hold on me. "Did you want to do it again, just to be sure?"

Kira chuckled in my ear. "So greedy."

"'S not my fault you're so hot," I corrected him.

He playfully bit my shoulder, then kissed where his teeth had been. "I have to go to work, babe," he said softly.

"Are you closing up?"

"Yeah."

I hated when he closed the gym at night. After the Tomic incident, where he'd been taken and tortured when he was closing the gym, I'd never been comfortable with it. It had taken Kira months and months of therapy, long after his broken arm had healed, for him to be okay with being there by himself at closing time. But he refused to live his life in fear, and after much discussion with his shrink, he'd told his boss, Chris, he wanted to get back into his normal routine.

Which was fine. I understood, I really did. But he didn't say I couldn't have a patrol do a drive-by every night just to make sure he was okay.

He must have taken my silence as disapproval. "Matt?"

"I can come by at eight thirty and wait for you to lock up."

He sighed. "I'll be fine by myself."

"We could grab something to eat after you finish."

He squeezed me in his arms and sighed again, resigned. "Okay." Then he added, "You know, you can't be there every night."

I pulled the pillow down under my head and smiled.

"Well, technically now I can. I'm a man of leisure, remember?"

He pulled his arms away and smacked my ass. "No you're not."

"Ow."

"I brought home some textbooks on anatomy and muscular development when training," he told me, as he rolled off the bed. "You can start by reading those."

I lifted my head to look at him. "Huh?"

"You're going to put your body through some fairly rigorous training. You should know why your body will respond in certain ways."

"Can you stop being a physical trainer for just a second?" I mumbled.

He ignored me. "When you were working on a case, you'd spend weeks and months examining the facts and researching everything you could, yes?"

"Mmm."

"This is no different," he went on to say. "I'll leave the books on the kitchen counter."

When I didn't respond, he knelt on the bed, pulled back the sheet, and bit my exposed ass.

I laughed and groaned at the same time. "Ow."

Then he slapped my other ass cheek. "Your mission, if you choose to accept this..."

I buried my face into my pillow. "I'm not *Mission: Impossible*."

He laughed as he got off the bed. "Some days I wonder."

I heard him get dressed as I started to doze off, and before he left, he kissed the side of my head. "See you tonight."

"Love you," I mumbled, just before I heard the front door close. I fell asleep with a smile.

I WOKE A FEW HOURS LATER, stripped the bed, changed sheets, did laundry, cleaned up the kitchen, and I even vacuumed the house. I played with my new phone for a while, entering in all the numbers I knew, and sent messages to the guys with my new, non-police-associated number. I even cleaned up the spare room, which we'd converted into a home gym, spraying and wiping down the kick-pads, stacking the weights, and straightening up the mats.

I did everything around the house I could think of, ignoring the textbooks on the kitchen counter for as long as I could. But by mid-afternoon, they got the better of me, and I parked my ass on the sofa and started to read.

It wasn't exactly interesting reading. But Kira had a point. This was going to be my job for the foreseeable future, and I should treat it as such. Learning about the metabolic responses to different physical exertion levels put a new spin on why Kira made me do certain exercises in a certain order, and I was beginning to see his point.

It wasn't as though I didn't take it seriously. I did. I knew what my body was in for, the high intensity, the physicality of what the next few months would be like. But *knowing* and *going through* were two very different things. I knew from years on the job as a cop that all the training amounted to not much in the field.

Kira had my body in the best shape it'd ever been, but I needed to get my head in the game. I needed to be in the right headspace, so when I stood against someone who wasn't Kira, I didn't get my head smacked in.

Kira pushed me because he didn't want me to get hurt. I understood that, even though I bitched at him for pushing me too hard. So with his good intentions at heart, I read the first textbook and reread the parts that applied to me and the type of high-intensity training I did.

I hadn't realized the time until my stomach growled. It was after seven, and daylight was starting to fade. I grabbed a quick shower, got dressed in cargos and a T-shirt, and headed into the city.

I walked into Kira's work like I'd done a thousand times. As always, there were other cops there, working out and finishing up for the night. They gave me a nod or smiled and called me "Elliot" just like I was still one of them. It was... nice.

Kira was running through some circuits with one of the guys from the fifth floor, but as he wrapped the session up and walked over to the counter, he smiled when he saw me. It was almost closing time and the few people there were finishing up. All the cops who went to the gym knew Kira and I were together. They knew if one of us was there, the other probably wasn't too far away.

No one had a problem with it. After they'd seen us spar, and after they'd seen Kira take down three out of four assailants on the CCTV footage from last year, no one would be game to have a problem with it.

I stood at the end of the service counter, flicking through some healthy eating magazine while Kira finished up, and when he locked the front doors, he looked up and down the street. "Hmm, no patrol guys tonight," he said. He turned to me and smiled. "Did they know you were coming in, or is the order you gave to have me babysat defunct now that you're not a cop?"

I smiled. I'd never admitted outright to requesting the patrol runs past the gym. "I did ask Mitch to make sure the other police officers were safe here."

Kira shook his head and grinned. "Right." He walked in behind the counter and picked up a client job card and wrote down his last session. "So," he hedged as he wrote, "did you have a chance to look at those books?"

"I did."

"I meant read," he amended. "Not look at the books, but actually read."

"Oh, ye of little faith," I said, stacking up the magazines into a neat pile. "I learned all about high-intensity interval training and how it causes specific metabolic responses by doing a range of exercises to utilize different muscle groups. Such as phosphocreatine, lactic acid and anaerobic glycolysis, and oxidative pathways."

Kira's eyes widened and he grinned. He was obviously pleasantly surprised. "Really?"

"Not exactly exciting reading, but yes, I read it," I told him. "It also helps I have a good memory for written details. Years of detective work will do that." He was still smiling, and I liked that he was proud of me. "Plus, I want you to know I am taking this seriously, and I appreciate all your help."

He gave me a nod and smiled. "You ready to go?"

"Yes. I'm starving."

Dinner was at a favorite haunt of mine not far from HQ. I chastised Kira for having carbs, and he rolled his eyes at me and told me not to lecture him about diet. It was his job to lecture me, he said. Not the other way around.

"How is that fair?" I asked as I stabbed my grilled fish with my fork.

"I never said it was fair," he said with a laugh. "And this pasta is divine, by the way."

He knew pasta was a weakness for me. "You really suck sometimes."

"You weren't complaining about that in the shower this morning."

I shook my head. "Definitely not."

He swallowed his mouthful of food and wiped his lips with the napkin. His shiny black hair was a beautiful, spiky mess, and his almond-shaped eyes shined. "Hey, I thought we might go shopping tomorrow."

"For?"

"Some new gear for you, before you start at the FC on Monday."

The FC was the fight center on Harbor Parade I'd organized to train at. Its actual title was the Harbor Fight Club, a name taken from the movie, but over time it had become known as the Fight Club, then been shortened again to just the FC. It had a reputation for taking amateurs to the next level. "I don't want to turn up looking like the new kid."

"You *are* the new kid."

"I've trained there before," I reminded him. "They've seen me spar."

He grinned. "I know, I was there. I think they were hoping you'd get flogged," he said. "You know, being a cop— a *gay* cop and all."

"But I did okay."

He nodded. "You did real good."

I took his compliment with a smile. "I'm still a bit nervous about Monday, though," I admitted.

"I'll be there," he said. "If that's okay with you? I don't have to work, and I'd like to see how you do."

"Sure," I said. Then I added, "You might need to drive me home anyway, you know, if I have black eyes or if I'm unconscious."

"Shouldn't joke about that," he said with a smirk. "You know, in case it happens."

I laughed. "Yeah, thanks."

He pushed his plate away. "No regrets?"

I rubbed my foot on his calf under the table. "Nope."

He looked at me for a long moment, then shook his head disbelievingly and sighed. "You ready to go home?"

"Only if you plan to have your way with me."

"Didn't you have enough earlier?"

"Never."

KIRA WASN'T JOKING when he said he wanted to go shopping. We walked into the sports gear shop that catered to just about every recreational activity you could imagine. Kira bought all his work gear from there, so he knew it well.

He headed straight to the back corner. There were rows dedicated to boxing, martial arts, and kickboxing, with everything anyone could ever need—kick pads, gloves, shorts, shoes, thigh pads, mouth guards, groin guards, punching bags, and even grappling dummies.

Kira collected a basket and just started throwing things in it.

"Kira, babe, I already have a mouth guard. Several, actually."

He shrugged. "You can never have too many." Then he held up a groin guard. "Or too many of these."

I chuckled and waggled my eyebrows at him. "God forbid." I left him to it and went to look at fighting shorts. I picked up two pairs and yelled out to Kira. "Black or white shorts?"

"Black" came his quick response. "White shows all the blood."

I frowned and put the white ones back and picked up a

second black pair. "As long as it's someone else's blood," I mumbled to myself, and when I looked at Kira, I found him in a different section, staring at something and biting his lip.

I crossed the three aisles to where he was. "What's up?"

"Um, these...," he said, and held up a jockstrap. "You wear these, right?"

"Yeah."

He swallowed. "Why have I never seen you in these?"

"Because you wouldn't come into the showers with me at the gym."

He groaned low in his throat. "Because I was working, and I know what would've happened if I did."

I picked up a black jockstrap with split straps, and imagined wearing them while he fucked me. "Mmm, you could really get your hands wrapped around these..."

He snatched them off me and threw them in the basket. Then he picked up a red pair. "These aren't for sparring."

I laughed. "Just two pairs?"

He bit his lip and looked at the rows of different jockstraps to choose some more. I laughed again, and putting my hand on his shoulder, I pushed him to the end of the aisle. "Two's enough, for now, anyway. I'm out of strapping tape."

A new pair of compression shorts, strapping tape, and ankle guards later, I finally dragged him out of the store. Not before he checked out other gear for work and bought himself a new sleeveless training shirt. Not that I minded, because he looked damn hot when he wore them.

"Am I all set now?" I asked him as we walked toward the car. "Have I got enough protective gear? Because I don't even use half the stuff I have at home."

"You will at the FC," he stated adamantly. "They won't be as easy on you as I was."

I snorted. "When were you ever easy on me?"

He laughed at me. "You might be surprised. I'm an amateur! These guys are the real deal. They're gonna work your ass."

I waggled my eyebrows at him, as he realized what he just said. "Not like you," I told him. "I can assure you."

He threw the car keys to me. "I should hope not."

I couldn't help but smile. "Speaking of working my ass, I think I need to try those jockstraps on when we get home. You know, just to be sure they fit nice and snug."

He looked at his watch. "We need to be at my mom and dad's in four hours."

I opened the car door and got in behind the wheel. "Plenty of time."

WE WERE LATE GETTING to Sal and Yumi's. We got *busy* and lost track of time, but the jockstraps fit just fine. So did Kira.

He loved them, very enthusiastically. I wore the black one first, and when he was hard again, I wore the red one. If his enthusiasm was any indication, the red one was by far his favorite.

I couldn't believe how much I enjoyed bottoming. Before Kira, I'd only done it once or twice, but with him, it was where I belonged. Not that he was some dominating top. Far from it. I just loved the feel of him inside me. I loved how he took care of me. I loved how he held me as he eased inside me. He'd spark fireworks in my blood every time and he'd give me the most intense pleasure. I'd never thought of myself as a true bottom. Until now.

"What's got you smiling?"

"Oh, nothing." I feigned innocence. "Though I might have to get a few different kinds of jockstraps."

Kira shook his head as he pulled the car into his parents' drive. "You're such a..." He trailed off, searching for the right word.

"Slut?" I offered.

Kira's mouth fell open. "I'd never call you that!"

I laughed. "It's true," I admitted. "And it's your fault."

"How so?" he asked as he got out of the car.

I got out and shut the door. "All this diet and exercise has me jumping out of my skin."

We walked up the front steps of his parent's house. "I'm not complaining," he said, as he opened the door. "But I think you might need a bit of a rest."

"I'll be the judge of that."

"You boys are late!" Yumi called out.

Kira grinned as he walked into the kitchen, and finding his mother stirring something on the stove, he kissed her cheek. "Matt's fault."

Yumi looked at me and pointed to her other cheek, which I promptly kissed. "Why is it your fault?" she asked. "And why you need a rest?"

"Kira works me hard," I said. "But I'm fine. I like it, actually."

Kira's eyes widened at my words, but the sexual innuendo was lost on his mother. She pointed her finger at her son. "You take it easy on him."

Kira glared at me, but ignoring the jibes at him, he changed the subject. "Where's Dad?"

"In his study," she told him, turning back to the stove. "Go let him know you're here."

Kira mouthed 'behave' at me and wandered off down the hall while I stayed with Yumi. "So," she said, not looking at me. "I saw you on the TV. It's really done, yeah?"

I nodded and waited for the little Japanese woman to look at me. "Yeah."

She nodded too. "You okay?"

I hated lying to her. I mean, I hated lying to Kira the most, but his parents had welcomed me into their lives, and now I was lying to them too. It was the worst part. "Yeah, I'm good." Then I changed the subject. "Start training tomorrow at the FC."

Yumi sighed. "You're crazy like Kira."

"Crazy like who?" Kira said, walking back into the kitchen.

Sal followed him in, offering me his hand, which I shook with a smile. "Hey, Sal." I faced him so he could he'd read my lips, then I looked at Kira. "Your mom thinks you're crazy."

Kira spoke and signed at the same time. "Crazy for putting up with you," he joked.

His mom turned around and threw up her hands. "You boys both crazy for kickboxing," she cried and walked over to the fridge to grab something else. She was forever on the move, a tiny little thing, but full of energy and always feisty.

Sal waited until Yumi had her attention diverted to the contents of the fridge before he signed that it was *her* who drove *him* crazy.

When she turned around and stood up straight, she eyed us three smiling men, then pointed her finger at her husband. "Don't think I don't know what you said."

I laughed and Kira smiled, and this was a typical dinner at the Franco household. Much laughter, much joking, much love.

I still wasn't fluent in signing, but I was learning. I could get by, though some conversations went over my head. Kira would normally narrate if I missed something.

Conversation at dinner was mostly about my leaving the police, but as I'd explained to them in the weeks leading up to it, it was time.

I needed to get out, I told them, while I was young enough to do something else. I didn't want to wake up one day, sixty years old and married to my job.

"Oooh." Yumi's face lit up. "You want to get married, huh?"

I looked at the faces around the table, my eyes landing on Kira's last, and I fucking blushed. "That's not what I meant."

Yumi bounced in her seat. "You see, Sal?" she asked her husband excitedly. "I told him I'll be the mother of the groom one day." Grinning, she got up from the table, took an empty dish with her, and darted into the kitchen.

Sal sagged with a sigh, then he signed something quickly, which I missed. I looked at Kira, wondering what on earth was wrong. Kira smirked. "He said thanks a lot, now she'll never shut up about it."

"I heard that!" Yumi yelled from the kitchen.

"Sorry," I signed to Sal. I looked to Kira. "That's not what I meant. I didn't mean I wanted to be married to you instead, I just meant that..."

Kira's eyes widened and his mouth fell open a little.

"...not that I don't ever want to get married, because I guess I probably would, but I just didn't mean I thought I'd marry you instead..." I stopped rambling, letting my words die. "I'll just shut up now and take these." I picked up the empty plates and bolted to the kitchen.

I put the plates in the sink just as the sound of Kira and Sal laughing echoed from the dining room. My head fell forward with a sigh, and Yumi bumped her hip into mine and giggled. I looked at her and smiled. "Well, if they're laughing at me, they're leaving you alone."

Yumi slid her arm around my waist and gave me a squeeze. "You're a good boy." Then she added, "And you be a good son-in-law."

"Kira?" I called out. "Time to go."

Yumi laughed and Kira appeared in the doorway. "Mom, are you scaring him?"

"Yes," she said with a grin. "But spring weddings are nice."

Kira looked at me, his eyes no doubt as wide as mine. "Yep, time to go," he said. He kissed his mom and grabbed my arm, pulling me away from her. "Thanks for dinner, but Matt's got a big day tomorrow, needs a lot of rest. We really should be going."

Now Sal was in the doorway, trying not to laugh. He signed something I didn't quite catch, and Kira signed something back to him with short, sharp hand movements that looked a little harsh.

Yumi gasped, and Kira signed something else.

I was really lost and a little bewildered. I hadn't meant for the conversation to take such a nosedive. "Um..."

Kira looked at me and explained. "Dad thinks it's hilarious to watch us tough guys act like scared little girls. I told him we'd see how funny it was if we actually agreed and asked Mom to organize it."

Now it was my turn to gape.

Kira glanced back at his dad and smirked. "Imagine how much she won't shut up about all that for a *whole year*? Not so funny now, is it?"

Sal was mortified. Yumi looked a cross between excited and pissed off and a whole lot of hopeful. "Really?"

I closed my still-gaping mouth. "Um..."

Kira huffed. "No, Mom. Not really. We're not getting married. Jesus." He let go of my arm to hug his mother.

I looked at Kira's dad. "I just came here for dinner..."

Sal smiled at me. Then he signed slowly for me. Though I couldn't be sure, it looked like he said, "Don't get married. Drive you crazy."

"I won't drive him crazy," Kira said. "He'll drive me crazy."

"See?" Yumi said. "It's like you're already married."

Kira took my arm again and dragged me to the front door. I barely had time to slip on my flip-flops before he pulled me outside, down the stairs, and to the car.

The trip home was deathly silent for a few blocks. Eventually, Kira mumbled, "Jesus Christ. That was weird. I'm sorry about that."

"It's fine." I laughed, probably a little maniacally. "Your mom seriously scares me."

Yep, that was right. I, narcotic detective, who'd been threatened with knives and bats, who'd been shot at, punched, kicked, who'd chased down crack-heads, was afraid of a tiny, wedding-wielding woman.

Kira changed gears, changed lanes, then looked at me and nodded. "Me too." But he took a deep breath and changed the subject. He started talking about going to the FC tomorrow and about starting with a new trainer and about being ready.

I agreed, of course, telling him I was looking forward to it and that I was ready. And for a moment, I almost forgot I was lying to him.

And the next day, it was easy to think this new 'career change' was all fun and games. But I was quickly reminded of the lie I was now living after I'd been at the FC for all of twenty minutes, when a certain guy walked in. A guy I'd seen a hundred photos of, seen reels of footage of, read dozens of reports on.

He was the reason I was there.

He was my mark.

He was the man I was there to bring down.

CHAPTER THREE

LEONARD TRESSLER, or Leon, as he was known, was five foot ten, with a stocky build and a shaved head. A flattened nose and hard brows told us he'd been in a bout or two, and his police profile told us he ran cocaine from his underground, illegal fight clubs.

That was what I was doing there.

He walked in through the back door and headed straight for the office. He had his usual entourage of two refrigerator-sized men with him, and a respectful silence fell across the busy club when strode past.

I'd met my new trainer, Max Bossari, or Boss, as he was called, a few times before today. After he'd seen me train and spar, he'd agreed to take me on as a new student. He was an older guy, and funnily enough, he reminded me of Ross Berkman. With short, graying hair and military-style discipline, he was a no-nonsense, no-bullshit kind of guy. Though the prison-style tattoos on his forearms told me that was about where the similarities ended.

But he'd agreed to take me on in his already busy schedule, and I was grateful. He was my foot in the door.

I was warming up and stretching out like Boss told me. "Who was that?" I asked, nodding pointedly to the door Leon Tressler walked through.

Boss didn't even turn his head. "That was the boss."

"Thought you were the boss."

The corner of his lip curled slightly in what I thought was supposed to be a smile. "I'm just Boss. He's *the* boss. The owner. Mr. Tressler." He said the name as though it was a privilege.

Well, that told me a few things. Tressler was respected, whether out of fear or not, I couldn't tell yet, but for Boss to address a man half his age as Mr. told me he respected him. It also told me there was a camaraderie here, not too unlike between my cop partners and me. These men stuck together.

Boss didn't even have to look to know who I was asking about. He knew from the silence around the room who had just walked in. And he seemed proud to be associated with him.

"Is your boyfriend gonna come every time you train?" Boss asked.

They all knew I was gay, but I was a little surprised he said the word 'boyfriend' so easily. He didn't seem to give a shit that I was gay. It seemed all of LA knew, following my very public outing after the Tomic ordeal. I wasn't going to deny it, but I also wasn't about to bring it up in conversation. I needed to fit in here.

"This is LA, kid," he said by way of explanation. "Not much fazes me anymore."

I smiled at him, then glanced over to Kira. He was watching some guys in the boxing ring. "Kira's a personal trainer. He's the one who got me started on this mixed martial arts," I explained, not stopping my sit-ups. "He wanted to see what I was getting myself into, but between you and me, I think he's jealous."

"Well, if he was your trainer, he did an okay job," Boss said. "You're in pretty good shape and I'd say about halfway there. I know most trainers work on endurance first, but I don't. No point," he told me. "You need strength, speed, and power first. Otherwise, all you'll be *enduring* is half-assed strength, slow speed, and no power. Get those three things up to the max first, and then we'll work on how long you can endure it."

I nodded. "Good point."

"You can start with these." He handed me a piece of paper with a list of exercises on it. "Complexes."

I read through the list. Eight different types of lifts, squats, and presses in sets of six. Kira did something similar.

"They might look easy," Boss said dismissively as he flipped through some other papers. "But don't underestimate this type of training. It's grueling. Doin' this twice a week, combining two reps in one set, and with one hundred pounds on the bar, you'll be lifting over twenty thousand pounds a week."

Boss's reputation for getting guys into the cage was good, so I had no reason to doubt him.

"Changing the weight you lift in each set will make you stronger, not bulkier. And take a look around." He scanning the training floor. "No machines. They do the work for you, so free weights only. Just you against gravity."

I didn't want to tell him Kira worked by similar principles, given I was his student now, not someone else's. "Fair enough."

He nodded. "Yeah, you probably know most of this shit already," he said. "But cage fighting will put demands on your body like you can't believe. You'll have excruciating levels of lactate in muscles you never knew you had, and this kind of training will condition your body for it." Then the older man sneered at me, not too kindly. "You'll fucking hate me every minute of the training I put you through. You'll fucking regret the day you walked in here."

I bit back the urge to bristle at his threat.

Then he smiled and tapped my face. "But after you've won your first fight, you'll thank me."

I grinned at him then, but he didn't give me time to relish the moment.

"Right," he barked. "Warm up. Skipping, standing sprint, push-ups. Three minutes a set, thirty-second rest."

Warm up?

Jesus.

"Whatcha waitin' for?"

Fuck. I knew eyes from around the room were on me. It was a large open warehouse-style gym with a boxing ring in one corner, a smaller-than-standard fighting cage in the adjacent, and open floor space for a range of various exercises and various punching bags, kick dummies, and a range of equipment. And there were seventeen men—yes, I counted them, and not including Kira—using the gym.

Most of them were pretending not to watch me. Some didn't even try to hide it, just stood there and blatantly watched me go through my 'warm-up,' which I had a sneaking suspicion was more of a test than anything.

And for all the times I'd bitched at Kira for the long, slow jogs, then the fast, intense sprints, I was grateful. This was what he meant by intense training. The short bursts of intense cardio, of anything up to three minutes, were the same duration as a round in fighting.

I knew other guys were watching me. I could feel their eyes on me. I was a cop, albeit an ex-cop, and I was certain they were hoping I'd fail miserably. Boss barked more instructions at me, and for the next hour, I kept my head down, my breathing even, and I ignored the burn in my muscles, trying to look like it wasn't hurting.

Boss picked up my towel and threw it at me and told me that'd do. He looked happy enough with me, surprised even. "Right," he said. "I've seen how you shape up. How 'bout we find someone to have a bit of a spar with. Nothin' fancy, just wanna see your form." He didn't wait for an answer. "I'll give ya a ten-minute rest, then we'll put you in the ring."

Well, shit. I leaned my hands on my knees to catch my breath and looked up at my new trainer. I wiped the sweat off my face. "Sounds good."

I walked over to where Kira was now standing and he handed me a fresh water bottle. "They're all watching you."

I took a sip and took some deep breaths. "I know."

"You look good," he said quietly. "I think they were hoping you'd fall in a heap. You know, see the great Matthew Elliott cry."

"I'm sure they were," I told him, still trying to get my breathing under control. "They might yet," I said. "Sparring next."

"Shit," Kira mumbled. "They don't mess around."

"Boss is trying me out to see," I explained. "Maybe see who he can match me against."

"He's testing you," Kira said. "That's what he's doing. He probably figured with that rigorous training straight up, you'd either sink or swim."

"To see if I'm a quitter?"

Kira gave me a small nod. "I'd say he'll be testing you out for the first few weeks to see if you've got what it takes."

"That's fair enough, I guess," I conceded. "He needs to

know I'm not wasting his time."

Kira pulled my gym bag over and handed me my gloves and mouth guard. The gloves were really only knuckle protectors. They weren't padded like boxing gloves, but rather thinner, fingerless gloves.

"Elliott!" Boss called out. I turned to see him walking over with a younger guy, who was about twenty years old, ripped, and fit. He was one of the guys I'd noticed training earlier. He had short blond hair and an old, yellowing bruise on his left eye.

"Elliott, this is Cody Kindella," Boss made somewhat of an introduction. "He said he'll stand against ya so I can see where you're at."

"Hey," I greeted him.

"Hey," he replied. "You're the cop, huh?"

"Used to be," was all I said, playing it down. I looked at Boss. "Ready?"

The older man smirked. "Yep, two minutes."

As I put the gloves on, Kira came up beside me. "Just do your thing," he said softly. "Remember, this is a test. Not just to see how you do in the ring, but so all the other guys here can see too."

I nodded.

"Keep your hands up, chin in," Kira added. "I've been watching those guys sparring over there. This kid leads with his left, kicks with his right."

"Got it."

"Go," he urged me.

I walked over to the ring where Boss was talking to some other guys. I climbed through the ropes and loosened up by bouncing on my toes, shaking it out. My muscles were starting to cool down.

By the time my opponent, Cody, climbed into the ring,

we had a bit of an audience.

"Right," Boss directed. "Spar only, no head shots, no body blows. I just wanna see strengths and weaknesses, that's all. We're not here to prove anything."

Like hell we weren't.

I slipped in my mouth guard, and Cody was in the center of the ring, smiling. He held out his fist, which I bumped with mine, and we began to circle around each other.

I kept light on my toes, kept my hands over my chin, and waited for him to move first. He jabbed a little with his right, and I deflected easily enough, but then he followed with a direct left, just like Kira said.

I blocked and jabbed back twice in quick succession, making him pull back just a little. There were some cheers and jeers from the little audience, and Cody came at me again, this time with a little more seriousness in his swing.

He landed a shot to my ribs, and as we were closer, he kicked with his right, but I countered with a hard knee to his side. He gripped my upper arm, bringing me into his body, and jabbed three or four quick shots to my ribs before striking up and landing on my cheek.

I pulled back and slipped out of his hold, snapping my right at his jaw a few times. It was hardly a serious bout, it was supposed to only be a spar session after all, but Kira was right. This was a test.

"Right," Boss called out. "Give me some high kicks. Show me your range."

I took a step back from Cody and bounced on my toes. He lifted his arms up to protect his face and I gave him two quick sidekicks to his head. He retaliated quickly with a sharp left while I was off balance, but I deflected his punch away from my body and gave him a knee to the ribs.

There were more jeers and cheers from the guys watching, and Cody stood upright and smiled. He lifted his hands to his chin but swept with his right foot, scoring me across the shin.

After a few more kicks, punches, deflects, and blocks, Boss had seen enough and called it quits. I held up my fist and Cody bumped his to mine, and by all accounts, it was rather amicable.

"You do all right," Boss said to me. "You'll be here every day, but you got three sessions a week, yeah?"

I nodded, trying to catch my breath. "Yeah."

"Good. I'll see you Mondays, Wednesdays, and Fridays for scheduled sessions," he said. "But I wanna see you here doin' slow training every other day. It'll help with soreness until your conditioning's up to scratch."

"Yes, sir."

He laughed. "Jesus. For fuck's sake don't call me that."

"Yes, Boss."

"That's better," he said as he was walking off. "Go shower, go home. You stink."

KIRA CHATTED ANIMATEDLY the rest of the afternoon. "You were so good," he said proudly. He gently pressed a frozen pack of peas to the corner of my eye. "You still could have blocked his shots a little better, but you kept your feet square, your shoulders straight. Your technique was good."

I smiled at him. My lip felt a little swollen, and I licked it instinctively. "Boss said I did okay, so I think that was a pretty good compliment coming from him."

Kira moved the frozen peas from my eye to my lip. "How are you feeling? He worked you pretty hard."

"I'm fine," I told him honestly. "I can feel my muscles tightening up, but that's expected."

"You need a hot shower."

"Then a massage," I added.

He tried not to smile, knowing exactly what kind of massage I wanted. "No more workouts," he chided me. "You need to rest your body tonight."

I pulled his hand and the cold pack of peas from my face and kissed him softly. "I'm wearing a jockstrap."

He groaned. "No. No sex tonight. You need to give your body a break."

I pouted. "You're no fun."

"I'm plenty fun," he said, putting the peas back to my eye. "I think you impressed them. They weren't expecting you to be that good."

"I was hardly *that* good," I told him. "Anyway, I think today was nothing. I think they'll throw everything they've got at me in the next few weeks."

Kira smiled that beautiful smile. "And you'll kick their asses."

I pulled my face back from the packet of frozen peas. I was starting to ache a little, my muscles were feeling tight and sore, and my shin hurt where Cody kicked me. But I wouldn't dare say that to Kira. So instead I said, "I'm starving."

"What do you feel like?" he asked. I smiled and he amended, "To eat. What do you feel like to eat?"

"Pasta," I answered quickly. "My favorite."

Kira kissed my lips. "With extra cheese."

"You know me well."

He threw the peas back in the freezer and opened the fridge door. "I'll make it. You go have a hot shower."

"Lots of cherry tomatoes?"

He walked over only to push me toward the hall door. "Don't start telling me how to make it. Go, get out of here, or there'll be no massage tonight."

I stood under the stream with the water as hot as I could for as long as I could stand it. I could feel it easing the ache in my muscles. While I was used to fairly rigorous training, today had been intense and I was feeling it.

It wasn't an unpleasant feeling. It was almost like a validation. I wouldn't say I *enjoyed* it, but I certainly didn't *hate* it.

When I walked back into the kitchen, wrapped in my robe to keep some warmth in my body, Kira's pasta was almost done. It was simply cherry tomatoes, sliced zucchini, peppers, with a dash of honey over pasta. I usually added a ton of Parmesan cheese to mine, but tonight, Kira added it for me.

We ate on the sofa in front of the TV, and when he was done, I took his plate and put it in the sink. When I came back into the living room, he was sprawled out on the sofa, so I leaned over the back of it and kissed him.

"Dinner was delicious," I told him. "As always, you're too good to me."

He slid his hand over my cheek and lightly traced my lip with his thumb. "I'm perfect like that."

I chuckled and kissed the palm of his hand. "You are."

"Are you being extra nice to me so I'll give you that massage?"

I stood up and stretched. "Maybe." I let the robe fall open, and as I turned around and started walking to the bedroom, the material slipped off my shoulders and fell to the ground. All I had on underneath it was a jockstrap. The red one.

He was behind me with his hands on my hips before I

got to the bedroom door.

Dear God, he massaged me. For what felt like hours of delicious torture, I lay face down on the bed and he straddled me, digging his fingers into my skin, the heels of his hands into the muscle of my shoulders, back, legs, and ass.

I could feel how turned on he was, and the more he massaged me, the more I moaned. He had my body all-languid, yet fine-tuned to his touch. My eyes were closed and my hands were gripping the sheets in anticipation. His lips soon replaced his hands, kissing and licking my skin, and when I heard the bedside drawer open, I smiled.

He readied me with slick fingers as he leaned over me and whispered in my ear. "I can't say no to you."

I lifted my ass for him. "I want you."

"You're insatiable," he whispered gruffly. "It's all you want, me in your ass."

I moaned. "Please."

"Fuck." Kira withdrew his fingers and when I heard the rustle of foil, I widened my legs for him. But he rolled me over and settled himself between my thighs. I hooked my legs around his waist, and as I pulled him over me, his arms slid under my shoulders, and ever so slowly, he pushed inside me. He whispered how good it felt, how deep he was, how much he loved me. He rocked us both. He made love to me until our bodies could take no more.

It was the perfect end to a good day.

I'd survived my first day at the FC, felt completely safe in Kira's arms, and I'd made a visual contact with my mark. I'd seen Tressler in the flesh, and he no doubt had seen me. He knew he had an ex-cop in his gym. An ex-narcotics cop. There was no doubt in my mind he knew I was there.

The wheels were in motion.

And I knew the game was about to change.

———

CHAPTER FOUR

THE NEXT WEEK WAS TOUGH. No, it wasn't long hours like I was used to as a cop, but it was physical.

More physical than I'd ever been.

Boss had me pushing limits I didn't know I had. It was intense and demanding. The majority of my time was training—circuits of complexes, grueling and unforgiving, but not much time in the ring.

I could feel the training making me stronger, even after just one week. I could feel it making me fitter. So as much as it was punishing me, I knew I needed to go through it. And I was surprised by how much I enjoyed it.

Boss had me write down everything I ate over the course of the week, and by the end of that first week, he had it broken down to proteins, carbs, and fats. What I ate was already pretty good, he said. "I presume your personal trainer has something to do with that," he said with a smile. "Because I thought cops just ate doughnuts." He looked me up and down. "You look like you don't eat that shit."

I laughed at that. "Yeah, eating doughnuts is in the how-to-be-a-cop handbook." I made a point of calling Kira by name. "Kira makes sure I eat pretty good. He does this for a living, so he watches his proteins and carbs and his water intake, and he includes me in that."

Boss nodded thoughtfully. "He trains fighting?"

"Not to this level," I answered. "He's good, don't get me wrong, but I needed more if I wanted to take it seriously. He understood that."

"Well, he's got good basics," Boss said. "There's nothin' worse than tryin' to unteach bad habits, but you're good."

I smiled. "Well, you can thank him for that."

Boss smirked and shook his head. "Uh, no thanks. You can thank him for me."

I chuckled at him. He had a dry sense of humor and seemed completely unfazed to be talking and joking with me about my boyfriend. After not expecting to be so readily accepted, it was a welcome surprise.

Well, Boss accepted it.

Not many of the other guys there training did. Whether it was because I was gay or because to them I was a lowly ex-cop, I didn't know. It could have been both. But there was a distinct distance they gave me.

They watched me train, they watched me with Boss, but they rarely acknowledged me otherwise.

I spent the week training, with my head down, doing everything I was told, and I never complained. I had no time in the ring until Friday afternoon, when Boss called over Cody again, telling us he wanted us to spar.

Only this time, not so softly. "No pussyfootin' this time," the older man said. "I want it clean, but I want it real. You're not in there to kill each other, you're in there for experience."

After I'd donned all the sparring gear, I climbed into the ring. Apparently this Cody kid hadn't been here much longer than me, so pitching the new guy against me, the newer guy, seemed fair. We were about evenly matched, in weight range, height, and ability, which I presumed was why Boss had made us sparring partners.

The FC was busier on Friday afternoons, so again, we had a bit of an audience, and it was pretty clear I had no supporters in my corner. It was probably a good thing—it made me try harder. I had more to prove.

"Three-minute rounds for three rounds," Boss called. He had a stopwatch in his hand. "Okay, boys."

Walking to the middle of the ring, I lifted my fist to Cody and he bumped his to mine. But there was no easing into it. He bounced on his toes a few times, jabbed with his right, looking to land with his left, and he kicked with his right.

I gave as good as I got. If he connected with one jab, I gave him two. If he kicked me in the thigh, I returned the favor. But the first three minutes of the first round seemed to take forever. The second round wasn't much better, though we danced around each other a little more, landing calculated shots.

I took a few shots to the ribs and the face, as did he. But I dominated with my feet. I kicked harder and I kicked higher and with more accuracy. It was one of my strengths. My other strength was reading people. It came from years of detective and police work, but I seemed to be able to read his moves and pre-empt his next.

If this was a scoring fight, going into the third round, I'd have been the clear-cut leader. But in the third round, he got me.

We bumped fists to start the round, and after we'd danced around each other a little, he made his move. He came at me hard and low, wrapped his arms around my hips and drove me into the mat.

Grappling had never been my strong point.

He pinned me to the ground with his weight on my chest and his forearm across my neck, in an almost-sleeper hold. But my legs and hips were free, so I twisted and spun underneath him, and while the pressure eased off my neck and I could breathe again, he grappled me, keeping me under his weight.

I lifted one leg and somehow wrapped it around his torso, pushing him off balance. I scrambled to my feet at the same time Cody got to his, but the bell went off and Boss called it.

Fuck.

Yeah, I'd done okay. Yeah, I'd won the first two rounds, but he'd got me in the last. And not only that, but every single guy watching us fight now knew my weakness.

I bumped fists with Cody, pleased he had a bit of a shiner already. He was panting, but he grinned at me. "Good fight, man."

"You too," I said, just as out of breath as him.

I took a mouthful of water, and Boss gave me a nod. I wiped my face down with my towel. "Need some floor work," I told him. "I'm okay on my feet but need some time on the mats."

"Yeah, you do," he agreed. "But you got out of it okay."

I climbed back through the ropes and jumped down to the floor level. "Just not my forte."

Boss looked at me. "Somethin' tells me you don't like to lose."

"Wouldn't be here if I did."

He grinned. "Go shower, go home." Then he said. "Good first week." He turned and started walking over to his next appointment and called out to me, "See ya Monday."

I couldn't help but smile as I walked into the showers. I ignored the hushed silence that preceded me, implying I was the subject of their conversation. I heard the words *cop* and *fag* being whispered before I rudely interrupted them, but I ignored it. I was bound to be the topic of conversation for a while. It was expected.

I wouldn't take shit off them if they confronted me with it, but while it was harmless whispers, I couldn't give a shit.

When I was done and walking out to the car lot, I pulled out my cell phone and checked the time. It was five-thirty. I thumbed the screen, ran through the contacts, found Mitch's number, and hit call.

He answered on the second ring. "Hey, asswipe!"

"Hey, shithead," I answered as I got to my car. "Did ya miss me?"

"If you're asking if I miss your ugly face and your bad jokes, then the answer is definitely no."

"Oh, fuck you."

He laughed. "What's up?"

"Still on for dinner at your place tomorrow night?"

"Yep," he answered. "Anna has everything organized. You just need to turn up, and for God's sake, don't be late."

"Wouldn't dream of it." I got into my car. Then I remembered my manners. "Does Anna want us to bring anything?"

"Nah, just yourselves."

"Sure?"

"If Kira cooks it, then yes, but if you cook it, then no."

"Thanks a fucking lot."

"You are most welcome," he said cheerfully. "Six

o'clock. Don't be late." Then the dial tone told me our conversation was over.

I contemplated going to Kira's work on the way home to see the other guys, given it was a Friday, but I knew Kira wasn't closing up and he'd be home not long after me.

It had been a full-on, physically draining week, and my muscles were all starting to stiffen up. I hoped Kira wouldn't be late, because I knew I needed another one of his massages.

"OH, MY GOD," Anna cried as she opened the door. "What happened to your eye? And why are you holding a frying pan?"

I smiled at her as we walked in. "You should see the other guy. And this is Kira's."

Anna slipped her arm around Kira's waist, and he bent down to kiss her cheek. "Don't listen to him. He's fine."

I turned so Anna could see me roll my eyes. Then I said, "I need to put this on the stove," as I walked through to the kitchen.

Anna and Kira followed me, and Mitch came in from outside. "Hey!"

God, it was good to see him. "Hey!"

He walked over to me and gave me a bit of a hug. "Shit, man, what happened to your eye?"

It wasn't actually my eye. It was a small cut on my cheek under my eye, but it was a little swollen and made my eye look puffy. "Sparring yesterday."

Mitch shook his head at me. "I hope you gave him one back."

"Yep." Then I sang for him, "My right foot's connected to his cheek bone."

Mitch laughed, then he saw the frying pan. "I told you not to bring anything. Oooh, is that..." He lifted the lid. "It is! Oh, man." Then he stopped and looked at me. "Kira made this, right? Not you?"

"Yeah, I can't make paella."

Mitch stuck his fingers into the pan and picked up a prawn. I smacked his hand. "No picking!"

"Oh my God," Anna mumbled from behind us. Mitch and I, both standing at the stove, turned to face them. Anna and Kira were watching us, shaking their heads. "You two are like kids," Anna said. "Go on, out the back. Sit out there so Kira and I can catch up before the others get here."

Kira and Anna were very close. Since going through the Tomic ordeal together, then going through counseling together, Kira had been teaching Anna some self-defense. And Rachel, Kurt's girlfriend, and Evie, Tony's wife. But he was closest to Anna.

They spoke on the phone, they met for coffee, and they talked about everything. They'd experienced something terrifying together and they'd bonded over that, but now they were like best friends.

So Mitch and I went out to their back sunroom while Kira and Anna chatted in the kitchen. It also gave us time to talk in private, before Kurt and Tony got there.

Mitch spoke quietly. "Seen him?"

He was asking about Leon Tressler. The reason I was undercover. "Three times."

"He's seen you?"

"Yep."

"He knows who you are?"

The way Tressler had eyed me when he walked in told me he knew exactly who I was. "Yes."

"Suspect anything?"

"Not that I'm aware of, but I'm sure he's looking into why I'm there."

Mitch nodded. "You doing okay?"

"Yeah. It's only been a week. Training's full-on. Jesus," I sighed. "I thought Kira was a hard trainer."

"They treat you okay?"

"My trainer is an older guy, bit of a hard-ass. The other guys at the gym are keeping a safe distance."

He looked at me seriously. "Watch your back in there."

"Always."

We heard other voices coming from inside and turned to find Kurt and his girlfriend, Rachel, had arrived, and not too long after that, Tony and his wife, Evie, walked in.

My God, it was good to see them. It had only been a week, but I'd really missed them.

We all hugged hello, then talked and laughed as we ate, and as the night got later, talk turned to some guys at the station, what they'd been up to, and what they'd done. But we didn't talk about work itself.

We couldn't.

And we sat around Mitch's backroom table, like we'd done a hundred times, but this was different. There were things we couldn't talk about, not in front of Kira or any of our partners, for that matter.

But the biggest secret of all—me being undercover—was like its own presence in the room. It was standing in the background, but I could feel it breathing down my neck.

It was the first time in my career as a cop that I felt a discernible shift in my life.

A separation.

Stepping away from my fellow cops, my brothers, and, of course, lying to Kira was something the police shrink had warned me to expect. She likened it to abseiling—taking that first step over the edge was the scariest, but the rest of the descent to ground level was calculated, measured, and with the safety precautions in place, it was just one foot after the other.

I'd thought I'd be fine with it. I'd known it would be hard, but I hadn't expected the rush of emotion. Maybe it was just an exhausting week, or maybe it was just the first time seeing them since I left, but it wasn't a pleasant feeling.

It felt like a step in the wrong direction, like everyone was walking one way and I was going the other.

I knew it was my decision to go undercover, but it didn't make it any easier. I knew they still considered me to be one of them, I knew technically I *was* still one of them.

But I wasn't. Not really.

"You look really good, Matt," Rachel said, grabbing my attention. "Whatever you're doing is really agreeing with you."

I slid my hand onto Kira's knee. "Thanks. It's good to know all that hard work is paying off."

"Yeah, Mitch, honey," Anna said. "Why can't you look like one of these two?" She waved her hand at me and she winked at Kira.

"What, a black eye?" Mitch cried. Then he defended himself by patting his stomach. "Anyway, I'm in shape!" Then he kicked me under the table. "Thanks a freakin' lot, Mr. Six-pack."

Kira grinned and took full credit. "You're very welcome."

I laughed, and looking at Kira, I patted his leg. "He's just jealous."

Mitch rolled his eyes and scoffed. "Not likely. I've seen how much exercise and training you have to do. No thanks."

Tony's wife, Evie, smiled at me warmly, though she seemed a little concerned. "How's it going?"

"It's good," I told her. "Very full-on so far."

She lifted her hand to her own cheekbone. "Your face..."

"Oh, this?" I poked my finger at the cut below my eye. "This is nothing."

Evie shook her head. "Do you miss it?" she asked. "Being a cop?"

I shrugged. "Yes and no," I answered honestly. "These guys, yes," I said, nodding at the cops at the table. "Being with them every day, yes. But the work itself, not so much."

Mitch looked directly at me and frowned for just half a second before he looked over to Anna. Then he cleared his throat. "While we're all here, we've got something we'd like to share with you."

There was complete silence around the table, and we all looked from Mitch to Anna, back to Mitch. "I asked Anna to be my wife," he said. "She said yes."

Kira was standing up before me, and he pulled Anna out of her seat and threw his arms around her, making her squeal. I got up slowly and Tony was already up, shaking Mitch's hand, then Kurt did, so I kissed Anna's cheek. "Congratulations, sweetheart."

Then I turned to find Mitch watching me, so I took a few steps over to him and hugged him hard. "So proud of you," I whispered.

He tightened his hold on me. "Goddammit, Matt," he spoke in my ear. "Wish you weren't gone."

I pulled back, and swallowing down my emotions, I gave him a pat on the arm and a nod. I hadn't been expecting this news, and I hadn't been expecting to be so moved by it. Anna had struggled this last year, dealing with the Tomic aftermath. They all had. And this was such a positive move forward for them, for all of us.

Except I wasn't a part of them anymore.

"Set a date yet?" Evie asked.

Talk turned to spring and getting Anna's grandmother's ring resized and wedding talk. Kira's hand was firm on my knee, like he knew I was struggling with it.

Not long after that, I finished my soda and said we should be going. I was exhausted, my body weary, and I was a little thrown by how emotionally affected I was by the night.

The car ride home was quiet, though Kira took my hand and held it on his thigh as he drove. I stared out the window at the passing houses, and when he squeezed my hand in his, he asked, "You okay?"

"Yeah," I offered weakly.

"Good news about Anna and Mitch..."

"Yes, it is," I said.

Kira looked at me, waiting for me to continue.

"I was supposed to be there for that, ya know?" I told him. "I'm supposed to be a part of shit like that."

"You were there for that. The others didn't know before you."

I shrugged. "I know. Just feels like it's all happening without me." I shook my head at how stupid that sounded.

We pulled up at the house, and when we walked in, I threw my wallet and keys on the hall cabinet. Kira walked right up to me without slowing and hugged me.

"Babe, you are a part of all that," he said. "It's not happening without you. You're still one of them."

I pulled out of his arms to look at his face, in his eyes, trying to judge exactly what he meant by that. "I'm not one of them anymore," I told him, testing to see how he'd answer.

The sweet man gently cupped my face in his strong hands. "You'll always have that bond with them. You're like brothers. You said that before, you're just like brothers. Just because you're not a cop anymore doesn't matter to them."

I tried to smile for him, though it was more sad than happy. There he was being wonderful and kind, and I was lying.

"Tonight was harder than I thought it would be."

"You knew it was going to be hard."

I nodded, my head in his hands. "I know. I just miss them."

Kira pulled me against him and kissed the side of my head. "You're a confounding man, Matthew Elliott."

I knew I confused him. My decision to leave the police department was something he'd never understand. I sighed against his neck. "I'm sorry."

"Don't apologize, baby," his deep voice rumbled in my ear. "Want me to take you to bed?"

I nodded. "No sex, if that's okay. But yes, I'd like you to take me to bed."

Kira pulled back and smiled. "No sex?" he repeated. "It's all you've wanted for the last two weeks, and now none?"

"We can if you want," I started.

He shook his head and gave me half a smile. "I'm fine. But *you* are a puzzling man."

I shrugged. "I aim to please."

He kissed my lips. "Yes, you do."

I chuckled, but then I yawned. "Tired, baby."

He turned my cheek and kissed the cut under my eye. "Come on, to bed with you."

Kira stripped me off, then himself, and climbed into bed with me. He tucked me into his side, wrapped his arms around me, and the next thing I knew, it was morning.

***

THE NEXT WEEK, again, was hard. The physicality of it was getting a little easier, but Boss never stopped pushing me.

It was less on the conditioning, now that he knew where I was, and more on the fighting. I sparred more, with Cody and another guy, Amil. And on Friday, Boss put me up against Amil for what I told Kira had become Friday Fun Fight—Boss liked to run full sparring sessions to wrap up the week. So, with the usual audience of other fighters who wanted to see me get taken down, I donned my mouthpiece, headgear, and gloves, and climbed into the ring.

It was a good spar with Amil. He was a Middle Eastern guy, shorter but more powerful, and his tactics were different to Cody's or Kira's—he seemed more of a street fighter than a technical martial artist.

He knew, like I presumed all the guys here now did, my weakness was going to the floor. If he grappled me, he could take me out. He tried, of course, and he did get me to the floor, but I was saved by the end of the second three-minute round. In the third round, Amil lifted me by my thighs and drove me into the mats. I managed to maneuver out from under him, and jumping to my feet, I gave him a quick left hook to the jaw.

He stumbled back a bit and I put my hands up, faced forward and called, "Time." I took out my mouthpiece and walked over to him. "Shit, man, I'm sorry. Didn't mean to connect so hard." This was just a sparring round, after all.

He put his hand up, waving me off. "Nah, s'all good. We're not here for haircuts."

I put my mouthpiece back in and held up my fist, which he bumped with his. He put his hands up defensively, as did I, and he smiled. Then he kicked me full force in the side of the thigh. I pulled back and bounced on my toes, knowing that kick would leave a mark. I smiled back at him. Tit for tat.

He came in close, connecting his fists with my headgear, rattling my brain a little, and I kneed him hard in the ribs. I could hear the air leave his lungs.

"Right, boys," Boss called. The older man was smiling at us, knowing we'd hit a little harder than we should have.

Amil stood up straight, raised his hand in a fist, and I tapped it with mine, acknowledging the session was over. He smiled at me and gave me a nod, in what was the first sign of acceptance I'd had here.

Our audience clapped Amil on the back as he walked into the showers, as though congratulating him for getting some decent shots on me. Boss called me over. "Better today. Between now and next Friday, I want you to practice your floor techniques. We'll be focusing on grappling, because you're shit at it."

Still breathing hard, I managed a laugh. "I know I am."

Boss nodded. "Practice with your personal trainer if you have to, get yourself a grappling dummy or put a punching bag on the floor and practice kneeing it, punching it, and different holds," he said. Then he threw my towel at me. "Next Friday you're goin' in the cage."

Fuck.

Boss grinned at my expression. "I think you're ready for it. You need to let loose, and I need to see what you really got."

"Not a sparring session?"

He smiled and shook his head. "Nope. Real fight." He tapped my face. "Scared, pretty boy?"

"Nope," I lied outright. "I want it."

He grinned at that and turned to leave. As he walked away, he said his usual farewell, "Go shower. Go home."

Fuck. I was going in the cage. No sparring, no being nice. It was ultimately what I was there for—the underground fights Tressler ran to dispatch his cocaine were all cage fights. I wondered who I'd get pitched against, and as I looked around the floor, I found most of the other fighters were gone, which was odd.

I picked up my water bottle, wiped my face down with my towel, and headed toward the showers.

I soon found where all the other guys had gone.

The dressing room was a large tiled room with rows of showers along the end wall, a urinal and two cubicles on one sidewall, and lockers on the other. There was a long bench seat that ran down the middle.

There were about fifteen guys, all the other fighters, all crowded around the center bench seat, watching something on an iPad screen. They all looked up at me when I walked in, parting like the Red Sea so I got a clear line of sight to the small screen that had them all so intrigued.

And my stomach dropped to my feet.

On the small screen was the soundless CCTV footage of my old gym, of Kira, fighting off two assailants, of Tomic using a stun gun to bring him to the ground.

These guys were watching the footage of Kira being beaten before he was dragged off the screen. This footage was later released and screened on the six o'clock news, and two seconds after that, it was on the Internet, so getting access to it wasn't an issue.

My initial reaction was to fucking let them have it, but years of being a cop had taught me to keep a level head in bad situations. And to look at things from all angles before reacting.

They were watching this, not for any insight into Kira's fighting ability, they were watching it so I'd walk in and see them. They were watching this to get a reaction out of me, so they could either give me a beat down in the showers, or so I'd quit.

Well, they obviously didn't know me very well.

I sighed and wiped my towel over my face, pretty much not reacting at all.

But then one of the men, a guy by the name of Abel Koczur, stood up. They called him Arizona, after the state he came from. He was a big, bulked-up black man, and he held up the iPad and sneered at me. "Fights pretty good... for a *fag*."

There were a few stifled chuckles from the guys watching, but the air was suddenly tense. I scratched the back of my head. "That's nothing," I told him. "You should have seen the footage from the plane hangar." There was complete silence now. I threw the sweaty towel into my locker and picked up a clean one, turned to them all, and smiled. "You should have seen how he still fought them with his hands and feet bound, how he still managed to stop those assholes from doing God knows what to three women, even after they'd snapped his arm with a metal rod."

Every pair of eyes watched me strip down, wrap the new towel around my waist, and walk over to the showers. It went against my instinct to be naked around them, making myself vulnerable, but I needed them to see I wasn't intimidated or even fazed by them.

I picked the last shower, so if they came at me, it could

only be from one side. But they didn't. After not getting the reaction from me they were after, they disbanded. Arizona stared at me for a long, disgruntled minute, but he turned, handed the iPad to someone else, and stalked out.

I quickly scrubbed soap over my body and even through my hair, pretending to wash it, but really so the last few guys in the room wouldn't see my hands shake.

KIRA GOT home about an hour after me. He came into the kitchen and directly over to me. With a feather-light touch, he touched the reopened cut on my cheek and kissed me sweetly. "What happened?"

"Sparring."

"No, what's bothering you?"

I pushed him against the kitchen counter and pressed against him. I needed him to not move, not until I'd finished saying what I had to say. I took his face in my hands and said, "I need you to let me finish before you interrupt."

He looked at me concerned. "Matt, what is it?"

I took a deep breath. "After my sparring match, I walked into the showers. All the other guys were in there, waiting for me—"

"Matt, you're scaring me."

"No, it wasn't like that," I said quickly. "They were all in there watching some footage on a small screen."

He blinked, confused. "What?"

"They were watching the CCTV footage of you. When Tomic took you from the gym."

He went to move, to push me away, which was why I had him pinned to the counter. "Matt," he said, with warning in his tone.

"No, listen," I said, trying to calm him. "I know it sounds bad, but they weren't doing it... it wasn't about you. It was to get a reaction from me."

Anger flashed across his features. "Of course it was to get a reaction from you. Do you think I give a flying fuck who's seen that footage? Half the fucking world has seen that footage."

"So what are you so mad about?"

"You!" he cried. "You walked into that shower room full of guys just waiting for you? Jesus Christ, Matt, you know better than that! They could have... fuck, they could have killed you!"

I held his face so he looked directly at me and shook my head. "You know me, Kira. If I'd thought I was in serious danger, I'd have gotten out of there."

"They're trained to kill people with their hands, Matt!"

"So am I!"

He took some deep breaths, gathering his thoughts, and finally, he sighed. "What did they say?"

"The main guy, Arizona, tried to goad me a little," I admitted. "Said you fight pretty good... for a fag."

Kira's jaw bulged when he clenched his jaw. "And?"

"I told him the scene in the gym was nothing compared to how you kicked their asses at the airport hangar. I told them even with your feet and hands bound, you still fought them."

He shook his head a little. "Matt..."

"No, fuck them," I said quickly. "They should know." I shook my head and exhaled loudly. "I don't care about the names. They were just looking for a reaction from me, and they weren't gonna get one."

Kira sighed again, and when he relaxed against me, I

knew he wasn't angry anymore. "So you just cornered me against the kitchen counter to tell me?"

I nodded and gave him half a smile. "I knew if you could pace, you'd yell, then I'd yell. But if I kept you still, you'd have to listen."

He growled playfully at me. "I still don't like it, that you faced them like that," he said. "But thank you for telling me."

And just like that, his absolute faith in me knotted in my chest.

He ran his thumb across the cut under my eye. "You got hit again."

I smiled at him. "Sparred against Amil today," I told him. "Oh, and next Friday I go into the cage."

Kira blinked, shocked, but his lips curled up in a smile. "Really?"

I nodded. "Yep. Boss said I've got a week to work on my grappling because my floor skills need work."

"But you've always said your floor techniques weren't your strongest."

"And it shows," I told him. "I mean, Cody and Amil have taken me down twice, and both times I've gotten out of it."

"We can work on it this weekend," Kira said. He double-checked his work roster, which was stuck by a magnet to the fridge. "I have to work on Saturday, but I'm off on Sunday and we can spend a bit of time on it every afternoon."

And that was what we did.

Kira got home mid-afternoon on Saturday and after he'd relaxed for a while and had some downtime on the couch, he suggested we spend some time on floor techniques in the spare room, which we'd turned into our own gym.

Which started out just fine. We moved the weights over to the wall and cleared the floor space, spread the mats down, and stripped off our shirts.

"Okay, first up, we'll practice you being taken to the floor and how to avoid it. So I'm gonna try and get you on the mat, and we'll run through some techniques to get you out of it." Kira's focus when he trained was impeccable. He took his job seriously, and I was really only now beginning to see why. "Because if being grappled is not your forte, then it makes sense to not get in that position."

We ran through different standing positions, where an opponent might try and take me down, and Kira demonstrated how to move my body to resist.

He was in such good shape. His body was taut and defined, and his muscles outlined him perfectly. It was different training with him. I could train with guys at the FC all day long and not feel anything, but as soon as a semi-naked Kira stood in the ready-to-fight position, as soon as his hands were touching me, his arms were around me, even pushing and shoving, tapping and kneeing, I was getting turned on by him.

I didn't know why, but these last few weeks, I hadn't been able to get enough of him. I wanted him all the damn time. I wanted *him* to have *me* all the damn time.

And training with him now was no different.

He was hot and sweaty, and although he was focused, he kept smiling at me. And I couldn't deny it—he turned me on. I tried to shake it off, ignore it. But it was hard.

I was getting hard.

Then Kira unhooked the punching bag and laid it on the floor but pushed it aside. "Okay, get on the floor."

"How do you want me?"

"Matt," he warned playfully. "I'm trying to teach you something."

"You are," I told him. "But it's not my fault you're so hot."

He grinned and pointed to the floor. "On your back."

Smiling, I got down on the floor like he asked. "Well, it is my favorite."

He rolled his eyes and ignored me. We went through some floor positions and how I could twist, elbow, move my head, and use my knees or my opponent's own weight against them to get out of being hammered into the floor mats.

He lay over me and I wrapped my legs around him. He put his forearm across my neck and pushed down. "How do you get out of it?"

I tightened my legs around his waist and lifted my hips into his so he could feel how hard I was getting. Kira raised one eyebrow at me and shifted one of his knees into my inner thigh, pinning my hips to the floor.

"You certainly won't do that to anyone else."

I chuckled. "No one else turns me on."

"Good," he said. Then changing the subject back to the training, he said, "Now use your knees to throw me off."

Just like he'd shown me, I pushed with my knees and used his weight to put him off balance. I followed with the momentum and ended up on top of him, wrestling him on the floor.

He rolled us again, throwing me off, and somehow I ended up face down. Kira was over me, lightly pushing my head into the floor, so I tried pulling his arm so he was covering me completely.

Except it didn't work.

"You're overthinking it."

I couldn't help but chuckle. "I was trying to get you on top of me."

"You're supposed to be pushing me away."

I wiggled underneath him. "Where's the fun in that?"

He pulled away and slapped my ass. "Bring the bag over," he said, nodding toward the punching bag on the floor.

I pouted at him but did as he asked.

He ignored me. "Now pin it down with your left forearm, and punch it with your right and knee the shit out of it."

I did as he said, but not correctly, apparently.

"Use your weight to hold your opponent down," he said. Then he was behind me and he tapped my left thigh. "This leg is too far out. Means your center of gravity is off and you'll get thrown too easily."

I could feel him behind me. He was on his knees.

"Put your hips down," he said. "Pin him completely." Then he pushed on my hip, flattening me into the punching bag.

I moaned.

"Fuck."

I don't know which one of us said it.

Kira's voice was gruff. "Straddle it."

I lifted my right leg and straddled the punching bag on the floor, my cock hard. He was quiet, so I prompted him. "Now what?"

He didn't speak, he just moved over and straddled the bag behind me. "Fucking hell," he said with a groan. He pressed himself against me. "You look so hot right now."

I laughed out a groan. "See? I'm not the only one."

He ran his hands over my back and down to my hips as

he kissed between my shoulder blades. Then he ground his hard-on against my ass.

I was horny as hell already, but to be straddling the punching bag on the floor and him behind me was a new sensation. Almost like there was a third body with us.

I arched my back, offering him my ass. "Fuck."

He started to grind and thrust, gripping my hips while he pressed me against the punching bag.

"Jesus," Kira rasped. "Matt, bedroom" was all he said before he was on his feet and lifting me to mine.

He didn't even wait to get me on the bed. We only got *to* the bed before he just pushed me, bending me over the side of it.

He kept one hand on my back, and I heard the familiar sound of the bedside table drawer opening. Then he pulled my shorts over my hips, exposing my ass to him, and with rushed, slick, clumsy fingers, he tried to ready me.

But I was too impatient. I was too turned on, too needy. I replaced his fingers with my own. "Fuck, Kira. Hurry."

I heard the foil tear, and he moaned, soon batting my hand away. He aligned his cockhead, pressed against my hole, then he was slowly sinking inside me. He gasped again and again. "Fuck. Fuck."

There wasn't a feeling like it, being filled by him. Having him take me, claim me, fuck me.

Still wearing my sparring gloves, with my shorts around my thighs, I let Kira push me up onto the bed. He dug his fingers into my hips and drove himself into me, over and over, brushing against my prostate until I came.

He followed soon after, pressing me into the mess on the mattress. As he came back to earth, Kira kissed the back of my head, my shoulder, my neck, and I couldn't help but chuckle underneath him. I felt him smile as he pressed his lips against my skin. "Something funny?"

"Just thinking we're lucky you don't train me at the FC, or we'd have given them something to talk about."

Kira chuckled and kissed my neck before pulling out and rolling to one side. He threw the used condom in the wastepaper bin beside the bed. "You were hopeless," he said with a smile and clicked his tongue. "Turned on during training."

I laughed. "I wasn't the only one, apparently."

"You started it!"

I stretched out and groaned. "And you finished it."

Kira moaned and bit me lightly on the shoulder. "I think we need to shower."

I peeled myself off the sticky bed cover. "I think we need to clean this bedspread."

"You throw it in the washing machine while I have a quick shower," he said. "Then you can get in while I order some dinner."

"Aren't we showering together?"

Kira's head lolled back and he groaned. "No! Jeez, Matt, you're insatiable lately."

"I can't help it! It's your fault for being so good-looking."

I swear I heard his eyes roll from the hallway.

But all showered, with dinner eaten and the bedspread in the dryer, we lay on the sofa and watched some TV. I was lying with my head on Kira's lap, while he traced his fingers through my hair. I was out like a light before the first commercial break.

MONDAY at the gym was normal. Boss had me working

out, then practicing boxing, wrestling, and Mauy Thai. It was physical and intense, but I enjoyed it. There was an excitement around the gym about the upcoming fight on Friday.

They were all excited to see me lose.

The guy I was scheduled to fight, Arizona, eyeballed me, trying to stare me down and intimidate me. I ignored him, and that seemed to piss him off even more.

I saw the owner, my reason for putting myself through this, Leon Tressler. He was standing at the door to the admin area, just watching me.

I pretended not to notice, or not to care, and kept up with my training. Boss was busy barking orders at me, so my focus was on my trainer, but Tressler was definitely watching me.

I wondered what he knew, what he'd found out. If he somehow knew my reason for being there wasn't to fight at all. I didn't doubt he knew. I just wondered what he'd do about it.

Tuesday was much the same. Though I didn't have a scheduled appointment, I went anyway and spent hours working out. Boss was doing his thing with other guys, but I knew he was keeping tabs on what I was routine I was up to.

On Wednesday, he put me in the cage for a sparring session with Cody.

It was actually my first time being in the cage as a competitor. I'd seen plenty, even done some sparring in one. But never actually fought.

It was daunting. The eight-sided structure had walls of black vinyl-covered chain-link fence. It was a standard size, with a diameter of thirty-two feet. The fence was about five foot eight and the cage itself sat atop a platform, raised four feet from the ground. The cage had two entry-exit gates opposite each other, and it sent a shiver down my spine when I walked into it.

It was a fucking rush.

I'd practiced up against the heavily padded wall in the sparring corner, but never against the cage wall, so Boss had me do that first, just to get a feel for it.

Arizona was there, of course, watching me.

Boss was fit for his age and strong as an ox. He put on thigh pads and held the kick pad and pushed me into the cage fence. It was my instinct to go easy on the older guy, but he gave as good as he got. He was a hard old bastard.

Then he had me pin him to the fence while he kneed and punched me to get away, but I held him. He called time and gave me an approving smile and held up his fist.

I bumped mine to his, and I thought he was starting to like me.

Even respect me.

Arizona, on the other hand, goaded me every chance he got. It started with simple name-calling, the ever-present glare, and the occasional shoulder if the opportunity presented itself in a hallway.

Oh, he threatened me. He called me 'fag' repeatedly, and promised to smack the gay right out of me, but I just smiled at him. He was doing it to psych me out, to get a reaction.

Which I had every intention of giving to him. Inside the cage.

I told Kira about Arizona's slurs and threats, and he surprisingly took the news okay. He didn't like it, but he understood the psychology of it all. He knew it was part of the game. Kira was more concerned that I'd watched Arizona practice and spar so I knew *his* game. I assured him I had, and it was really nothing to worry about.

But he told me he was coming to watch, whether I fucking liked it or not.

We ran through practice shots, breathing techniques, and even more floor grappling which usually ended in the bedroom. It was physical, rough. It was perfect.

I needed it.

Kira seemed to know it. He always knew what I needed.

I GOT to the club on Friday, nervous but excited. I was ready for my first bout in the cage. I was ready to prove myself. I went through my normal training routine and Boss kept me focused. He knew I was nervous, but he knew I was up for it.

But with about two hours to go before the fight, Leon Tressler stood at the admin door, watching me. One of his fridge-sized men came over and told me Mr. Tressler would like to see me.

I looked to Boss, and upon his nod, followed the man into his office. I knew the second I walked in that there were two henchmen, possibly armed—one at the right of Tressler, one in front of the door we'd just came through. There was a chair I could use as ammunition if required, the window was big enough for me to get out of if it came to it.

It was ingrained in me to assess every room I walked into, knowing I had an exit plan if needed.

I had been called in here for a specific reason. It was a good development, but it made me nervous. I looked at Tressler expectantly and gave him a smile.

He stood, leaning against his desk, and his face was stoic. "What exactly are you doing here?"

Every cell in my body was on alert, though I made sure

my face gave nothing away. This was a very good first step to where I wanted this case to go. "What do you mean?"

He smiled like he was explaining something to a child. "I want to know what a cop is doing training in my gym."

"*Ex*-cop," I told him. "I got out."

"Why?"

I shrugged. "I... I had some issues that weren't *conducive* to police work," I lied convincingly.

"Issues with what?"

And here it was. The first stepping-stone. "I have a tendency to be violent."

He stared at me for a long moment. "So you thought cage fighting was what, an outlet?"

"Yeah. My division boss sent me to a therapist, who suggested I try using the sport as an outlet for aggression management," I half-lied. "I found that it was a better fit for me than police work."

He tilted his head. "Aggression, you say?"

I nodded. "I was on my last warning for touching up some collars."

Tressler's eyebrow flickered. "That's not how the media portrayed you."

I laughed. "The media portray what they're paid to sell."

He smiled. "They sure do."

"Is that all, sir?" I said, adding the 'sir' as a show of respect. "I have a fight in a few hours and Boss will have my hide if I'm not ready."

Tressler smirked. "Who are you fighting?"

"Arizona."

He lifted one eyebrow, pleasantly surprised. "I'll make sure I watch."

I grinned. "I'm looking forward to it."

He stood up straight from leaning on his desk. "I can't wait to see these 'violence issues' in action."

I grinned at him, turned, and walked out. *Fuck, fuck, fuck.*

Boss eyed me cautiously when I walked over to him. "Everything cool?"

I gave him a smile and a nod. "Yeah, it's cool."

"Okay," he said dismissively. "You're as ready as you're gonna be. You need to get in the dressing rooms, get some rest. You'll warm up for about half an hour beforehand."

One hour to wind down sounded easy, but Arizona shared the same dressing room, separated only by one wall. It wasn't exactly soundproof. So for one hour, I had to listen to him.

"Ready to tap out, fag?"

"Did ya kiss your boyfriend goodbye this morning?"

"Not gonna be so pretty when I'm finished with ya."

It went on and on until I put in my earbuds and drowned him out with music.

When I was dressed and getting strapped, Boss told Arizona to cut it out and told me to ignore him. I laughed. "Don't worry about it, Boss," I said. "I got him covered."

Boss looked at me seriously and spoke quietly. "Keep your head down, your hands up. Don't let him take you to the floor."

I nodded and took his warning.

"Right, boys!" Boss called out, making sure Arizona heard him. "Fight time."

I walked out into the main gym floor, surprised by the number of people there to watch. No doubt they weren't there to see me win.

Except one man. Kira sat at one side and gave me a nod as I walked to the cage.

Walking into the cage, knowing it was to fight, was almost surreal. There was a buzz in the air and people were talking. We had about ten minutes or so before the bell went. I spent the time bouncing on my toes, keeping my adrenaline pumping.

Arizona was relaxed and cocky as he mouthed off, something about fighting fairies. I looked to Kira, saw his jaw bulging and gave him a smile.

When the referee called us into the center and warned us about fair fights and how long the rounds would be, I wasn't too concerned. I had no intention of letting it go that far.

The bell rang, the referee called, "Fight," and Arizona came back to the middle of the cage, all smiling and smug.

I bounced out on my toes, keeping light on my feet, with one thing on my mind.

Tressler wanted someone with violence issues? Then that was what he'd get.

So without warning, in the first few seconds of the first round, when Arizona was expecting a few test jabs, I round-house-kicked him in the side of the head.

But I didn't stop then. I followed him to the ground, pinned his chest with my knee and punched his face until the referee pulled me off him.

I looked around me. Arizona was an unconscious, bloody mess on the mats, the crowd was in shocked silence. Kira was on his feet, wide-eyed and stunned.

Tressler, who was standing in his usual spot at the far wall watching the fight, looked at me and smiled.

CHAPTER FIVE

____

I WAS SITTING on the physio table in the dressing rooms, letting Boss unwrap my hands. "Well." He shook his head, still shocked. "I wasn't expecting that."

I smiled. "Neither was Arizona."

Boss chuckled. "Nope. Don't think they'll be giving you a hard time again," he said, pulling the tape off my hands. "Not now that they've seen you in action."

I shrugged. "We'll see."

He unwrapped the last of the tape and held up my right hand. "Sore?"

I open and shut my hand and wiggled my fingers. It was a little sore. "Not really."

Then Boss picked up my right foot and peeled off the ankle guard. "How's the kicking foot?"

"It's fine."

"Because you fucking kicked him hard."

I laughed, and there was a soft knock on the open door. Kira stuck his head in. "Can I come in?"

Boss looked at me and smiled but answered Kira, "Yep,

come in." He pulled off the left ankle guard and said, "I'm done."

I smiled at Kira. "Hey."

"Hey."

Boss rolled his eyes at us but asked Kira, "What did ya think of the fight?"

Kira looked at me and shook his head. He still seemed stunned. "Um, it was quick."

Boss laughed. "Quick? It didn't even start!"

I chuckled. "It started just fine. It just ended sooner than anticipated."

Boss smiled and clapped his hand on my thigh. "Right. I'm off. See you Monday," he said. He nodded to Kira. "Next time."

Kira was quiet for a long moment. I watched him trying to find the right way to say whatever it was he had to say. "You, um," he started. "You okay?"

"I'm fine."

"Jesus, Matt," he said quietly. He shook his head. "You were a little scary out there."

I gave him a smile. "It was always my game plan," I told him. "I needed to prove something to these guys. I needed them to take me seriously. I couldn't let him take me to the floor."

"Fuck," he said with a loud exhale. "You smashed his nose in."

"Before he could do it to me."

Kira nodded. "I know." He picked up my hand. "Is it sore?"

"A little," I answered honestly. I wriggled my fingers. "Nothing broken."

"Good."

I jumped off the table. "You ready to go?"

"Yeah."

"Good. I'm starving. I can shower at home, but I just need to grab my bag. Come on, it's through here." I lead the way.

I walked through to the main dressing room where there were quite a few guys. They stopped their chatter and looked at me, then to Kira, who had followed me in. I waved my hand toward him. "This is Kira," I told them. "The one you watched in the CCTV footage beat the crap out of those three guys." There was a silence, so I looked at each of them. "Yes, we're together. Does anyone have a fucking problem with that?"

They collectively shook their heads. Didn't think they would.

Then Cody stood up, walked over to me, and held out his fist. "Fucking awesome fight, man."

I grinned at him. "Thanks."

"Not gonna do that to me, are ya?" he asked. "We just spar, right?"

I laughed. "Nah, you're all right."

Then Amil, who I'd only sparred with a handful of times, stood up and clapped his hand on my shoulder. "Good fight."

"Thanks." I looked around. "Where's Arizona?"

One of the other guys gave a pointed nod toward the back room where the medical gear was stored. I walked over and stuck my head around the door. Arizona was sitting on a bench seat that ran along the back wall with a bag of ice over his face. There was a pile of bloodied swabs in the trash and bloodied towels on the floor.

Jesus.

"Hey," I said. "Up for visitors?"

Arizona lifted the bag of ice from his face. His nose was

swollen and had a new dent. Both eyes were already blackening. "Yeah," he croaked.

"You okay?"

"Yeah."

"How's the nose?"

"Broken."

"Sorry."

"Don't apologize," he said. He looked at me, then to Kira, who was behind me. He took some deep breaths and after a while, he nodded. "You know, you fight okay."

I smiled at his compliment. "You mean, for a fag."

Arizona smirked then winced in pain and groaned out a laugh. He put the ice back on his face and mumbled, "Yep."

I considered this a victory—that he'd admitted I 'fight okay' was an admission of respect, no matter how small. But I wasn't sure what else to say. "Anything I can get for you?"

He took a while to answer. "A time machine."

Kira laughed behind me and even I chuckled. "Huh?"

Arizona mumbled from under the bag of ice, "Then maybe I might get to see your foot comin' at me."

I laughed at that, but then I walked over to him and held out my hand. He took the ice off his face and gave me a nod and shook my hand.

"See ya next week," I said.

He put the ice back on his face and let his head rest on the wall behind him. "Yeah, I'll be here."

I walked back through the dressing room with Kira, though instead of silence or snickers, I got the occasional nod of acceptance. And as I walked through the main gym floor, Boss was already going through the motions with his next student. But Tressler stopped talking to two other men in suits, smiled at me, and watched me leave.

WE WERE EATING dinner at the kitchen counter. "Did you want to talk about it?" Kira asked.

I swallowed my mouthful of food. "Talk about what?"

"Matt," he said softly. He stood up, walked over to me, and took my hand. "Tonight, when you were in that cage, you were... different."

"I told you," I said again. "I couldn't let him get me first."

"You were a little frightening."

I kissed the palm of his hand and took the emphasis off me. "Now you know how I feel when I see you train."

He smiled and shook his head. "You know what I mean. You were brutal tonight. The referee had to pull you off him."

I looked away and speared another forkful of food and shoveled it into my mouth. I knew he saw through me. He knew me too well.

He played with my fingers. "What aren't you telling me?"

I pushed my plate away. "Nothing," I replied a little sharply. *Fuck.* I sighed and started again. "Nothing, babe. I was keyed up for my first fight, that's all. It was an adrenaline rush." And just like that, the lies got easier. I got up and put my plate in the sink. "Plus, like I told you before, I needed to prove myself out there tonight. If I got hammered, I'd be the laughing stock of the whole club."

Kira leaned against the counter and looked right at me. "They're not laughing at you now."

I smiled at him. "No, they're not."

Kira shook his head and couldn't help but smile back at me. "Well, you looked good."

I walked over to where he was, stood in front of him, and leaned my hips into his. "Scary, but good," I repeated his words.

His beautiful almond-shaped eyes, dark brown and all-seeing, stared into mine. His perfect lips parted, and he nodded. I gently cupped his face and pressed my lips to his. Kira's ability to be fierce and lethal and equally gentle had always amazed me, and I wanted to be the same for him.

I didn't move to deepen the kiss. I kept it soft and sweet and my fingers were feather-light on his cheek. "Thank you for being there tonight."

"You're welcome."

I was just about to apologize for how erratic my life had been these last few weeks when his cell phone rang. Kira pulled the phone from his pocket, saw who was calling, and answered with a smiling eye roll. "Hey, Mom."

I heard Yumi's muffled voice through the phone and Kira nodded, waiting for his window of opportunity to speak. "Well, it wasn't exactly what I'd call a fight... No, Mom, he's fine... Stop, Mom. Listen, he's right here..." Kira gave up with a sigh and just handed the phone over to me.

"Hi, Yumi."

"Oh, Matt," she started. "How are you? Kira say there was no fight. I thought you were fighting tonight. That's why I call. To make sure you're okay."

I took a deep breath, listening to her speed-talk, and lifted myself so I sat on the kitchen counter with Kira between my legs.

I explained to Yumi that the fight had been over in less than ten seconds and I'd been the one who ended it. I reassured her he'd never touched me; I was completely unharmed.

Kira rolled his eyes and sighed at how protective his

mother was of me, but truthfully, I loved it. I'd never realized how much I missed my mom until I'd met Yumi. I lifted my knees higher and wrapped my legs around Kira's hips, pulling him into me.

"Oh, no, Yumi, not a scratch, not a bruise, not a mark," I told her. Then I hooked my ankles around each other and wriggled against Kira, putting my hand over the mouthpiece, and whispered to him, "Not yet, anyway."

He shook his head at me, but as Yumi explained that she and Sal were worried sick about me, Kira started to kiss my shoulder, my collarbone, and up my neck.

"I could come around to check on you," Yumi said, and I could imagine her already grabbing her handbag, ushering poor Sal out the door.

Kira licked my neck up to my ear. "No!" I barked gruffly into the phone. "Yumi, that's not necessary. Thanks, but Kira's looking after me just fine."

Maybe it was the husky tone of my voice or Kira's too-close chuckle, but there was a silence on the phone, then, "Oh. Ew, I not want details. You two be here for lunch tomorrow." The phone clicked off in my ear and I slid it across the countertop.

Kira laughed and slipped his fingers under the elastic of my lounge pants and skimmed the skin of my ass. "You're not too sore?"

I pulled his hips harder into mine. "No."

Kira groaned. "Then maybe I'm not fucking you hard enough."

I knew he said it as a joke, but his words sparked a fire in my belly. I released my legs from around his waist, jumped down, and dragged him toward the bedroom. "Challenge accepted."

———

THE NEXT WEEK at the FC was good. I'd wondered how I'd be received when I turned up on Monday, but there were nods and smiles, even the occasional hello. The other guys took me seriously now, and that was half my battle.

Boss still trained me one-on-one, but he threw me in with the group round in the second week. I sparred with some of the other guys, even talked a bit, and for all intents and purposes, they treated me like one of the boys.

Kira said he wasn't surprised I thrived on their acceptance. "Going from one boys' club to the next. You loved being with the Fab Four, and now you've got another group of soldiers," he said with a loving smile and told me there was nothing wrong with that. It was just who I was, he said. I needed to be accepted, to be liked. I didn't know if there was any truth to that theory, but I certainly couldn't argue it.

But the more I got to know the boys I sparred with, the deeper I got. No, they weren't clean-cut, model citizens like Mitch, Kurt, and Tony. They'd lived very different lives, some with street stories that, even for a cop, were harsh to hear. But they were a band of brothers.

Just like my fellow police officers, these guys I fought with were loyal, respectful to-the-death kind of men.

Leon Tressler, on the other hand, was a different story.

Over the two weeks after he'd watched me fight Arizona, he'd been eyeing me. Keeping tabs on my training, on my sparring sessions, on how I interacted with the others.

I pretended I didn't notice. I pretended not to see the looks, not to hear the murmurs of excitement about something going down.

I pretended not to give a shit.

But halfway through the second week, he called me into his office. "Saw your anger management issues the other night," he said.

I nodded but chose to stay silent.

"I was surprised."

I treated that as a compliment. "Thank you."

He nodded thoughtfully. "I've done some asking around about you. Some cops aren't as loyal as you might think."

Fuck. I acted like I didn't care. "Huh."

"Mmm, don't get me wrong," he said. "I have no problem with you wanting to fight here." He stepped closer to me and looked me in the eye. "But I have to wonder if there's an ulterior motive."

"I just want to fight," I told him like I was bored with this conversation. "If you don't want me here, then I'll go somewhere else."

Tressler stared at me for a long, quiet moment. "Hmm, you can stay. For now," he said, and dismissively went back to his desk.

I got to the door and stopped. "Tell me it wasn't O'Rourke you asked for all the dirty secrets on me, because he hates me."

Tressler looked at me and cocked his head, waiting for me to explain.

"He hasn't liked me since the Christmas party two years ago when he asked me to tie him up and spank him, and I turned him down. So yeah, he never liked me after that."

Tressler's eyes widened just a fraction before he composed himself. I needed him to know I wasn't threatened, and I behaved like I had nothing to hide. So I gave him a huge grin and walked out.

I chuckled to myself and made a mental note to tell

Mitch that if he heard any rumors about O'Rourke, they hadn't come from me.

When I walked back out, Amil eyed me a little cautiously. I knew he wanted to say something, but considering the four other guys in our sparring group, he chose not to.

"Everything okay?" Boss asked me in front of the others. He was a no-secrets, no-nonsense kind of guy. "That's twice he's called you in there."

"Don't think he trusts me," I answered as honestly as I could. "You know, he just wanted to know why I was here, being an ex-cop and all."

The other five guys in our group stopped and looked at me, but it was Boss who spoke. "What'd you tell him?"

"I told him I'm just here to fight. That's all I want to do."

One of the other guys, a tall black man who I guessed was in his early twenties, Isiah, asked, "Why did you stop being a cop?" He looked at me unapologetically. "I mean no disrespect, just wanna know what made you give up a job like that? With full medical, full benefits, full retirement."

They all waited for my answer, Boss included. "Besides getting shot at? Besides having my partner tortured?" I asked rhetorically. I jabbed the punching bag a few times before holding it still and looking at them. "I didn't want it to be the only thing I ever was." I shrugged. "I didn't want it to define me."

"I thought it was 'once a cop, always a cop'?" Benji asked.

I smiled ruefully. "For some, maybe. The ones who are in for life. But not me." I sighed and figured I'd show the human side of me. "I joined young, when my mom died. They were like my family, but then they found out I was gay…" I let my words hang in the air. "Even my old partner, he was a great guy, but things were never the same with him after that."

My little audience all nodded, probably not too sure what to say.

I jabbed the punching bag a few times, looked at them, and gave them my best smug smirk. "And then there were my anger management issues."

Boss laughed at that. "Yeah, we've seen those."

I grinned at him and went back to my practice jabs and strikes. The other guys, Amil, Cody, Benji, Isiah, and Jamaal, all smiled and went back to their training too.

And just like that, the lies became easier.

It scared me just how easy it was.

I hit the punching bag a little harder, trying to beat down the feeling that, with every lie I told, there was no going back.

CHAPTER SIX

ARIZONA LOOKED LIKE SHIT. Actually, he looked like he'd been kicked and punched repeatedly in the side of the head. Over the two weeks after the fight, his bruising and swelling faded, but he never stopped training.

He was a hard man. A good man. Kira had been worried Arizona might try and get some revenge for the beating I gave him, but it was the opposite of that. I'd won his respect.

I was scheduled to fight again on Friday, and Arizona had even helped with talking me through techniques. Yes, I'd beaten him in one fight with the element of surprise, but he had more experience for the long haul.

The guy I was fighting I hadn't seen fight before. He was a white, blond man, not particularly good looking, or even friendly looking, for that matter. I'd seen him spar a little bit, and I'd seen him around the FC but had no idea of his game plan.

I had no idea what his real name was, but they called him Truck. Apparently, the name was derived from how he hit. Like a truck.

When I stepped into the cage again on Friday night, I

knew I had no element of surprise. This Truck guy had seen me fight Arizona apparently, so he was expecting me to try and take him out early, to avoid going three rounds.

It was a more tactical fight. We danced around each other, sizing the other up. He was taller than me, so his reach was longer, which meant my best option was with my feet. I took a lot of punches to the ribs and kicks to the thighs, and the first round was more of a tester.

But his namesake served him well. And as we broke at the end of the first round, I was sure of one thing. I didn't want to go another fucking round with him.

So when we bumped fists to start the second round, I swept his leg out from under him and took him to the floor. It was risky because if he got out of it and pinned me, it was all over, but I bent his leg around in a direction it shouldn't strictly bend. He had to tap out, or I'd snap his leg.

He pushed against me and tried to punch me in return, so I changed angles and not long after he tapped the mat.

I'd just won my second cage fight.

I had a cut eye, a bruised thigh, and a skull-cracking headache to show for it. But I was now officially two wins to nil losses, and my place within the FC as a new fighter was pretty well established.

SITTING AT THE DINING TABLE, Kira bathed the cut at the corner of my eye and iced my thigh. His concern and attentiveness should have warmed me, should have reinforced my love for him.

But the nicer he was, the harder the guilt was to wear.

I told him he didn't have to baby me, but he shook his head. "I like doing it," he said softly, with a kiss to my swollen eye. "Anyway, you look kinda sexy with some war wounds."

"I'll keep that in mind next time I'm getting right hooks to the face."

Kira shook his head, then put a bag of ice on my thigh. "Your leg is gonna be sore as hell tomorrow."

"So is my head."

Kira frowned. "I'll get you some Tylenol," he said, putting my hand on the bag of ice on my thigh. "Here, hold this."

He came back with two tablets and a glass of water, sat down, and took over holding the bag of ice.

"You don't have to be so nice to me," I said.

Kira blinked. "Why wouldn't I want to be nice to you?" he asked.

"I signed up for this," I said, as an excuse. "I knew there'd be injuries."

Kira studied the cut at my eye again and smiled to himself. "Doesn't mean I can't *be nice* to you." Then he shook his head a little. "I can't believe you said I shouldn't be so nice to you. Of course I'll be nice to you, I'm your boyfriend."

I chuckled at him. "Okay, I apologize. Wrong choice of words."

"I should think so," he said, happier. "Now take your tablets like a good boy. I'll go run you a bath." And with that, he kissed the side of my head and walked to the bathroom.

I was lying to him, every second of every day, and he was so nice to me. So loving. So perfect.

I swallowed down the two tablets he gave me, then swallowed down my guilt. I needed to compartmentalize. I needed to do my fucking job.

"Bath's almost ready," he called out from the bathroom.

With a pounding head and a heavy heart, I hobbled down the hallway.

***

OVER THE NEXT WEEK, there was whispered talk at the FC of an upcoming fight. An unscheduled, unsanctioned fight. The exact type of fight I needed to be invited to.

But it was still too early, and if I asked too many questions or even *any* questions, I could risk raising suspicion. So I kept my head down but listened to the buzz around me.

From what I could understand, it was scheduled for Saturday. No one knew where or exactly what time, but I heard one name mentioned.

Arizona.

I needed to let Mitch know, not that I knew anything in detail or had any proof, but I needed him to know things were happening. But I was also concerned for the man who would fight. He still had some bruising, and I worried his face wasn't healed enough.

After our sparring session on Friday, I cautioned him as vaguely as I could. "Sure you're ready? Your eye socket's not a hundred percent."

He smiled like I had no idea, and he rubbed his thumb against his index and middle fingers in the sign for money. "Got a wife and kid, man," was all he said.

And I understood. He was trying to support his family the only way he knew how. By fighting. By putting his body, his life, on the line in underground, dangerous cage fights.

Just like Cody who lived with his unemployed parents, or Amil who had a wife and two kids, or Jamaal who lived with his two school-aged brothers. They were just people trying to get by.

Underground fights were unsanctioned and very dangerous. There were no rules in underground cage fighting. It wasn't fight-to-the-death, but there were no UFC guidelines. It was a mixed martial arts free-for-all where bets were made on the man likely to still be standing at the end of three rounds. And it was against the law.

But nabbing the likes of Arizona and other fighters was not my concern. I had bigger fish to fry. Tressler had been using these underground fights as dispatch centers for trafficking his supply of cocaine. That was who we were after. Whoever fell in the crossfire when we brought Tressler down was not my concern.

Well, it wasn't supposed to be my concern. But I liked these guys. The more time I spent with them, the more vulnerable they were to me. They were just guys trying to make a living to support their families.

And the realization that I felt empathy for these men should have been warning to get out then.

But I was in. I had a foot in the door. I was close.

I just had to find out when and where without looking like I was fishing for information.

"Look, Arizona," I said. "I get that you need money. Hell, we all do. But your eye's not great." It was still bruised and the eye itself was still a little bloodshot. "You sure it's worth it?"

He shrugged one shoulder. "It'll be all right. Might try your tactic and not let him get one on me."

I gave him half a smile, very aware I was probably not supposed to know he was scheduled to fight. I had to tread carefully. "Do you know who you're fighting?" I asked casually. "You seen him train? Know his tactics? What his background is, whether he's a jujitsu, boxer, wrestler?"

Arizona smiled at me. "Nah, I don't know. Normally find out on the night," he said. "But thanks. I like the way you think."

I snorted. "'Bout time all that cop training paid off, huh?"

He nodded thoughtfully and was quiet for a moment. "How ya finding it? I mean, the change. Do ya miss it?"

I sighed. "Kind of. Not the work. But I miss the money. Going from full pay to none is hard. My savings won't last long."

He snorted sarcastically. "You got savings?"

I chuckled. "Had, but it's disappearing pretty quick."

Then Boss called out, "Elliot?" He was across the gym with his clipboard in his hand.

"Yeah, Boss?"

"You're up!"

"Who you fightin'?" Arizona asked me quietly.

"Marco, apparently."

"Watch his left foot," he murmured.

I smiled. "Yeah, he sweeps. I've seen."

He turned, and as he walked away, he said, "Thought you might have."

MY FRIDAY NIGHT fight was a little earlier than normal—I presumed because of the underground fight—and Kira had to work. I offered to pick him up from the city, but he said he'd just see me at home.

He had the weekend off, and I was thankful. These last few weeks had been crazy and I just wanted some downtime with him. I wanted to curl up on the sofa, lie in bed, go for a walk, to the movies, whatever. I wanted to connect with him.

When he came through the door, he found me in the kitchen, trying to cook dinner. He walked straight up to me and gently touched my eyebrow. "Is it sore?"

The concern and love in his eyes made my heart thump. I shook my head. "No." I took his chin in between my thumb and forefinger and pulled his lips to mine.

He kissed me soundly, and when he pulled away, his tongue swept across his bottom lip and he hummed. Then he looked at the mess. "What are you making?"

"Dinner."

"Oh, really?"

"Don't sound so disappointed."

Kira chuckled and pecked his lips to mine. "It looks more like a mess than dinner."

"The mess I have perfected," I admitted proudly. "The dinner, not so much."

He looked at the various ingredients strewn across the counter. "You know, stir-fries aren't *that* difficult."

"Well, it is when I'm trying to chop up vegetables and my hand's a little sore."

Kira grabbed my right hand and inspected the knuckles, then looked into my eyes, just as concerned. "What happened?"

"I won my fight," I said with a smile. "Just bruised my knuckles, that's all." I flexed my fingers to prove nothing was broken.

He shook his head. "Matt..."

I took back my hand. "Hey, can you grab the noodles out of the fridge? I've got them soaking. They should be separated by now. Are you hungry? Because I'm starving."

"Did you want to talk about the fight?" he asked, opening the fridge door. "Tell me how it went."

"I'll tell you about it later," I conceded. "But I was thinking about this weekend. I thought maybe we could rip up that old garden bed like you wanted to, and maybe have your parents around for a cookout on Sunday."

Kira put the bowl on the counter. "Why?"

"Well, your mom called..."

He rolled his eyes. "Did she threaten bodily harm if she didn't see us?"

"Pretty much," I said with a smile. "Here, taste this." I offered him a spoon of marinade. "I can't get it right."

Kira gave me a warm smile, the type that crinkled the corners of his eyes. He tasted my stir-fry sauce. "Needs more soy."

"I can't make it like you," I mumbled, turning back to my mess and adding a dash more soy to the bowl.

Kira wrapped his arms around my waist and kissed the side of my neck. I melted into him and sighed. "I've missed you," I whispered.

"Missed me?" he questioned, teasing my skin with his lips. "Matt, we've been going at it like rabbits for weeks."

I turned in his arms. "No, I've missed *you*."

His eyes searched mine. "What do you mean?"

I shrugged a little. "I just miss you. It seems like forever since we've just been... I don't know, us."

Kira agreed. "It's been kind of crazy since you started at the FC."

"It has," I conceded. I slipped my arms around him and just held him against me. I kissed the side of his neck. "I just want to spend some time with you this weekend. No fighting, no training."

"Unless it's floor grappling," he joked. "You don't seem to mind how that goes."

I pulled back, smiling. "I do like it when we're... *on the floor*. But this weekend," I told him quietly, "I just want us."

"Okay," he said, clearly concerned. "You sure you're okay?"

I traced my thumb along the scar that ran through his eyebrow, the scar Tomic had given him, and nodded. That scar was a daily reminder of what I'd put him through. "I'm fine," I lied. "I just need some us time."

He took my hand and kissed the finger I just touched his scar with. "Sounds good."

"Now can you fix this sauce for me?" I asked. "I'll heat the wok."

As I cooked, with his help, and as we ate, I told him about the fight earlier that night. I told him how it had gone two rounds, but mostly just jabs and a few kicks, but in the second round my opponent tried to take me to the floor. So while he was bent down with his arms around my waist, I'd taken hold of his head and kneed him until he fell to the mat.

Yeah, it was brutal, but it was tactical, measured and deliberate. And Kira was a kick-boxer. He understood exactly that MMA was a sport, not street-thug brutal. It wasn't like I was involved in random violent attacks on unsuspecting strangers. These were other fighters, who had signed up for the same as me. MMA was a regulated, strictly ruled sport. It was a simple case of hit or be hit. Thankfully, I didn't have to explain that principle to Kira.

After dinner, we stayed on the sofa. We were kind of lying back and I had my head on Kira's chest, feeling his heartbeat thump in my ear while he played with my hair. I couldn't tell you what was on TV. I was lost in the sound of his heart, and how mine beat out a tempo with it. Sometimes they'd thump in time, together, then mine would speed up and I'd have to take some deep breaths to get it to slow down, trying to get it back in time with Kira's.

I felt his voice rumble in his chest, rather than hear the spoken word. "Matt?"

I lifted my head from his chest to look at him. "Yeah?"

"You sure you're okay?"

So I didn't have to lie out loud, I nodded and pushed up his body so I could kiss him. I settled my weight over him and he wrapped his arms around me. I got lost in him, in his strength, his taste, his everything.

I pulled back from him only to peel his shirt over his head, then mine, desperate to feel his skin on mine. I fell back over him, needing to kiss him, to feel him. But he drew his hands from my ass, up my back to my face so he could pull my lips from his.

He never said a word. He just stared at me. I could see his love for me, I could feel it thumping heavily in my chest. He was completely open, honest and true. I could never doubt him.

It should have warmed me through. It should have made me happy. But it made every lie I'd told him tighten my windpipe and constrict around my heart. I wanted to tell him. I wanted to spill everything. I wanted him to know. And he saw it. He knew there was something I wasn't saying. Of course he did. He *knew* me.

But I couldn't say a fucking word. For his safety, for mine. I choked back the words I wanted to say, and he spoke instead. Just a whisper. "I love you."

My heart rate spiked and my breath caught in my throat. Words that should have comforted me only made my guilt worse. I leaned in and kissed down his jaw so he couldn't see the struggle in my eyes. "Take me to bed."

––––––––

I MANAGED A LITTLE SLEEP, but well before the sun came up, while Kira slept soundly, I crept out of bed and went to my closet. At the back of the top shelf was a pre-paid cell phone only two people had the number for—Mitch Seaton and Ross Berkman. The phone was off and set to mute, so I pressed the On button and typed out a text to my partner and my boss about the next underground fight.

Next meeting is on tonight or tomorrow night. Don't know when or where. But I will be at the one after.

It wasn't confirmed that I would be. I just had to do everything I could to make sure my name was on that list.

We knew each bout was about two months apart, and we knew each venue and time was different. So giving them the date of this fight gave them a fairly good guide for the next one and a goal to work toward. I just had to trust they'd work with any information I could give them, and make it all happen behind the scenes without me.

I turned the phone off and stashed it back where it was. Kira never went to my side of the closet. He had no reason to. He hadn't rifled through the piles of clothes at the top shelf in the twelve months he'd been living with me, so I had no reason to think he would now.

I considered climbing back into bed but knew trying to sleep was futile. So I grabbed my keys and headed to the grocery store. I wanted this weekend to be all about us, about Kira, so I figured his favorite breakfast was a good way to start.

Thirty minutes later, I knelt over his still-sleeping form

and kissed his shoulder and his neck. "Muesli, yogurt, fresh fruit salad, croissants, and coffee in the kitchen."

"Mmmm," he mumbled. Then he pulled the sheet down to reveal his naked ass.

I groaned. "Fuck. Keep that up and we won't be having breakfast."

He laughed sleepily into his pillow.

I smacked his ass and walked to the door. "Get your sexy ass into the kitchen."

He did exactly that. Without a stitch on.

I ended up feeding him his yogurt and muesli, watching his full lips close around the spoon. He put my coffee to my lips and let me sip it, but after I fed him strawberries and melon, I had to lick the juice from his chin and neck. He was still far too sticky, I declared, and it was only right we shower together to save water. Total body washes and soapy hand jobs later, we finally made it out of the house.

It was so good to spend the day with him. To laugh and talk with him. Even the comfortable silences, no matter how brief, were nice.

I almost forgot I was lying to him.

We went to the nursery first, bought enough plants to start our own nursery, and spent the day outside, cleaning up the yard, ripping out the old vegetable patch, and planting a new one. Kira had been wanting to do it for a while and I'd never really seen the point. Kira had done a lot around the house since he'd moved in and had really worked at fixing it up and making it a home.

I was just happy he was there. For me, it had nothing to do with painting or new kitchens—the fact he was living there made it a home for me. But he mentioned his next project would be the back yard so I decided to join in. Was it my guilt eating at me? Probably. But it was the best day I'd spent with him in a long time.

After dinner and separate showers, we collapsed on the sofa, only this time Kira lay down with his feet on my lap. He shuffled around a bit and fidgeted and even tried stuffing a cushion behind his shoulder. "This couch is so uncomfortable," he mumbled.

It was my old sofa. I'd had it since forever, and we kept it in front of the TV because it was longer than the two Kira had brought with him when he moved in. "Yours aren't much better," I said, nodding toward the smaller ones along the other wall. "But we could try moving them around if you'd prefer."

"Nah, it's okay," he said kindly. "I'll survive."

"Let's buy a new one tomorrow!" I said excitedly. "We can get rid of all this other mismatched stuff and buy new ones."

Kira's eyebrows rose toward his hairline, but he smiled. "Buying plants together, buying furniture together..." He waggled his eyebrows. "What's next? A house?"

I knew he was joking, but I wasn't. "If you want. I already think of this one as half yours anyway. I can call my lawyer and have him change the deeds, if you want."

His eyes stayed wide, but his smile died. "Matt, you can't do that," he said. "This is your home."

I shook my head. "It only became a home to me when you moved in."

Kira's eyes softened. "I know," he said quietly. "It was your mom's house. It must have felt empty for a long time."

I nodded. "But not anymore."

He waggled his toes. "I'll settle for a foot massage and some new furniture tomorrow," he said. "We can work on the house idea later."

I took his foot in between my hands and dug my thumbs into the arch of his foot, and I smiled at the TV. I could feel him watching me.

"What are you smiling at?" he asked.

"Just imagining what your mom would say if we told her we'd bought a house together."

Kira groaned. "She'll be bad enough when we tell her we bought a new sofa." He looked at me, somewhat concerned. "I'm being serious. She'll have the wedding invitations picked out by tomorrow night."

I laughed. "And the color theme."

Kira raised one curious eyebrow. "Weddings have color themes?"

I patted his leg and clicked my tongue. "Anna will be disappointed in your gayness if you don't know that. She's going to want her gay best friend's advice."

Kira's lips curled up beautifully. "She knows me better than that."

I laughed again at him. "Yeah, right. Anyway, it'll be good experience for when you have to go through it with your mother."

Kira jumped up and straddled me, taking my hands and pinning me to the couch. "If I'm going through all that shit, you are too."

I was laughing at him, so he started to tickle me, which ended up with us wrestling, which led to us both lying down on the sofa, playfully fighting for dominance, which of course ended up with us sweaty, sated messes in bed.

It wasn't lost on me that we'd just discussed our own possible wedding, not in a *what-if* sense, but in a *when* sense. And it wasn't lost on me that neither of us seemed opposed to the idea.

That night, wrapped up in his arms, for the first time in what felt like months, I slept like a baby.

WE WERE at the furniture store when it opened. We'd agreed on a budget, more or less, but hadn't really discussed what type we'd wanted. I went straight for the corner suite, figuring the size would benefit both of us, but Kira wanted the leather sofa with built-in recliners, right or freaking wrong.

The sales assistant watched us argue about it for twenty minutes before he spoke up. "We actually have leather corner suites that have recliners," he said, seemingly a little intimidated by us. "They're in that section." He pointed to the far corner. "They're at the higher end of the market…"

Kira gawped at him. "Why didn't you say so?"

The sales assistant looked up at both of us. We were taller than him by almost a foot and were both obviously a lot more muscled than him. Then I remembered my cut, bruised eye. We must have looked a little frightening.

"Can we see them?" I asked with a smile. I took Kira's hand, and as the sales assistant walked ahead, I whispered to Kira. "I think we scared him."

Kira rolled his eyes. "Well, it would save a lot of time if you just agreed with me at the beginning."

I slid my arm around his waist. "And where's the fun in that?"

The sales assistant stopped and turned to see if we'd followed. He eyed us, at how I was now standing with my arm around Kira, opposed to the snarky compromising he'd just witnessed. I gave him a smile and glanced at Kira, but he was distracted by something else. He was smiling.

There was a chocolate-brown leather corner suite, with built-in recliners, or so the sign said. He walked over, planted himself into the soft, pillow-top sofa, and grinned. Then he almost scrambled up to the end, pressed some button, and the footrest slowly lifted out and the back of his seat reclined. Kira sighed contentedly and the smile he gave me warmed my chest.

So much for the budget. If Kira gave me a smile like that, I'd buy him the moon. I looked at the sales assistant. "We'll take it."

"It's six thousand dollars," the sales guy added.

I smiled at him, a little annoyed at his attitude. "I said we'd take it." Then because he was an asshole, I added, "With cash."

He stumbled off to start paperwork or whatever, and Kira patted the seat beside him. I sat down and he pressed the recliner button, and soon I was lying back like him. "It's expensive," he said quietly.

"It's worth it."

"Don't let that guy get to you."

"I won't," I said. "So, should we look at new dining tables too?"

Kira barked out a laugh. "I think a six-thousand-dollar sofa is enough."

"I would have paid ten thousand to see you smile like that."

Kira blushed a little. "Is that why you said we'd take it?"

I nodded without shame. "Yep. Anything that makes you happy is worth it." Then I pet his arm. "Anyway, you're paying for half, remember?"

Kira laughed just as the sales assistant walked back over.

"Is there anything else, gentlemen?"

I looked at Kira and he rolled his eyes. A new dining

table and chairs, some canvas prints, a hall table, and a coffee table later, and we were done.

At Kira's insistence, the sales assistant reluctantly organized transport, even on a Sunday. We left, substantially poorer than when we arrived, but happy. We called into the market to pick up some things for the dinner we were having with his parents, and all in all, it was a fantastic day.

This was what I missed. Just doing everyday things, just normal things.

And dinner with Sal and Yumi was the perfect way to end a great weekend. They loved the new furniture, of course, and true to form, Yumi thought the fact we'd purchased furniture together was a prequel to a walk down the aisle.

The sign language conversations behind each other's backs were still as funny as always, even when they talked about me. My sign language still wasn't perfect, but I caught most things.

I got that Sal chided Yumi about pushing us to get married, and I also understood that she told him to mind his own bloody business. Yumi was concerned about the cut near my eye, and Sal asked Kira all about my fighting.

Most people would probably hate being talked about behind their backs while they were in the same room. But I liked it. In fact, I loved it when they spoke and chuckled about me because it made me one of them. They loved me enough to treat me like one of their own.

It had been years since I'd been part of a family, and now I had Kira's.

"What will you do with the old furniture?" Yumi asked.

"I'll put a flyer up at the FC tomorrow," I answered. "I get the feeling some of those guys don't have much. Figured someone could probably use some free furniture."

And that was what I did. I wrote a simple 'Free' ad on a piece of paper, and before I could pin it to the bulletin board at the FC, I saw Arizona. He looked like he'd been through hell. Twice.

The right side of his face was swollen, his eye completely shut, and he had a nasty-looking egg at his temple. I'd say at a glance, he had a fractured eye socket.

"Jesus, Arizona," I gasped. "What the fuck happened?"

He was quiet. "I didn't win."

"Fuck! Are you okay?"

He gave me a defeated nod. "I'll be all right."

"You can't fight," I told him. "You shouldn't even spar. What the hell are you doing here?"

The left side of his mouth lifted, just a fraction in what I thought was a smile. "Need to be here." He cleared his throat. "Need to practice, so next time I can get some cash."

I nodded but didn't really know what to say.

"Whatcha got there?" he asked, nodding toward the piece of paper in my hand.

"Oh, just a flyer," I said. "Got some furniture to give away."

"Oh," he said, his tone a little more involved than before. "Anything interesting?"

"Two couches, a dining table, chairs, and an old coffee table. You want them?"

He shrugged, trying to decide what he wanted more—the second-hand furniture or his pride.

I decided to help him out. "If you want it, it's yours. We can deliver it, just need an address."

He seemed to appreciate not having to ask outright. "You sure?"

"Hell yes," I said like it was no big deal. It wasn't like I could tell him Kira and I went out and bought all brand new stuff when this man was clearly not well off. "We kinda collected two of everything when Kira moved in," I said by way of explanation.

"Maybe Lashona won't think she married a loser if I give her new stuff for the house," he said. I doubted his wife thought he was a loser. It was more like *he* thought he was a loser.

"No problem, man," I said with a gentle pat on his back. "It's all yours."

He gave me his address, which I knew to be a not-so-nice part of town. It wasn't too far from the FC or from the city, but from my time as a cop, I knew it to be a problem area. High unemployment, low income, gangs, and troubled kids.

As we pulled up in front of Arizona's and I noticed the rows of houses and the people who watched us arrive, it really dawned on me the three-sixty I'd done. I used to bust places like this. I used to bust people in places like this. Now here I was, friends with them, dropping off furniture, doing them a favor.

I liked Arizona, and we got along. Sure he'd taunted me early on, but it was just a fight tactic. He meant no harm. He was an ally. I'd even consider calling him a friend.

I'd done training for undercover work. I'd read reports, case studies, I'd been through psych analysis for this.

But I had no real concept of what it would really be like.

I had no concept of how bad it would get.

AND WHEN KIRA and I dropped off our unwanted-but-still-good furniture to Arizona's, it was a shock for me to see how he lived. His tiny house was an old townhouse, and there was barely any furniture.

A young woman with dark skin, tight curly hair, and wary eyes, who I presumed to be Lashona, with a little baby girl on her hip, smiled at us when Arizona introduced us.

"Thanks," she said with a smile. "Means a lot."

"No problem," Kira said, making a start on lifting the chairs off the back of the rental truck. "Where do you want them?"

As we unloaded the few things and took them inside, I noticed they didn't have much—of anything. There was one ratty old sofa, old yellowed curtains, and aged stains on the ceiling. But the living areas were clean and uncluttered, there were a few photos on one wall, and a small plastic cross on another. The kitchen was old and tiny, but it was sparkling clean and pleasant, and what few things they had were for the baby. No, they didn't have much, but they were proud of what they did have.

Lashona offered cold tea for our trouble, but I kindly told her not to worry about us. When we were done, their little house looked more lived in. Lashona already had a small empty fruit bowl on the center of the table and she was grinning as she sat on her new sofa with her baby on her knee.

Arizona smiled as he watched his wife and daughter. Even with a bruised and swollen face, it was easy to see he adored them. I bumped my fist to Arizona's as we walked out, and he offered his fist to Kira, which Kira bumped in return. It was an acknowledgment of acceptance, of friendship, and I returned his smile at the gesture.

I liked Arizona. He was just a young family man, trying to live the only way he knew how. "See ya tomorrow," I called out as we got in the truck and drove away.

"Jesus," Kira mumbled when we were halfway home. "They had nothing. Makes you realize just how lucky we are to have what we have, doesn't it?"

I looked at him and at his words, which had two meanings for me. "It sure does."

ARIZONA SPARRED with me all the next week. He held the pads for me and bravely wore the protective guards over his already bruised thigh so I could practice my kicks. Boss seemed pleased Arizona had taken me under his wing. He was a seasoned, well-respected fighter in the FC. Sure, we'd had a rocky beginning—which was simply an establishment of pecking order—but we'd become unofficial sparring partners.

We also trained with Cody, Amil, Jamaal and Benji, but Arizona and I were now pretty much inseparable. We were an odd pair—me with my 'golden boy' blond hair and blue eyes and him being African American and a hulking six-foot-three. But we gelled.

Boss said Arizona respected me because I stood up to him. Normally he'd heckle the new guys so they feared him and posed no threat. But I didn't. I gave him as good as I got, and apparently that earned me some credit with the big guy.

I was scheduled to fight on Friday, and Arizona wasn't allowed to get back into the ring or the cage until his eye healed, so he took it upon himself to get me ready. This was going to be a different fight. We were going up against another fight center, which meant I was going toe-to-toe with someone I'd never seen.

"Do you know anything about him?" I asked Boss. "Is he five foot tall? Six? Right-handed? Left-footed? Anything?"

Boss tried not to smile. "I know you like to know how your opponent fights, but this will be a good test for ya," he said. "You haven't lost yet."

"I'd like to keep it that way."

Boss must have felt sorry for me. "Look, all I know is you're both listed as new fighters. He's been registered at that club for as long as you've been here. That's why you were matched."

"That doesn't mean much," I challenged. "He could have spent five years registered somewhere else."

Boss smiled at his clipboard and nodded. "Could've."

"Do you *want* me to lose?" I asked, because it was starting to feel like it.

He looked up at me, his smile was gone. "No. But I don't want you gettin' an ego either. It's good to get knocked on your ass every once in a while. Reminds you that you're human. I've seen guys with egos step into a cage thinking they already got it won, only to get their face rearranged." Then he smiled at me. "God forbid anything happen to your pretty mug."

I snorted. "Thanks. Anyway, I have someone at home who'd threaten to knock me on my ass if I let my ego get away from me."

Boss chuckled. "Good. Keeps it real." Then he checked his watch. "You got about two hours till your fight. Go inside"—he nodded toward the dressing room—"get cleaned up, and rest for an hour before you go over town."

"Yes, Boss," I said. The old tough guy was used to me addressing him like he was my leading officer. At least I hadn't called him 'sir' in a while.

I grabbed a quick shower, changed, and took my phone from my bag. I sent Kira a quick message.

Fighting at Jackson's on West tonight. Six thirty.

I knew he was working and wouldn't get a chance to check his phone until he took a break or even the end of his shift. So I figured I'd put my feet up and rest as Boss suggested and read the paper.

I started at the back, checking out the sports section first, and once that was read, I flipped to the front. That was when I saw the article on page three titled, 'Meet the Newest Member of the Fab Four'.

There was a photo of Mitch, Kurt, and Tony, all smiling. And some guy called Ricky Collins.

Not two months since Detective Matthew Elliott quit the Fab Four, the LAPD has found his replacement. Detective Ricky Collins officially stepped up for the job two weeks ago, but the decision was made to keep it quiet while he found his feet.

And found his feet he has. Already a key player in the team, he helped nab his first collar just one week into the job.

"I had very big shoes to fill," Collins goes on to say. "But the boys have welcomed me into their team, especially my direct partner, Mitch Seaton..."

I stopped reading after that. Well, my brain stopped seeing the words.

I'd been replaced.

I wasn't even officially fucking gone.

I was under-fucking-cover, risking my fucking life and sanity, and they'd gone and found someone to replace me?

Was it all part of the plan? Was it for public show? Maybe it was, but I fucking doubted it.

And for two weeks? Two fucking weeks and no one told me?

I'd had dinner at Mitch's place with all of them a few weeks before. Surely they must have known a replacement was in the cards. I spent years with them. I was still one of them! Mitch was my best friend, and I found out he had a new partner by reading it in the fucking newspaper?

Did this Ricky sit at my desk? Did he pick Mitch up on his way to work? Did he have Mitch's back when it all went down? Did he joke with them like I did? Did they like him like they liked me? Did he go to the bar with them, to the gym with them?

The gym...

Fuck. No fucking way.

If he did go to the gym, then chances were Kira knew him. Surely Kira would have told me. He didn't keep secrets from me. He wouldn't lie to me.

Not like how I was lying to him.

It was different. This was for my job.

He wouldn't keep that from me.

Would he?

"What's up?" Arizona said from behind me, making me stop walking. I wasn't even aware I was pacing.

Realizing I was limited to what I could say, I exhaled through puffed cheeks and pointed to the open paper. "I knew they'd replace me at some point," I said, kind of pathetically. "But they could have fucking told me."

Arizona didn't look at the paper for long. I wasn't sure if it was because he could only see out of one eye or if he didn't really care, but he no doubt saw the photo. "What'd they do?"

"It's not the fact they replaced me," I told him, probably confusing him more than clarifying. "But they fucking lied to me."

Arizona nodded but didn't say anything for a long moment. "Do you still talk with them?"

Shit.

I shook my head. "Nah, only once since I left," I told a half-truth. "It's not the point though," I said, my anger spurring me on. "I would have taken a bullet for any one of those fuckers, and they..." I raked my hands through my hair. "You know what? It doesn't fucking matter." I started pacing again.

Arizona nodded again, slower this time, eyeing me carefully. "You know those anger management issues you said those cops thought you had?"

I stopped walking and looked pointedly at him.

"Well," he continued. His lips twitched in an attempt not to smile. "I think they might've been right."

I huffed out a laugh and smiled, despite how fucking irate I was.

"You need to get your shit together before you get in that cage," Arizona said. "If you're angry, you can't focus."

Then he looked me up and down. "Or knowin' you, you're likely to kill the guy."

I huffed again and stretched the tightened muscles in my neck. He was right. I needed to get my head in the game before this fight. I needed to focus. Or I'd end up with a fractured eye socket like Arizona, or worse.

"Come on," he drawled. "Get your stuff, it's almost time we weren't here."

"We?"

He picked up my bag and threw it to me. "Yeah, you'll need someone who knows what they're doin' in your corner."

I rolled my eyes at him but was glad he'd be there.

ME AND THE other five guys who were fighting that night arrived at Jackson's, and we walked in as a team. Dressed in our training gear, we arrived ready. There was silence as the entire floor stopped to stare.

I couldn't help but smirk. I was itching to fight. I wanted to smack the shit out of someone.

The floor set-up wasn't too different from the FC's. There was a training area with mats and pads, and there was a small boxing ring in one corner and a cage in the other. There were even some chairs in rows, so I presumed there'd be more of an audience than just other fighters.

I was the second fight on, so while Boss took time out to go over last-minute prep with Cody, Arizona stuck with me.

I got dressed, and after I'd put on my ankle guards, Arizona strapped my hands. He talked me through the usual pre-match psych-up and we went out to watch the first fight.

More people had come in, and I certainly wasn't expecting Kira to be there, but my eyes picked him out of the crowd as if they were automatically trained to. He smiled when our eyes met, and he left his seat and came over.

"Hey."

"Hey," I replied.

"I'm only here for your fight. I have to go back to work to close up," he said. Then he looked me up and down, taking in my naked chest, fighter's shorts, and fingerless gloves. "You look good. You look ready."

I gave him a nod. "I saw the paper today."

His eyebrows almost met. "What?"

"Mitch has a new partner," I explained coolly. "Did you know?" I was unable to keep the bite from my tone. "Have you met him at the gym?"

Kira looked at me, then at Arizona, then back to me. "Matt, I don't think this is the time."

His non-answer was answer enough. I nodded. "Of course you have. Why didn't you tell me?"

Kira looked confused and hurt. "Tell you what?"

I couldn't say anything more. Not here. Not now. "Never mind," I said dismissively. I knew it wasn't rational to be angry at him, but I was.

A little voice inside me, deep in my head, knew my anger was misdirected. I should have been aiming it at me. I was the one who was lying. I was the one who was risking it all.

But in that moment, I didn't fucking care.

I was fucking pissed off.

"Right," Arizona said, stepping in front of me and effectively ending my conversation with Kira. "You got two minutes to get out of your head." His face was just a few inches from mine. "Get out of your head." Arizona half turned, half pushed me toward our team. "Get over there."

He stayed and spoke to Kira for a little while, no doubt talking about me, but I couldn't watch. I kept adding layers of fucking guilt over more layers of guilt, and it was starting to suffocate me.

It was then I noticed a young guy on the other side of the cage dressed and ready to fight, bouncing on his toes. The guy *I* was about to fight.

He was young, maybe nineteen. He had a military style buzz-cut and a tattoo on his shoulder. He was about my height, and he looked strong.

Good. I wanted to fight.

And when I walked into the cage, I was fucking psyched.

The ref called the rules, then called the fight to start, and we went through our usual dance of sizing the other up. He jabbed a few times, and each time he connected with my mouth, I smiled at him.

It felt... good.

I felt alive.

I traded punches and a few kicks, and gave him a decent knee to the ribs. I did wear one good right jab to the mouth and could taste blood, even with the mouth guard in. I smiled at him and almost dared him to do it again.

He took me to the fence and pinned me there. It was a common tactic in cage fighting. He tried to get me off balance and use the cage wall to his advantage, but I held my footing. But it was frustrating, and I was losing my patience for it.

The bell rang to tell us the first round was over. I deliberately never looked at Kira and went to my corner, where Boss and Arizona were quick to join me. They iced my face and the back of my neck, all while giving some pep talk about tactics and keeping a level head.

But I didn't hear a word of it.

My head wasn't where it should have been. I kept thinking about what I was doing, what I was risking. And why? I think in that very moment, I could feel myself losing it. Losing something. Losing myself.

"Elliott?" Boss snapped at me, bringing me out of my head.

It was time to get back into the fight. "You know what?" I said through my mouthpiece.

Boss and Arizona both looked at me.

I smiled at them. "Fuck this shit."

I bounced up to my feet, bumped fists with my opponent, and when the bell rang, I fucking let him have it.

I kicked him so hard in the ribs I swear I heard them crack, and when he recoiled to the side, I swung through with my elbow and connected with his jaw. He was unconscious before he even hit the floor.

I only looked at Kira in the crowd when the ref held up my hand as the winner. He was staring at me like he didn't know who I'd become.

I turned to Arizona and Boss and crowed my victory to them instead.

KIRA WAS quiet when I got home, and I knew he was worried about what he'd seen in me tonight. I acted like nothing was wrong, of course, and I'm sure he saw through me.

But he said nothing.

I smiled at him and he tried to smile back, but it looked

so wrong on his face. Gone was the genuine, all-consuming happiness that made my heart thump funny. There were no crinkles at the corner of his eyes.

Just worry and concern for me.

I was starving, so I cooked up some pasta, and I talked while we ate. I babbled on about the guys at the FC, the jokes and the stories they told. Kira barely said a word, and I knew I was trying too hard to prove there was nothing wrong.

And after dinner, when we sat on the sofa, he looked as though he was about to launch into the whole "tell me what's going on or we're through" conversation. He looked at me and opened his mouth to speak, but having that conversation was the last thing in the world I wanted to do.

So I flung my leg over him, grinning as I straddled him, grinding my ass on his hips.

"Matt…"

His words were cut off by my mouth over his, by my tongue tasting his. I pushed his head onto the back of the sofa, my hands holding his face, in his hair.

He groaned long and low, and the sound spurred me on. I kissed down his jaw and took his earlobe between my teeth. "I need you," I told him.

"Matt…"

"I need you to fuck me."

He gripped my hips and I thought he would hold me still and stop me, but he pulled me down onto his hardening cock, then he shivered and moaned.

I almost came right there.

I climbed off him, took his hand, and dragged him to our bedroom. I stripped out of my clothes, and after undoing his cargos, I slipped my hand in his briefs and freed his cock. I grabbed a foil wrapper and the lube from the dresser drawer and quickly opened the condom and rolled it down his long cock, giving him a good squeeze.

"Matt," he gasped.

I quickly grabbed the lube, and pouring some on my hand, I pumped him a few times, slicking him. Then I leaned face down over the edge of the bed, and with my already slick fingers, I rubbed my hole. "Kira, please."

"You're not ready," he whispered.

"Yes, I am," I said, knowing I wasn't. I wanted to feel this. I wanted it to stretch and burn. I wanted it to hurt.

But he didn't move. So I took his hand and pulled him over so he stood behind me. I stretched his arms forward so his front was flush against my back, and I wiggled and spread my legs so his hard cock was pressed into the crevice of my ass. "Kira, fuck me, please."

Kira pulled his hands from mine, only to push on my back so my ass lifted to meet him.

The blunt head of his cock pushed against my hole, and I pushed against him, feeling him stretch me, breach me, push inside me.

My back arched at the sensation. I gritted my teeth and absorbed the pain.

It was what I wanted.

What I needed.

And when he didn't thrust hard enough, I bucked back onto him, slamming my ass to his hips. I wanted it to burn.

I deserved the pain.

Kira growled and gripped my hips, starting to fuck me how I wanted him to. It didn't take long before I came, and with a strangled cry, he followed soon after.

Even as we fell onto the bed, he kept his arms around me. He kissed my shoulder and the back of my neck but never said a word.

I scared him.

So to alleviate the tension and as a distraction from the things that needed saying, I turned in his arms and laughed. "Jesus," I said, pecking his lips. "That was amazing."

Kira's eyebrows flinched. "Did I hurt you?"

I smiled and looked down to the sticky mess on me, on the sheets. "Definitely not. You were just what I needed."

Before he could start any conversation I didn't want to hear, I rolled on top of him, smearing the mess between us. "Oh dear, now we both need to shower," I joked. He smiled despite himself, and I jumped off him and started to strip the bed. "You go run the water, I'll be right in."

Then, cleaned up, dried off, and with a freshly made bed, I lay with Kira against me and I traced patterns on his back until his breathing evened out and he slept.

I stared at the ceiling until he was sound asleep, then I crept out of bed to check the cell phone I had stashed in my closet. My only connection to Mitch and Berkman, to the case I was drowning in.

I was hoping there'd be a message from Mitch to explain why he had a new partner or to tell me they'd found some important link and almost had the case against Tressler wrapped up. Or even a message to see if I was okay.

There wasn't.

CHAPTER EIGHT

THE NEXT FEW weeks flew by.

I was now pretty much one of the boys at the FC. After my last fight, I'd earned respect from even the guys who at first wouldn't give me the time of day. Arizona's eye was healing nicely, and we trained well together.

Tressler would smile and nod when he saw me. I was fairly certain he lived by the 'keep your friends close, your enemies closer' rule, but that was fine with me. I knew the rough date of the next underground fight, but was yet to be given a green light to fight in it. I'd also earned a bit of a reputation outside of the FC, on the fight circuit, as the golden boy ex-cop, now fighter, who had yet to lose a match.

And that combination put a price on my scalp. Apparently other guys at other clubs were itching to get into the cage with me, to be the one who beat me. And *that* was my ticket to the underground fight.

Maybe that was why Tressler pretended to like me.

I just had to keep my head down, my ear to the ground, and keep winning fights.

My time at home with Kira was better. I was making a

real effort so he wouldn't worry about me. I'd make dinner, make jokes, snuggle on the sofa instead of pushing for rough, almost-violent sex, as much as I wanted it.

I was being the old me: the version of me he loved. Not the new me: the version he couldn't make heads or tails of.

I wasn't being fake with Kira. I was just being someone who made him happy. This whole case, the whole concept of going undercover was about living a lie. I'd known that before I agreed to it. I'd known it would be hard on my relationship with Kira, but we were rock solid. We'd already been through hell together. I was just making him a priority.

I kept telling myself it wasn't guilt that made me try a little harder. I was doing it because he deserved it.

It wasn't guilt at all.

***

IT HELPED that I didn't fight for those next two weeks after my last fight. I trained and sparred every day but didn't match up against anyone in the cage.

We were scheduled to fight another club on Friday night, but this time it was at the FC. Boss had been adamant all week through training that he wanted to see me fight with a tactic other than take the guy out with a TKO in the first round.

I wiped the sweat from my face with a towel and gave him a smile. "It's a pretty good tactic," I told him.

"It is," he agreed. "But you're not conditioned for three five-minute rounds. If you can't take him out and it goes the distance, you won't have the strength to make the final bell."

"Isn't that what all this training's been for?" I asked. "Conditioning me for endurance?"

Boss smiled at me. "Exactly. Now instead of taking this

guy's head off in the first ten seconds, let me see if all this training's been worth my time."

"Ten seconds..." I scoffed. "The last guy lasted *at least* thirty seconds."

Boss looked back to his clipboard. "Don't make me put you on your ass, Elliott. These other guys might not be able to," he muttered as he waved his pen around the room. "But I certainly could."

The man was at least sixty years old, all of five feet, four inches tall, two feet wide, and with a balding head, and yet I somehow didn't doubt he could knock me on my ass. I grinned at him and he didn't even look up at me but said, "Stop your smilin'." Then he called out, "Arizona, try and smack some sense into this kid before I do."

Arizona laughed and threw a medicine ball at me. "Don't push him, Elliot," he said. "I've seen him take down men bigger than me."

I threw the heavy ball onto the ground and proceeded to do push-ups with one hand on the ball and the other on the floor.

Then Arizona added, "He might look decrepit and slow, but he moves pretty quick for an old guy."

I had to stop mid-push-up because I was laughing and I looked up to see Boss close his clipboard and stare at the both of us. He pursed his lips together so he wouldn't smile and tapped his pen on the clipboard he never put down. "Do I need to separate you two?" He shook his head at us, then held up three short, stubby fingers. "Three rounds tonight, Elliott," he reminded me. "No KO's in the first two rounds or you will see how fast I am."

Arizona laughed at me. "Do you have to actually fight tonight and not just pummel some guy into the ground in the first round?"

I rolled my eyes. "Apparently."

And before the fight, Kira walked in, followed by Sal and Yumi. They wanted to support me, apparently. I was dressed in my fighting shorts and gear, ready to fight, standing with the FC team when they walked over to us.

"They wanted to see how you did," Kira said apologetically.

I shook Sal's hand in greeting and kissed Yumi's cheek. "Glad you could make it," I told them, belying how nervous it made me having them here.

Arizona walked over and held out his fist to Kira, which he quickly bumped with his own. "Hey man, good to see you here."

Kira smiled back at him, then introduced his parents. Sal signed hello, then shook his hand, and to Arizona's credit, he never batted an eyelid. He said a quick hello to Yumi, who, though probably only half his height, shook his hand fiercely and said hello with a curt nod, telling the huge man with the bruised face in front of her she was here to watch her boy.

I loved watching people's reaction when they met her for the first time. She was an amazing woman, and the fact she thought of me as 'her boy' made me smile.

"I'm not allowed to KO in the first two rounds tonight," I told them.

"Why not?" Kira asked, looking concerned.

Arizona answered with a smirk. "Boss wants to see if it's possible for him to even make it to the third round."

"Who say that?" Yumi asked.

"Boss. My trainer," I answered.

"That not make sense," she said. "Where is he? Someone should tell him."

Arizona bit back a laugh, and I reassured Yumi. "It's okay. It's all part of my training, apparently."

"Okay," Kira said warily. "Well, we'll go take a seat. Good luck." He put his hands on his mom's shoulders and led her over to the rows of seats.

Arizona chuckled. "Would she really have words with Boss?"

"Oh, you have no idea. Kira's a lot like her." Then I added, "And don't start with the mother-in-law shit. She's already on us to get married. To make an honest man of her son."

"And I thought my mother-in-law was bad." Then he impersonated a woman's voice. "When you gettin' married? When you havin' my grandbabies?"

I snorted. "Oh, hell no. Don't even *suggest* kids to Yumi. Jesus."

Arizona threw his head back and laughed, and I shook my head and smiled at him. It was then I noticed a familiar face in the small gathered crowd.

There was a guy, looking rather nondescript, with a few other guys I didn't know. It took me a second to place him, but he was a cop on the third floor of HQ. I almost didn't recognize him. Wearing a sleeveless shirt that showed his tattoos and with a baseball cap on backwards, he looked remarkably different out of uniform.

I kept my eyes to the cage, watching Amil fight while keeping tabs on the other cop in the room. He never looked at me; he never made eye contact. But I knew without a doubt, he was there to check on me.

Maybe something had happened and they needed to verify some of the information I'd sent them. Maybe he was there to see if I was still doing my job.

I simply didn't know.

"Elliott." Boss's voice startled me. "Three minutes. Get your shit together."

Three minutes later I walked into the cage.

My opponent was a guy they called Juarez from the LMA Club, who was about my height with cornrows in his hair. I had no idea about his ability or what his strengths or weaknesses would be. What I really wanted to do was to step out there at first bell and surprise him with a foot to the jaw but wasn't allowed to.

I'd never been one to go against my superior's orders. No matter how fucking stupid the order seemed at the time. And while I was at the FC, Boss was, well, my boss.

The first round, I spent the full five minutes sizing Juarez up, taking jabs and a few thigh kicks and giving them back two-fold. There were a few calls from outside the cage, from Juarez's team, telling him to take the 'faggot cop' out.

When the ref called corners, Boss came in with a short stool and sat me on it, and Arizona was there with water and an icepack on my face. "Don't listen to the bullshit they're talkin'," Boss said. "It's just a distraction."

I pulled out my mouth guard. "He's right-handed but left-footed. He drops his left all the time," I said, panting. "I could drop him so easily."

Realizing their slurs didn't mean shit to me, Boss smiled. "No, third round."

The bell went again, I put my mouthpiece back in, and moving to the middle of the cage, I bumped fists with Juarez. He hit harder in the second round, he kicked and kneed me, and while I deflected most of his shots, I still wore more than I'd have liked. My right cheek was starting to swell, and my left thigh and shin had taken a few hard kicks.

But the calls from his team were worse, and louder.

"Make the pig squeal."

"Smash the faggot."

"Make the cop fuckin' sorry."

I gave Juarez a neat right to the nose, and when he took a step back, I said, loud enough so they'd hear me, "That's *ex*-cop, asshole."

Juarez's team erupted in jeers and slurs. I just smiled at my opponent and gave him another two quick jabs to the face. He grabbed hold of me, trying to take me to the ground, making his team yell more profanities. So I kneed him in the ribs, then gave him an elbow to the face, just about ready to unload on him when the bell rang, declaring the end of round two.

"Don't get angry," Boss warned. "You let your emotions get the better of ya out there and he'll take you down. You're holding your own. He's gettin' tired, so use that to your advantage."

Arizona held an icepack to the back of my neck while Boss held one to my cheek. I took out my mouth guard and sipped some water. "Can I take him out now?"

"I'd like to see you go the three rounds," Boss said.

"Are you fucking kidding me?"

"You're nowhere near as tired as him," he told me. "You'll beat him on endurance."

I put my mouth guard back in to stop from saying something I shouldn't to Boss. The other team was pissing me off with their slurs, and Boss expected me to take it on the fucking chin? I wanted to fucking smash this guy. And his entire fucking team.

But the third round started, we bumped fists, and the guys in Juarez's team wasted no time. "Give it to the faggot!"

I looked to Boss, but he shook his head. So I let fly with

my foot and kicked Juarez in the ribs. He took a step back, so I followed in with a few hard jabs to the same ribs I'd just kicked.

He went backwards again, over toward where his team was standing, and they cheered their teammate on while letting fly with more insults at me. "Come on, Juarez. You can take this cop faggot."

I slammed Juarez into the cage wall, and with my forearm across his neck, I yelled out, "Now, Boss?"

"No," he called back to me.

So I bounced back on my toes, and Juarez jabbed me in my already swollen cheek. We danced around each other for a bit and he smirked at me.

"The little faggot needs someone to give him instructions."

"Wonder if that's all his coach gives him."

"Maybe they're all faggots."

I now had my back to Juarez's team and could see Boss on our side of the cage. I put my hands out. "Now?"

"Yes, now!"

With all the frustration, the anger I had, and for every fucking 'cop' and 'faggot' comment they said, I let him fucking have it.

I gave him a front kick to the chin, knocking him out right there, and as he fell backwards I went with him, smashing my fists into his fucking face.

The ref pulled me off an unconscious Juarez, and I faced his team who were all looking a little stunned and silent at the prone, bloodied man on the floor. I pulled my mouth guard out so I could speak properly. "*That* was the instruction I was waiting for," I told them, then I cupped my hand to my ear. "Don't seem to have much to say now, huh, assholes?"

Boss and Arizona were in the cage by then and pulled me back to my corner, telling me to shut my mouth.

Arizona was holding more ice to my swollen face while Boss put gel over a cut on my cheek. I couldn't feel any of it. I felt good. It felt good to let loose. It'd been weeks since I'd smacked the shit out of something.

It was freeing.

I inhaled deeply, catching my breath. "You might want to tell them to find a different tactic," I said. "Saying that kind of shit doesn't distract me, it just pisses me off."

Arizona laughed. "Yeah, I learned that the hard way too."

Boss chuckled as he smoothed more gel over my face. "Your anger issues might not have done you much good as a cop, but they're fucking beautiful to watch in the cage."

The ref called me the winner by knockout, which made six wins, zero losses.

The other cop in the audience was now standing up, talking to the guys he was with, but he watched as I walked out of the cage over to my team to a reception of high-fives and fist bumps. He saw how assimilated I was in this group, how accepted I was.

Without a word, without a nod, without so much as a look to me directly, he left not long after.

Kira walked hesitantly up to where I was, with Sal and Yumi not far behind him. I thought he might have been alarmed or worried at my burst of anger, but then he smiled. "Good fight."

"Thanks," I answered.

Before I could say anything else, Yumi hugged me. I was all sweaty, but even with some of Juarez's blood on me, she didn't care. "You okay? Oh my gosh, you fight so good. But three rounds when you could take in one round? That's crazy!"

Sal pulled her off me and couldn't help but grin. But then she saw my face and she gasped. "Oh!" And her hand went straight for my swollen eye.

While she fussed over me, Sal signed behind her. I missed what he said, but Kira quickly signed something back to him, which Yumi caught the end of.

"I don't mind, Kira," she said.

"Mom," he whisper-shouted. "You don't need to come home with us. I can look after him, he'll be just fine."

Sal laughed, and Kira glared at him and signed, "Not funny."

I laughed, but then I heard Boss call my name. I turned to see him motion me to the dressing room. "I have to go," I told them. "Thanks for coming tonight. We'll come visit on Sunday," I said to Yumi. "And you can fuss over me all you like."

She beamed, and Sal rolled his eyes and signed, "You're a brownnoser."

My gaze darted to Kira's, and I grinned and nodded. "I know."

Kira smiled but put his arm around his dad. "Not complaining," he mumbled, and as he ushered his parents toward the door, I saw Sal push Kira's arm and Kira laughed as they left. Sal was deaf, but he still understood the brown-nosing, rimming innuendo.

I was still smiling when I followed Boss into the dressing rooms, though he grumbled at me to stop being so damn happy. He wanted me to be seen by the medic to check my face. I could feel it now. It was swollen and felt hot and tight. There was a sting in my cheek and my eyebrow had its own pulse, but nothing major.

The medic put butterfly bandages on the cut on my cheek, then checked my cheekbones, my nose, and felt along my eyebrows. "Nothing broken, but I want ice on that thigh tonight," the medic said, indicating to the reddened strip from my knee to my hip. He looked at Boss. "No matches for two weeks."

The medic walked out and Boss took his place, pulling my gloves off, then the strapping tape. "Well, if they didn't want your head before, they sure as hell will now," he said, like he was making a general observation.

I shrugged. "They were assholes."

Boss nodded and half-shrugged. "Yeah, probably. But I'm pretty sure you've just put a target on your head for your next fight."

"Let them. But no more three-round matches," I told him. "If I can take him in the first round, I will."

"Fair enough," he said, pulling my ankle guard off. "I think you'd have gone three full rounds easy enough."

"He wasn't their strongest fighter," I said. "Some of those other guys on their team looked stronger."

"Rest assured, you'll meet one of them next time."

"Speaking of next time," a voice said from the door. Boss and I both turned our heads to find the man who spoke standing in the doorway. Tressler.

He walked in, and one of his bodyguards stood behind him, pretty much filling the door frame. The owner of the gym smiled, looking smug and out of place in his suit. Tressler gave me a sly smile. "Did well tonight."

"Thanks."

"You can go three rounds and then still pummel the guy into the mats," he said. "I like your style."

I took his compliment and knew better than to say anything smart in return. "Thanks, sir."

He smiled at the word 'sir' and clapped Boss on the shoulder. "I think this boy needs to really show me what he can do."

Boss nodded as though it was message received and understood, though I did notice Boss never looked at Tressler and had yet to say a word to him, which surprised me.

As soon as Tressler was out the door, I asked Boss, "What did he mean show him what I can really do?"

Boss glanced at the empty doorway and sighed. "You just got listed to fight for the FC."

Although I had a pretty good idea what that meant, I needed to act like I didn't have a clue. "I thought I already fought for the FC."

"You do," he said and threw my ankle guard on the seat next to me. "But this is..." He exhaled through puffed cheeks. "Look, I know you're an ex-cop, and Tressler knows that too. He's not stupid, so I'm presumin' he's done some homework on ya if he wants ya to fight..." he said, as though he was thinking out loud.

"Boss?" I cut him off. "Tressler told me he'd done some snooping into why I was here. I told him, just like I told you, I'm not a cop, not anymore. I'm here to fight. Now just tell me, what do you mean I'm listed to fight?"

"There are some organized fights that aren't entirely legal..."

He trailed off, so I prompted him. "Like the one Arizona fought in?"

Boss nodded. "Yeah." He looked at me, then he really *looked* at me. "You get what I'm sayin' to ya?"

Illegal. No rules. Dangerous.

I nodded. "We can earn some cash, yeah?" I asked,

going along with the lies I'd told, giving him my motive to want to do this.

Boss nodded. "If you bet on yourself." He threw the used strapping tape in the trash and put the icepack on my thigh. "Before you ask, there's some things you should know. Yes, like that fucking movie, you don't say nothin' to no one. No, I don't know when, I don't know where, so don't ask. The date and the time aren't given till the actual day of, so you gotta be ready. But I'd say you got about three or four weeks to get ready." He looked me square in the eye. "Being picked to fight is a bit of a privilege. It means Tressler sees some talent in ya, but," he said warningly, "if you don't want to do it, tell me right now. Once you say yes and get in that cage on the night, I can't help ya."

I smiled. This was what I was here for. "I get to punch the ever-living shit out of someone *and* earn some cash?"

Boss rolled his eyes. "Yep."

My smile became a grin. "Then I'm in."

CHAPTER NINE

I GOT home and Kira was already there. By this time, my muscles had cooled down and the aches and pains were settling in.

My face hurt, my ribs grabbed a little, and my thigh felt like it had been corked. Kira looked at me walk in, and his lips curled into a sympathetic smile. "Do you want a bath?"

I shook my head, and as I limped over to him, I pointed to my lips. "Kiss first."

"At least they're not swollen," he said. "Well, one side, anyway." He leaned in and gently kissed the corner of my mouth. "Have you eaten?"

"I'm starving."

"Mom gave me some dinner to bring home for you," he said.

"God, I love your mom."

Kira smiled warmly. "I'll heat it up for you, and when you've eaten, your bath will be ready."

I put my forehead on his chest and exhaled slowly. "You're so good to me."

He kissed the top of my head. "So you keep saying."

Kira went to pull away, but I slid my arms around him and held him. "Stay here, just for a minute."

He gently wrapped his arms around me, and I almost melted into him. "Three rounds," I mumbled into his chest. "I told Boss next time I can take a guy out in the first round, I will."

He sighed. "Watching you go three rounds wasn't easy," he said. "I thought it was hard watching you punch someone's lights out, but at least it's not drawn out like that. I'm not sure which is worse—watching you smash some guy into the floor, or watch you go toe to toe for three full rounds."

I sighed into him. "I'm sorry, babe. Hopefully it won't happen again."

"It better not," he said. "I don't think my heart can take it."

I tightened my grip on him. "What did your mom and dad think?"

"Dad thought you fought well, but he was a bit shocked to see you go off at the end. He's never seen you like that."

I sighed into his chest but wasn't real sure what to say.

Then he added, "But Mom, well, she wanted to give those guys yelling stuff out at you a piece of her mind."

"They would have deserved it," I said with a bit of a laugh. "Your mom wanted to give Boss something to think about too."

"They love you, you know."

I nodded and tightened my hold on him. "I know," I whispered. "Your mom called me 'her boy' tonight," I told him. "And your dad... I've never had a father before... Well, there was Berkman, but not a real dad. Not like your dad."

Kira pulled back, gently cupped my jaw, and kissed the

non-swollen side of my face. He looked at me for a long moment, then studied my bruises. "Food, bath, bed."

"Sounds good."

Later that night, when Kira was asleep, I took the phone from my closet and sent a text message to Mitch and Ross. I told them I was in, that the fight was three to four weeks away, but no set date.

Over the last few weeks, I'd given them details as I knew them. Nicknames of Tressler's men, known associates in other fight centers, physical descriptions of other men in suits I'd never seen before and the times and dates I'd seen them. I'd told them of rumors I'd heard, without knowing if there was a lick of truth to any of them. All I could do was send on what I knew, what I'd heard, and have faith in them to put it all together. It was like working by remote control, trying to give instructions to someone who was flying blind.

And not getting any responses in return was even harder. I didn't even know if they were getting my messages. I was risking everything and was left completely in the dark.

I had no way of verifying, off the record anyway. But I asked Kira if he saw Mitch at the gym very often anymore, to which he replied, "Yeah, just like normal."

I nodded, ignoring the sting that everything was 'normal' for them. But very not normal for me. "Ask him if his phone works."

Kira smiled but looked at me confused. "Why? Don't you talk to him?"

I shook my head. "Not really." I sounded pathetic, even to my own ears. "I know he's busy, and I know I'm not one of the boys anymore..." My voice faded away.

"Have you tried calling him?"

I shook my head. "I don't feel like I can, know what I mean?"

"Because you left?"

His words stung. Because *I* left. It was *my* choice, it was *my* decision to put myself through this. It was *my* fault. "Yeah."

"Matt," Kira said softly. "Don't shut them out of your life."

"It's like they've just forgotten about me." I didn't know what made me say that. Yes, it was true, that was how I felt. There I was, out on a limb, still a part of their team, but very, very removed. But I also told Kira because as much as I needed to talk about it, he needed to hear it even more. He knew there was something bothering me, so in a way, it was for him too. He needed to feel like he was helping me.

"Oh, babe," he said. "They've not forgotten about you. Mitch misses you, I'm sure he does."

I nodded, not really believing it. "Anyway, just have a shot at him about picking up his phone once in a while."

And sure enough, when I was at home by myself the next afternoon, my cell phone rang. Kira's name scrolled across my screen, so I answered with, "Hey, babe."

"You freakin' wish," came the reply. It was Mitch.

I smiled at the sound of his voice and at the realization he'd gotten my message. By speaking to me on Kira's phone, Mitch was making sure that if my incoming and outgoing calls were monitored by Tressler, as far as he knew, I was talking to Kira.

"Hey," I said with a laugh. "How's that beautiful fiancé of yours doing?"

"She's still beautiful," came his reply. "Frankie here said you were bitching about me not calling, so I took his phone. Figured you'd be more likely to answer if you thought it was him calling not me."

I heard Kira mumble something in the background and I knew this call was for show.

"You got my messages?"

"Yep." Then he quickly covered with, "They're okay. Berkman still yells, and Kurt and Tony are still a pain in my ass."

I heard both Kurt and Tony interject in the background, and Mitch laughed at them. I knew he was calling to let me know they were getting my messages and that everything was okay, but I could imagine them at the gym, all laughing and joking around like we used to, while I was digging myself deeper into a hole.

"How's Ricky doing?" I asked, unable to keep the bite from my tone.

Mitch stopped laughing then. "He does all right," he said quietly. There was a silence between us then, until he asked, "How's the MMA career going?" I knew there must have been people around, so he was unable to speak freely. He wanted to know how I was feeling.

I found it suddenly hard to speak. "It's hard," I croaked out. "Harder than what I thought it'd be. The lies are killing me."

"Listen, come and have a few drinks on Friday night, like old times," he said cheerfully, for the benefit of listening ears. "It'll be good for you."

"I'm not fighting on Friday," I told him. "But I need to be there for Arizona's fight. So I guess we could meet you there later."

"Good," he said. "See ya then."

There was a muffled exchange on the phone, then Kira's voice was the next I heard. "Hey," he said. "I gave Mitch your message, obviously."

"Yeah, thanks," I said with a chuckle. "What time do you finish on Friday?"

"Eight."

"I could meet you at your work and we could swing past the bar and say hello to the boys," I said as a suggestion.

"Sure," Kira said brightly. "Sounds good. I gotta go, I'll see you when I get home."

I could tell by the tone of his voice he was glad I was getting out to see the boys. I felt so fucking bad for putting him through this whole emotionally fucked-up rollercoaster ride, and he'd been so worried about me. I could tell he was smiling when he said goodbye.

Now I wasn't strictly undercover in the sense other agents were. I hadn't assumed a new alias, a fake name, and a made-up past. I'd gone into the FC as *me*. We'd just fabricated the reason for my being there.

So if I was meeting up with my ex-partners at a cops' bar, I was doing it as me, as well.

I had no doubt Tressler would know I'd been to a bar and spent time with cops, so I made no attempt to hide it. In fact, Mitch had an even better idea.

***

MY HEART WAS RACING and I had butterflies in my gut when I walked into that bar on Friday night. There was the familiar noise and laughter, the smell of stale beer, and bullshit that I was no longer a part of.

Through the crowd, I saw Mitch at our old table. He was laughing at something, and when he caught sight of me, he smiled at me like he'd missed me as much as I'd missed him. He said something to the other guys at the table, and they turned to see me making my way through the other cops.

There was a noticeable silence as I weaved through the crowd. Before when I walked through, I would get claps on the back and smartass comments. Now I was lucky to get a nod of acknowledgment.

But when I finally made it through the crowded bar, Mitch stood to greet me. He gave me a one-armed man-hug, then Kurt and Tony did the same, then they said hello to Kira, who was behind me.

Then all eyes fell on the one man at the table I didn't know. I'd seen his picture in the paper, but I'd never been introduced to him. As far as replacements went, he looked the part. He was younger than me, had blond hair like me. He was even sitting in my fucking seat at the table.

"Matt," Mitch said, breaking the awkward silence. "This is Ricky Collins. Ricky, this is Matthew Elliott."

"Of course," Ricky said, standing up to shake my hand. "Nice to finally meet you in person. I've heard a lot about you."

I took his outstretched hand and probably squeezed it a little too tight. "Wish I could say the same."

Mitch cleared his throat and yelled out to the bartender. "A round of drinks for the table."

"Just a soda for me," Kira called out.

Mitch looked at me. "Beer?"

I hadn't had anything alcoholic to drink for a while, so I knew it would go straight to my head. But I thought, *Why the hell not?* "Sure."

We took a seat and general talk started, though it was mostly questions about my newfound fighting career.

I told them some stories of my new partner, Arizona, Boss, and the other guys and boasted a little—or a lot—of my no-loss status, which they disputed of course, saying my shiner was proof enough.

I shrugged. "I said I've never lost a fight, not that I hadn't ever been hit. Black eyes and cut cheeks are all part of it," I told them. "Anyway, you should see the other guy."

Though I knew he was older, Ricky *looked* all of twenty years old and was a lot younger than I'd imagined him to be. He watched and listened like he was sitting at the big kids' table. His eagerness and innocence reminded me of how I probably was when I first made detective.

I kind of ignored him all night, but I wanted him to see I had a history with these boys. That they were *my* boys first. That he was on my team, keeping my seat warm. He was just temporary where he was, because when this was done, it'd be back to the old Fab Four.

At least that was what I told myself.

Kira sat next to me, smiling and laughing as we talked, and I could see me being out and socializing outside of the FC made him happy. I think it was his way of reminding me, even though I wasn't a cop anymore, I still had friends. Kira had always thought it was like I'd wandered off on my own the day I left the police, and maybe this was his way of showing me I didn't have to take on the world by myself.

And every time I realized just how much he loved me, how much he tried to help me, every lie I'd told him tied knots in my stomach.

Talk at the table soon turned to Kira and how he was teaching Rachel, Evie, and Anna self-defense, and when Mitch caught my eye, he gave a pointed nod toward the bar. We left the others talking and laughing, and when we were perched up against the bar and out of earshot, he asked me how I was doing.

"I'm okay."

"Really?"

I shook my head. "It's... hard."

"You knew it would be."

"Not this hard. I feel like I'm flying blind. I feel very alone in this." Jesus. Nice way to ease into the conversation. "Sorry, it's just that I can't talk about this to anyone else."

"Don't apologize," he said softly. "We're pulling it together. The info you give is invaluable. We've got a team on this. You're not alone in there."

I nodded. It was comforting to know he still had my back, but it somehow didn't feel like enough.

"I saw your man in the crowd last Friday night."

"Perez, from the third floor," Mitch said. "Said you fought like a machine. Actually, he said you went off."

I nodded. "They wanted to know why I left the force. I told them though the media made it look like it was my decision, I was basically fired because I have anger issues."

Mitch smiled. "How they treating you?"

"The guys on my team are good men. They're not involved in this, Mitch. They're just trying to make a living. It's Tressler. From what I've seen, not even Boss, who's my trainer and like his second-in-command, knows anything. He knows about the illegal fights, but not the drugs." I sighed. "Boss is a good man, Mitch. He reminds me of Berkman."

Mitch gave me a half smile and turned to face the bar more than me. "Don't get attached to them, Matt."

I ignored that.

"How's your new partner?"

Mitch looked over at the table to where Ricky was still sitting. "He's all right. He's young, but he's got a good head on his shoulders. He's got a long career ahead of him." Mitch took a sip of his beer. "He reminds me a lot of you."

I watched as Kira searched for me, and when he saw me talking to Mitch, he smiled. I tried to smile back at him but couldn't quite make it work.

"He's worried about you," Mitch said so only I could hear.

"I know he is," I mumbled. I turned to face the bar, away from Kira. "He deserves better."

"No, he doesn't," Mitch replied quickly. "He deserves you."

I shook my head, and instead of saying anything, I finished my beer.

"Matt, I wanted to see you tonight because the other night on the phone, you sounded... off," Mitch said softly. "Kira told Anna you've been distant lately. He's worried about you. Don't push him away. Not after everything you've been through. Not for this."

I looked away from him. "Some days I feel like the lines are blurring, know what I mean?"

"Just say the word, Matt," Mitch said in a stern whisper. "Just say the word and you're out of there."

I shook my head. "I'm close now."

"Fuck, Matt, it's hard to watch you struggle like this."

I laughed, but it was without humor. "Hard to *watch* me struggle? You should try stepping into a cage sometime with a guy who wants to kill you."

Mitch was quiet for a long while. He looked at me, and I know he was hurting to see me like this. "For what it's worth, Matt, I wish you'd never asked for this job." He put his hand up to get the attention of the bartender and ordered two more beers. "I know you were the best man for the job. I get that. It made sense. It just doesn't make it any easier."

I picked up my third beer and took a mouthful so I didn't have to say anything.

"But we're watching everything," he said in a hushed murmur. "We've got your back. Don't think you're in this alone. Yeah, you're the front man, but there's a team behind you, you hear me?"

I nodded. "Yeah, I gotcha."

"Good. Feel better?"

I smiled at him. "Yeah. Tonight's just like old times, huh?"

Mitch gave me a sad smile in return. It was hard to watch. "Back to the grindstone tomorrow, huh?"

Which translated as, *Good as it's been to see you, you're on your own again tomorrow.* "Yeah."

"Does Tressler know you're coming here?"

"I have no doubt he knows."

"Then we need to make sure you stay on that team," he said. "If you get booted out of the underground fight because he doesn't trust you, you may as well walk away now."

"I know."

"So you know what we have to do?" he whispered. "It's to protect you when you go back there, you know that, yeah?"

I nodded.

Mitch picked up his beer. "Just don't fucking kill me, okay?"

I tried to smile and failed miserably.

Mitch put his hand around my neck and pulled me in close so he could whisper in my ear. "I love you like a brother. Don't forget that."

Then he slammed his beer bottle on the bar and pushed

me as hard as he could. "What the fuck, Elliott!" he yelled at me. "You're not a fucking cop anymore!"

And it was one second of utter silence before the room erupted.

I lunged for Mitch, and he tried to swing at me, but there were suddenly about twenty cops between us.

There were arms holding me back and men in front of me. Faces I knew, of men I'd known for years, the faces of men who should have stopped me, soothed me, but didn't. They were protecting Mitch, protecting one of their own.

Not me.

To them, I wasn't one of them anymore. Part of me realized in that moment, I *wasn't* one of them anymore.

The rage I'd tried so hard to contain these last few weeks was back in full force. I threw off two or three men, then swung at another, and I saw it on their faces.

Fear.

They were scared of me.

They knew what I could do. They'd seen me fight, they knew the damage I could do.

It was loud and there was yelling and it was all happening so fast, but then Kira stepped in front of me.

And it stopped.

The noise, the voices, the commotion, my entire fucking world. Everything.

I realized I still had my fists raised and the look in his eyes nearly killed me. Behind him was Mitch, surrounded by Kurt and Tony, but most surprising was Ricky. He stood right in front of Mitch, his partner, glaring at me with his hands up.

If I wanted Mitch, I'd have to go through him first.

His partner.

A true fucking partner.

I looked back at Kira as I was being shuffled outside and saw him say something to Mitch, but then he followed me out. And they basically threw me out onto the street.

Kira came out, wide-eyed and with pure disappointment written all over his face. He threw his arm around my shoulder and led me forcefully to his car. He opened the door and gritted his teeth. He was so fucking angry with me. He was so angry he couldn't speak.

The entire trip home was quiet. Not a word, not a sound, nothing but my pulse hammering in my ears. When we got home, I followed him inside. He threw his keys on the kitchen counter, turned to me, and finally he spoke. "Want to tell me what the fuck that was all about?"

I shook my head. "I don't even know," I answered, louder than I intended. I tried again, quieter. "I don't know. We were just talking about work—" Then I corrected, "*his* work, and I said something about him having a new part-ner..." I shook my head at how easy the lies just spewed from my mouth.

"You might not work with them anymore, Matt," Kira spit at me. "But I do. I have to face those guys every day! What the hell am I supposed to say to them when I walk in to work tomorrow?"

"I'm sorry."

He shook his head, still too angry with me. I didn't blame him one bit. "And Mitch?" he cried. "Your best friend! What the fuck am I supposed to say to Anna on Monday when I see her for class? You just tried to take her fiancé's head off."

"I'm sorry."

He threw his hands up and stopped pacing to look at me. "Just what exactly are you sorry for?"

"I had my fists up at you," I answered, on the verge of fucking tears. I shook my head. "I would never hurt you."

His head fell back and he sighed through a frustrated groan. "Not physically, Matt. I know that. You put your hands down as soon as you saw it was me. I know you'd never physically hurt me," he said with a calmness that scared me. "But emotionally... well, I just don't even know what page you're on anymore."

"I'm dealing with everything the best I can," I told him. Probably the first honest truth I'd said in far too long. Then like the idiot I was, realization hit me that he could be trying to tell me goodbye. I gasped as a sudden pain ripped through my chest, and tears sprang to my eyes. "No." I shook my head. "No, no."

Kira looked at me, even more confused.

I sucked back a breath. "You can't leave me."

Kira's eyes widened and his mouth fell open. "I'm not leaving you, Matt. I'm fucking mad at you, but I'm not leaving."

I almost sagged and my heart seemed to start beating again. "I'm so sorry."

He walked over to me, and sliding his hand around my head, he pulled me into his chest. "I'm worried about you."

I nodded. "I'd be lost without you."

"Matt, I said I'm worried about you," he repeated. "Did you hear me?"

I nodded again. "I'm sorry."

When he realized I wasn't saying anything else, he said, "I'm going to bed." It wasn't an invitation, it wasn't anything of the sort. It was a quiet, resigned, "I don't know what else to do" thing to say.

And he left me standing alone in the kitchen.

I knew then, as much as I'd tried to deny it or wish

otherwise, I really knew then I'd crossed a line somewhere. And even though the whole fight at the bar was staged so Tressler wouldn't discredit me, when I thought back to Mitch, Kurt, and Tony in the bar and the way they looked at me as I was being dragged out, I saw it on their faces.

Something I think I'd known for a little while.

I wasn't a cop anymore.

CHAPTER TEN

I WASN'T EXACTLY in the best mood when I got to the FC the next morning. I kept my head down and my mouth shut, and decided unloading on the punching bag was a safer option than on some unsuspecting person who asked me the wrong question at the wrong time.

Arizona seemed to understand, and while he trained alongside me, he gave me distance and silence. I was grateful.

I'd been there for about an hour when one of Tressler's men walked over. "Elliott? Mr. Tressler would like to see you in his office."

Arizona eyed me cautiously, and I gave him a shrug as I followed the walking fridge in to see his boss. But I knew what it was about. I had no doubt in my mind it was about the altercation last night at the bar.

I stood in front of Tressler's desk. "Sir?" I felt like a probationary getting disciplined by a sergeant.

Tressler looked for a noticeably long moment at my still-gloved hands like they were loaded weapons, then he looked at my face. "Seen the papers this morning?"

I looked at his desk then, to the *LA Times* opened to page two, to the blurry pictures of me being thrown out of the bar, shirt torn, looking very pissed off. I looked back to the wall above Tressler's head. "Seems anyone with a phone these days can sell pictures to the media."

His eyebrow flinched as though he agreed with me. "It's an interesting article."

"I haven't read it." Which was a lie. Of course I'd read it. Kira had left it open on the kitchen counter for me this morning when he'd gone to work.

"It says you got into an altercation with your old partner," Tressler said, reading over the article. "'Ex-detective Matthew Elliott was thrown out of The Regent's Arms bar, the local cops hangout, last night after fighting with other members of his old crime-fighting team, the Fab Four. It's believed an argument started between Elliott and his ex-partner, Mitch Seaton, and Elliott was thrown outside before any damage was done. A source said Elliott is now training in Mixed Martial Arts, hoping to make it to the UFC, which is a far cry from his squeaky-clean career in the LAPD.'" Tressler looked up at me from reading. "My favorite part is next," he said, then continued to read. "'Our source goes on to say that things weren't as they seemed between the Fab Four and had been strained since the highly publicized Rajko Tomic incident a year ago. Our source said Elliott has been dealing with anger management issues and his departure from the LAPD was not as amicable as made out to be, just three months ago.'" The press article had Berkman's stamp all over it.

Tressler looked up at me and smiled. "What were you doing there at this cops' hangout?"

"Kira thought it would be a good idea."

"And what does he think of it now?"

"Don't know," I said quietly. "He's not talking to me."

Tressler's lips twisted into a smug smile. It took every ounce of my self-control not to clear that desk and take his fucking head off for even speaking to me about Kira. Maybe that was why the walking fridge was still beside me. "And it seems your *ex*-cop friends aren't talking to you either."

I stared at the wall above his head and gritted my teeth. "They're not my friends."

Tressler leaned back in his chair and smiled. "I don't know if you heard, but there was a press release from the LAPD on the ten o'clock news on the radio, to officially say the officers involved had no comment on the matter. That it was a misunderstanding, nothing more." Tressler paused a moment to look at me. "It seems they've washed their hands of you."

I didn't know about the radio comments. I'd been inside the gym all morning. So my nostrils flaring was an honest reaction. "The only thing they misunderstood was me telling them to go to fucking hell."

Tressler smiled more genuinely this time. "It seems you've generated a little public interest in your position here," he said. Which to him meant more dollars in the betting pool. "I like you, Elliott. I like your 'fuck everyone' attitude. You've got a fire in your eyes that tells me how bad you want it." Then he stopped smiling. "But I'm keeping an eye on you. Fuck up once and you're out. Speak to the media about anything you see or do here, and—" He stopped mid-threat and changed tack. "—and well, I don't recommend you do that."

I gave him a hard nod. "Understood."

"Good."

And with that, I was dismissed. When I walked back

out to the main floor, Arizona gave me a nod and picked up a punch pad.

I liked how he didn't make a scene, even though a lot of eyes watched me leave Tressler's office, all wondering what the hell had just happened. Arizona didn't make a fuss, just threw the punch pad to me, and without a word, told me we were cool.

I held the punch pad for him, so he practiced rib shots and short jabs, and it wasn't for a good fifteen minutes until he spoke. "You good? Still got my sparrin' partner?"

"Yeah, I'm good," I told him.

He never stopped throwing punches into the pad. "Talk about it?"

"I got into a bit of trouble last night," I told him. "Made the papers, and Tressler just wanted to clear up a few things."

Arizona laughed and threw two quick jabs into the pad. "Does it have anything to do with a bar fight?"

"Uh, yeah. How'd you know?"

He smiled. "Boys were talkin' this morning." He threw a few rib shots into the pad. "Said you got thrown out of a bar for trying to punch your old partner."

"Can you hit harder?" I goaded him. "You couldn't bust a grape with that left."

He laughed again but struck the pad I was holding with his left fist with more force. "I take it they weren't no rumors."

I shook my head. "Nah."

Arizona dropped his hands and stood up. "For real?"

"Didn't you see the picture in the papers?"

He scoffed. "What the hell would I do with a newspaper?"

I chuckled at him, at how different he was from most of

the guys I knew. I think that was part of his charm for me. I knew not having came with its own troubles, but he was also blissfully unaware of what was on the news or in the papers.

I envied him that.

He took the punch pad off me. "Get on the floor," he said. "And don't think you're special, Elliott. I ain't that way inclined."

I laughed, and he threw the punch pad at my head.

"You're runnin' out of days before you fight for real," he said. "And you still don't stand a chance if they take you to the floor."

We practiced floor maneuvers, and he certainly didn't take it easy on me. But his choice of words wasn't lost on me. He said 'fight for real' like every fight I'd had and won wasn't real or serious enough.

Two weeks later I found out why.

I WAS SCHEDULED to fight in-house, meaning it was a planned fight with someone from our team. In this case, it was Jamaal. But when Arizona came into the dressing rooms when I was getting changed into my fighting gear, he stopped me.

"It's on," he said with a hushed excitement. "Tonight. You, me, and Cody. Get dressed and ready to fight, but wear your sweats on top. Leave your phone and wallet here—no phones allowed where we're going. Come on, we're leaving now."

Shit, shit, shit. I had a pretty good idea what was going on, but I had to act otherwise. "Where *are* we going?"

"Don't know yet," he answered, getting himself dressed into his gear. "We'll find out on the way. We need to pick up some gear for Mr. Tressler and we'll get told where to go from there."

Well, that didn't sound exactly fucking legal.

It was perfect.

We took one of Tressler's vans because we'd need the room in the back, apparently. Arizona took the driver's seat. I didn't argue. The truth was, I didn't care. Once a stickler for even the smallest of laws, now I didn't give a shit.

Six months ago I would have. Hell, three months ago I would have.

But walking out to the van with an unlicensed driver to make an illegal pickup before an illegal fight, I called shotgun.

"I've only been to this place once," Arizona said as he navigated his way through the side streets. "Instructions were to pull up out back and ring the buzzer."

Great. It was already getting dark, and we were walking into God only knew what.

I certainly wasn't expecting Arizona to stop the van at the back of a sports equipment warehouse. "This is it," he said, pulling on the handbrake.

"Here?" I asked.

"What were you expecting?" he asked as he was getting out.

I got out with him. "How the hell would I know? I don't even know what it is we're picking up."

Cody got out with us and laughed at us. "You two fight like my parents."

Arizona walked over to the large shutter door and stopped. He looked at Cody. "I'm the dad, right?"

I pushed his shoulder. "Fuck off."

Cody laughed again and shook his head. "Nope. You'd both give my momma a run for her money."

So I pushed his shoulder too. "You can fuck off with him."

All joking aside, by the time Arizona pressed the buzzer to alert whoever was on the inside of our presence, I knew the makes and models of the three cars up the side street, that there were two silhouettes of people two buildings down, and that neither building next to us had lights on.

Some habits die hard.

It was ingrained in me to know what I was walking into.

And as the roller door slid up, I wished to God I had my gun. I could almost feel where it should have been in my shoulder holster. Fuck.

I shoved Cody to one side, away from Arizona, and stood on the other side as the door came up, spreading us out. So if some shit was about to go down, the three of us weren't an easy target.

I could feel Cody's glare eating into the side of my head, but I didn't take mine off the two men who were revealed by the opening door.

"Hey, we're from the FC," Arizona introduced us, almost cheerfully. "Here to pick something up for Mr. Tressler."

"You Arizona?" one of the men asked.

"Yep, that's me," he told them. "This here is Elliott and Cody," he said, pointing his thumb to each of us.

"Over here," the other guy said. "There's a bunch of stuff." Then he looked the three of us up and down. "But you guys are big enough to load it, yeah? It's heavy as hell."

"No problem," Arizona said. He pointed to a section of fighting equipment, all brand new, all wrapped in plastic with the labels on them. "This us?"

"Yep," the other guy said, ticking off an inventory sheet. "Three punching bags, three sets of kick pads, four punch pads, a box of strapping tape, and six floor mats. Got enough room in that van?"

"Yeah, we'll be all right," Arizona said.

I was a little confused. This was all sparring gear. I wasn't exactly sure what I thought we'd be picking up, but picking up new gear for the fucking gym was not it. But Arizona collected the thigh pads, looked at me and Cody, and said, "Don't just fucking stand there."

We put the larger floor mats in first, Arizona and I grabbed one end each of the punching bags and threw them in, and we piled everything on top of them.

One of the warehouse guys gave me the inventory sheet to sign for, and the invoice itself looked legit. It was all straightforward. Every item accounted for, every item had a product code and a price. I scribbled something illegible on the paper and handed it back to the guy. "That it?" I asked.

"Oh, wait," the other guy said. "Delivery address. West El Segundo."

"Thanks," Arizona called out as we got into the van.

"Is that the address where we're fighting tonight?" I asked.

"Yep," Arizona answered. "Instructions were to pick up the gear and we'd be given an address. Simple, huh?"

Mmm, too fucking simple, I thought.

Cody sat forward and tapped my shoulder. "What the hell did you push me for?" he asked. "When they were opening the door?"

"I was eliminating their target range if the person on the other side of the door started shooting," I answered. "If we all stood together, they'd have a better chance of taking us all out, but if we're spread out, they'd only get one or two of us before the last guy could stop them."

Both Arizona and Cody stared at me, wide-eyed and gaping mouths.

I smiled. "That shit is ingrained in me, sorry."

Arizona looked from me, to the road, then back to me. "You would have let them shoot me?"

I smiled at him. "I had your back."

"Fat bit of fucking good that is if I get shot in the front."

The look on his face made me laugh. "You know, for a big tough guy, you do a lot of fucking whining."

Cody sat back in his seat. "Yep, definitely sound like my momma."

AS WE TURNED on to El Segundo Boulevard, Arizona asked, "You been down here before?"

"Yeah. It used to be a containment yard for the old ship-ping district, where they'd hold all the imported cars on and off ships."

There were rows of huge warehouse-style buildings, but they were now half-neglected, rusted and falling down. Except tonight there were cars and people everywhere, seemingly oblivious that they were breaking the law, or they just didn't care.

Arizona pulled the van up to one of the doors.

When we got out, I grabbed my bag from the backseat and indicated to the gear we'd just picked up from the sports warehouse. "Are we bringing that in?"

"Nah," Arizona shrugged. "One of the others'll grab it."

And true to form, as we were walking in, Tressler's two henchmen, the two walking fridges, met us on their way out.

Arizona threw Fridge One the keys, and in return,

Fridge Two pointed back to the way they'd walked. "We're on the left side, bottom corner."

I followed Arizona, who seemed to know where he was headed or what he was looking for, at least. But taking in details, even under the darkness of night, I knew where my exit points were and roughly how many men were between me and each of those exits.

Like I said, some habits die hard.

It was like a maze of old offices or storerooms, long abandoned, and we followed the sound of a crowd. We soon walked out into an open floor space, where they once stored imported cars under cover in huge warehouses, about the size of half a football field.

Except now there was a cage in the middle of the floor.

There were groups segmented along the outer walls, which I realized were other fighting clubs, as guys were strapping, sparring, and psyching themselves up. There was also a ring of punters, there to make money on who'd be the last one standing.

Arizona headed left, as told, and soon found two familiar faces of guys from the FC—one was one of the trainers by the name of Pete, and the medic, who was only known as Doc.

"Boss not here?" I asked.

Arizona shook his head. "Won't have no part of it."

That surprised me. "Fair enough."

We walked over and hadn't even put our bags down before Pete started. "Arizona, you tape Cody for me. Elliott, put your bag down, put your hands up." I threw my bag on the floor, took off my sneakers and socks. And when Pete started to wrap tape around my hands and knuckles, that was when I started to get nervous. This was about to happen. I was about to step into a cage and fight without rules. Well, without any *real* rules.

And when I saw Doc's supply bag of the medical equipment he thought he'd need to treat just three guys, I started to get real nervous.

Pete finished my left hand, then started on my right. "First time, huh?"

I nodded. "Yeah."

"Some nerves can be good," he said. "It keeps you on your toes and your eyes wide open. But don't let it cloud your head. It's just another fight. I've seen what you can do, you'll do just fine."

Arizona finished strapping Cody's hands. "Do we know the roll call yet?"

Pete nodded. "Twelve guys, six fights. They've not done the draw yet. Won't know if there's a second round till they tell us."

"Wait," I said. "We have to fight more than once?"

Pete grinned. "Only if you win."

"Well, I don't plan on losing."

"Sometimes they'll do the draw till there's one winner," Pete said, finishing off my right hand. "Depends on how much money there is in the pool." He looked around the dim arena. "There's a good crowd here tonight. Word is, they're here to see you fight."

"Me?" I asked.

Doc, who was sitting against the wall and hadn't said a word yet, finally spoke. "Out of the twelve guys here to fight tonight, you've flattened four of 'em."

Oh, fuck.

"Let me guess," I said flatly. "They're not here to see me win, are they?"

Arizona laughed and clapped his hand on my shoulder. "I'm thinkin' no."

Fuck.

Pete smiled. "Hope you got your game on tonight 'cause they're itchin' for a shot at you."

"A shot at who?" someone said behind us, and I spun to see it was Tressler. His two men were behind him and carrying the protective kick pads from the back of the van, which they threw down near our bags.

"A shot at Elliott here," Pete answered. "Word is there's money here tonight."

A smug smile crept over Tressler's face. "You boys want a wager tonight?"

Playing ignorant, I held up my hands. "No wallet, no phone, sir."

He smiled knowingly. "I should hope not. I place your bets for you, put the cash up for ten percent of your win in return," he said, then looked at Arizona. "How much?"

"Five hundred," he answered. "On me to win."

One of Tressler's eyebrows rose. "That's a lot of money. You don't even know who you're up against yet."

"Need to recoup my losses from last time," Arizona told him.

Cody put himself in for a hundred bucks, then Tressler looked at me. "How confident are you?"

Fuck. "Five hundred," I answered, not trying to think about how many laws I was breaking tonight.

Tressler smiled, rather pleased with himself. "You boys get ready, they'll be calling the draw soon. Good luck," he said. Then as he was walking away, he said, "Don't let me down."

Finally dressed in our protective gear, we took turns

holding the sparring pads so we could loosen up and get ready to fight.

My nerves settled down a bit when the first fight started. The noise, the hype, and the energy in the arena turned my nerves into adrenaline.

Out of the three of us, Cody went in first and was evenly matched against his opponent. Another young kid, same weight class, same division, and he fought well. The match went the distance, and Cody won on points, but he had one hell of a bruised cheek and his ribs down his right side were red raw.

But his busted-lip smile was huge.

Arizona was the next one of us to fight. He fought against one of the guys I'd fought before from Jackson's fight club on the south side. He matched Arizona's height and weight class, but it was a different kind of fight.

It was the first time I'd seen a no-rules bout, and it was brutal. MMA is a brutal sport, but there is always an underlying respect for the martial arts, and when the ref says to break apart or to stop the fight, the opponents always listen.

But not in this. The bell went, the referee—if that was what you'd call him—was in the cage, but it was a free-for-all. Normally not allowed, dirty kicks, illegal knees and stomping were fair game in these fights.

Arizona fought fucking hard, and he gave as good as he got. When he sat in his corner at the end of round one, Pete and Doc got into the cage to tend to him, while I spoke to him through the cage.

"He's jujitsu trained," I told him. It was easy to tell from the way he stood, from the way he fought. "He's waiting for you to get off balance, so use your hands, not your feet. He leaves his left wide open, take him with shots to the ribs."

Arizona nodded, and like I said, unloaded with his fists

to his opponent's ribs, keeping his feet on the floor. But about halfway through the round, he took a chance with a kick and paid the price.

He got taken to the floor, and while they wrestled for the dominant position, his opponent's arm slipped, and Arizona grabbed him, rolled him and put him in the choker hold. Five seconds later, his hand tapped the floor, declaring defeat. Arizona won.

It was all class.

It took the next two fights for Doc to get Arizona wiped down, iced up, and stitched up, but even with a banged-up face, he grinned the entire time.

The guy I was getting in the cage with was listed as Ray, who I presumed was the guy on the other side of the cage staring me down. He was with the same guy who'd been mouthing off at me the other night at the FC, when Kira and his parents had come to watch me fight. The guy who kept calling me *faggot cop*. He was trying to bore holes in my head with his eyes.

I grinned at him.

"I would say don't let him get to ya," Arizona said with a fat lip. "But the more pissed off you are, the better you fight."

I chuckled at him, bouncing on my toes, shaking out my nervous energy.

"You ready?" Pete asked. "'Cause you're up next."

"Yeah." I gave a nervous nod. "I'm ready."

"I've seen this guy fight," Pete said. "He's a kick-boxer and has a mean left foot, so watch for it."

I nodded again and put my mouthpiece in.

"He's gonna try and make an example out of ya," Pete said. "It's not gonna be easy. Remember, there's no grace in this cage. It's not like other fights. There's no respect here, ya understand?"

"Got it."

Then Arizona was beside me. "Remember what we talked about, what we practiced. If he takes you to the floor, do whatever it takes to get out of it. There's no rules here."

I nodded again, but truthfully, if this Ray guy took me to the floor, it was game over for me. "Yeah, I got it."

Arizona looked at me and shook his head. "You have no intention of letting it go that long, do ya?"

I smiled around the mouth guard. "None whatsoever."

He grinned at me just as the bell went and my name was called.

Stepping into that cage was a fucking buzz. The noise was incredible. There were people yelling and cheering. And I was scared out of my mind. I had flashes of Kira in my head and what I'd tell him if this fight ended badly, and I had flickering thoughts of what Mitch and the boys would do if I ended up in the hospital.

I could hear Arizona, Cody, and Pete yelling out to me, that I could do this, I could beat this guy, I could take him down. But I could also hear Ray's team telling him to kill the ex-cop faggot. They were mocking me more than encouraging him, calling me names, jeering the crowd to take their side.

I figured I was the underdog in this fight. No one expected me to win. In fact, they'd come to watch me get beat. They had bet against me, wanting me to get smashed and beaten to a pulp. Which meant this Ray guy had to be pretty good. They wouldn't pitch me against some unknown, unrated starter.

So as the referee stood between us and waited for the last bets to be taken, I shut out the noise, and never took my eyes off Ray. The ref spoke to us about five five-minute rounds, but I wasn't listening. This fight wasn't going that long—either he was being carried out, or I was.

The bell went, the ref called, "Fight," and I put my fist out for Ray to bump with his, the way all fighters did. But he ignored my fist, and while I was undefended, before I'd even started, he jabbed me in the face.

And the crowd erupted.

The noise was deafening, louder than any fight there that night. We danced around for a little while, sizing each other up. I watched him, how he stood, which foot he lifted, which foot bore his weight, which hand he held a little higher, which side he left unprotected. I threw a few jabs and kicked at his thigh a few times just to see how he reacted.

The men in his corner were yelling at him to take the faggot out, to take me down, to make me sorry.

And I welcomed it.

Because the more insults his team screamed at me, the more they called for my blood, the more eager he'd become, the more mistakes he'd make.

And the angrier I got.

I could feel the acidity of it in my gut, and I welcomed it. I sought that familiar anger and rage that lived buried in my belly, and I let it out to play. Normally, they'd warn against fighting out of anger because it clouded your judgment and reaction time. But not me. I thrived on it. Maybe it was years of detective work, having to think under stress, keeping personal feelings in check regardless of the situation, yet being able to react on instinct. I let my emotions rule my fists and my feet.

Fear, adrenaline, and anger were a dangerous mix.

"You got thirty seconds, Elliott," Arizona yelled out over

the noise.

Someone on his team yelled, "Take him down now, Ray. Take him down now!"

And I knew then this was it.

He lunged at me, down low, to take me around the legs and slam me into the floor, but as he bent low to grab me around the waist, I elbowed him in the back of the head, spun my hips, and kneed him in the face.

I didn't need to watch him slump to the floor. I knew he was unconscious by the sound of his nose breaking on my knee.

The crowd was stunned at first but exploded in a mixture of cheers, applause, and insults. I faced the ref and bowed my head, then stepped over the prone, bloodied man on the cage floor like I was stepping over a piece of trash on the ground and walked to the cage fence so I could bow my head to the crowd.

I almost forgot what I was really there for. For one second, I wasn't a narcotics detective. I wasn't undercover. I was a fighter.

Arizona and Pete were suddenly beside me in the cage. Both men were grinning, and Arizona hugged me. "Great fight, man."

Ray's teammates came into the cage from their door and went straight to the man on the floor. The leader of their team, the most vocal guy, eyed me like he couldn't wait to kill me, so I smiled at him.

While the ref and their team's medic checked over poor Ray, Doc climbed into the cage. He put his gloved hands up to my face, looking for damage, and shrugged. "You're good."

Then Arizona laughed. "Come on, we gotta get outta here."

He wasn't joking. I didn't even get to put on shoes or a shirt. We literally picked up our bags, the few kick pads, and made our way back to the van, and Arizona left the abandoned lot like a bat out of hell.

From the passenger seat, I pulled on a shirt, and when I looked at Arizona and Cody, they were both grinning. "We fucking won!" Cody cried. He sat forward in his seat and held out his fist. "The three of us!"

I bumped my fist to his, as did Arizona, and I laughed. "That was fucking awesome!"

"Oh shit, you should have seen that guy's face," Arizona said. "The one who has a lot to say about you? He was fucking ang-gry."

Cody laughed. "Yeah, I don't think he likes you very much."

Arizona laughed as he drove. "*Like* you? He wants your fucking head."

"Well, I'll just have to politely tell him there's only one man who gets my fucking head, and it ain't him."

Arizona's mouth fell open, but then he busted up laughing, but Cody didn't get the joke at all.

We were still on a high when we got back to the FC, and we were still in the parking lot at the back entrance before we relayed our evening to the boys who were waiting to hear how it went.

I told them how Cody went the distance and won on points. "The boy's got skills," I said with a laugh. "And Arizona here won his fight on pure technique. The other guy tried to take him down dirty, but our man here was too good. Pure. Fucking. Class."

Arizona, with his bruised and swollen face, obviously wasn't used to compliments. He brushed it off and shook his head. "Elliott here did his usual first-round KO."

As we talked about our night, we unloaded the gear from the van and carted it into the back storeroom. The other guys helped and we had it done in no time, and it was only when Arizona and I were carrying in the heavier stuff that I realized something was different.

"Wassup?" Arizona asked as we stacked the punching bags against the wall.

"Nothing," I replied. I pretended to stretch my back and groan. "Just, they feel a ton heavier at the end of the night than they do in the afternoon."

"One hundred forty pounds is one hundred forty pounds," he said.

It wasn't the weight of them that bothered me.

"Come on," Arizona said, dismissing me. "You need to go home and go to bed, old man."

"Old man?" I joked. "Did I look like an old man in the cage tonight?" I pretended to punch the air a few times.

He rolled his eyes at me, but we went into the dressing rooms to collect our wallets from our lockers. I checked my phone and had a message from Kira.

Locking up tonight. Don't worry, Chris is here with me. See you when I get home.

I bid Arizona goodnight with a fist bump and a one-arm man-hug and the promise to see him on Monday.

I needed to get home before Kira. I had a fucking lot of information to relay back to Mitch and Ross. I walked inside, dumped my gym bag on the floor, and headed straight for my closet.

I pulled out the little phone, and instead of texting messages, I dialed.

Ross Berkman answered. "What's wrong?"

I smiled. "I know how Tressler's taking delivery of the coke."

CHAPTER ELEVEN

"I FOUGHT in the underground circuit tonight," I said quickly.

"You what?" Berkman yelled down the line.

"Just shut up and listen," I said, not really caring if he liked my tone or not. "I need to tell you this before Kira gets home."

I heard the line click and the sound echoed in my ear. "You're on speaker," Berkman said. "Now what the hell did you do and why the hell didn't you let us know?"

"Because they walked in, told me to get dressed to fight, and we left. I didn't have a chance. I had to leave my phone and wallet at the FC. I had no way of contacting you without making it obvious."

"Where did you go?" It was Mitch's voice. "Where did they take you?"

"The old storage yards off El Segundo," I answered. "But we made a delivery pickup on the way."

"Of what?" Berkman interrupted.

"If you'd shut up and let me finish, I'd tell you," I whisper-shouted into the phone. I'd never spoken to him that way before. I could imagine his face reddening and Mitch trying not to smile. "We took the FC van to the back delivery door of the sporting goods warehouse on South Western, off West Manchester in Westmont. We picked up new supplies for the club—mats, pads, gloves. I was surprised, but when I saw what we were collecting, I didn't think anything of it," I admitted. "Not until after the fight. When we were unloading the van, I noticed the punching bags had been switched. The bags themselves were exactly the same—same brand, same weight—but the manufacturer's packaging was sealed different."

I let them absorb this news.

Then I continued, "Tressler's bringing in cocaine inside the punching bags. It's not the Fight Club or any of his staff or even the fighters. It's coming from the manufacturer. Wherever he's getting these punching bags, it's coming from there. The underground fights are just a distribution point. No one looks twice at punching bags at a fight club. They're a dime a dozen. He's doing it all in plain sight. The unsanctioned fights are just a distraction from what's really a drop-off point. There were three punching bags last night that got switched. One hundred forty pounds each, that's a fucking lot of coke."

Then I said, "So, someone else signs for the delivery of the bags, physically drops them off, and his dispatch mules take it from there."

"Yeah, so?" Tony asked.

"He doesn't touch it," I said. "If the drop-off goes bad, his hands are clean."

They listened as I gave them the details of the fight arena, told them how Fridge One and Fridge Two were never far from Tressler, how they were armed with Ruger

9mms, and what I estimated the crowd to be, and how much money was bet.

"Your fight," Mitch interrupted me. "You hurt?"

"Nah, I'm okay. But I tell ya, I've got a target on my back," I told them. "There's a guy at the LMA club, I think his name is Yuan. He wants me dead. Find out what you can on him. If I get into the cage with him, I don't think one of us is walking out, understand what I'm saying?"

Mitch's voice was tight. "Next fight's in two months?"

"Underground, yes," I told them. "Thereabouts. No way of knowing exactly. But I think I'm scheduled to fight his club in a couple of weeks at the FC."

Berkman's gruff voice was next. "If you're in danger and you fear for your life, you need to—"

"Need to what?" I cut him off. "Put my hand up and say 'Don't hit me too hard because I'm really an undercover cop'? Because fuck, that'll end well." I scoffed sarcastically. "I fear for my fucking life every time I step in that cage."

"Matt, we'll be watching you," Mitch said. "We've got our ear to the ground, okay?"

I rolled my eyes. "Just keep an eye on Kira," I said quietly. "That's all I want. Make sure no one follows him, no one from any other fight club goes near him, you hear me? Just make sure he's safe."

Alarmed, Kurt asked, "Do you think he's in danger?"

"No," I answered honestly. "But none of us thought that with Tomic, did we?"

No one answered.

"Just watch him," I repeated. "I can look after myself."

"Matt, are you okay?"

I didn't answer Mitch's question. Instead I said, "I've told you all I know. I'll have no way of letting you know when or where this next drop-off is, so this will probably be our last communication until the fight. You guys are just gonna have to figure out what you can without me. But I'll tell you this," I said flatly. "You've got less than eight weeks to blow this fucking case open. The next underground fight will be my last. Then I'm out. Either someone will kill me, or the lying to Kira will. Either way, I'm done."

I heard the front door open, and Kira called out, "Hey, you home?"

I turned off the phone and yelled back, "Yeah, just in here." I slid the phone to the back of the shelf and darted to the bathroom to flush the toilet. Kira met me at the door as I pretended to wash my hands. "Just got home before you," I lied again.

"How'd your fight go?"

"Good. KO'd him in the first round."

Kira shook his head and smirked. "Work was kinda quiet. Mitch's team is working on some big case, apparently. They're pulling all sorts of hours so they weren't at the gym tonight," he said. "Of all the things, I certainly don't miss you working those kind of hours." He smiled and kissed me. "What did you want to do tonight? It's still kinda early."

I slid my arms around him and sighed at the familiar scent. "I will do whatever you want," I told him. "I'm completely at your mercy."

"Mmm," he hummed. "Let's go grab a bite to eat," he said. Then he pushed me back into the bathroom. "But shower first, you stink."

I laughed and pulled him into the bathroom with me. "Better make it a late reservation."

We eventually went out for dinner, spent the night talking, both of us pretending I wasn't trying too hard to act normal. I knew by the way he looked at me he knew I wasn't telling him something. But he never asked me outright, and I certainly didn't bring it up.

But the guilt wormed its way into my chest, and now instead of fearing fighting in a cage, I was starting to fear Kira finding out even more.

Later that night, I took the memory card out of the phone, bent it until it snapped, and threw them both in the trash.

I really was in this alone.

MONDAY at the gym I was still on a bit of a high from winning the underground fight. After a day of training and recuperation, I was talking shit about the fight with Arizona when Tressler called us into his office.

He looked rather pleased. "You boys fought well Friday night," he said. "Here." He reached into his breast pocket. "Your dividends." He pushed a wad of notes across his desk to Arizona, then slid a considerably larger wad of notes to me. "Lot of money on your fight, Elliott. Not many had you to win," he said with a sly smile. "So the purse was in your favor."

Shit. There must have been eight or nine thousand dollars in that wad of hundred dollar bills. Like I hadn't broken enough laws already, I took the money and gave him a nod as thanks. I'd just received illegal money.

"I took out the five hundred I put down for your bets," Tressler said. "Plus my ten percent loan fee. But it's all there. You can count it if you like."

To count it would mean I didn't trust him. Only a fool would count it in front of him.

Arizona pocketed his winnings and smiled. "Thank you, Mr. Tressler."

He gave us a nod, dismissing us, and when we were in the dressing room packing up and getting ready to leave, I handed Arizona half the money Tressler had just handed me. Not that I counted, but it was probably a couple of grand.

He stared at me with wide eyes. "What's that for?"

"I wouldn't have won a cent without your help," I told him. "I figured me adding that to what you earned makes us equal, dollar wise anyway."

He held the money out to me. "I can't take this."

"Yes you can," I said. "I wouldn't have won without you, and today we take home equal money."

His brow pinched and he frowned. "I don't need no money out of pity."

"Pity?" I asked. "Who the fuck said anything about pity? I told ya why I wanted you to have it. Do what you want with it. Give it away, I don't care. But it's yours." I pulled my bag from my locker and shut the door. "Buy Lashona some flowers or something. Or buy that cute kid of yours a new toy."

He smiled at the mention of his wife and daughter. "My girl was so proud of me when I told her I won." He shook his head in wonder. "Don't know why she puts up with me. She deserves nice things. I want to be a good husband to her, and I want my little girl to have a good life, ya know. Both of them."

I sat down beside him. It was the first time I'd seen him so... vulnerable. "You're a lucky man."

He nodded. "I know," he said with a smile. "How 'bout you and Kira? Did ya tell him how good you did the other night?"

I sighed. "I, um... I told him I won my fight, but not that I didn't fight here," I said quietly. How could I explain this? "He... he doesn't really understand..."

"But he's a kick-boxer, yeah?"

I nodded. "Yeah, trained in karate as a kid, went on to kick-boxing as he got older. He's a personal trainer but teaches boxing as a type of fitness. So he understands the love of it as a sport, he just... he just struggles with why I'm doing this, why I left the police..." I stopped talking before I said too much.

Arizona looked at me for a long second. "Why's he struggle with it?"

And I said out loud what I'd only ever told myself. "I'm doing this for him. I've not told him that, but I think he knows. I mean, he's not stupid..."

"You've not talked about it?"

I shook my head. "No. He'd feel guilty if I got hurt," I said. "I don't want him to worry." Then I took a deep breath and exhaled slowly. "I don't want him at risk because of what I did for a living. Doing what I did, being a cop and being in the public eye, put him at risk. I couldn't put him through it again."

"He's okay though, isn't he?" Arizona asked quietly. "And the girls he was kidnapped with? They're all doing okay?"

I nodded and kind of shrugged. "They're all still in counseling, but yeah, they talk openly about it."

"And you?"

"Me, what?"

"Talk about it? With Kira, with anyone?"

I shook my head. "No."

Arizona picked up the backpack at his feet and stashed

the money I'd given him inside it. "Man, you need to talk about shit like that or it will eat at you."

I nodded, and pushed down the knot in my stomach. "I know."

Arizona stood up. "I'm going home, man. Gonna take my girls out for ice cream."

"Sounds good."

"You need to go home and talk to Kira."

I nodded. I knew I did. I wanted to. I *needed* to. But I couldn't.

I couldn't tell him. Not any of it. If I started to tell him one little thing, I'd end up telling him everything and expose this whole case.

I wouldn't put him at risk like that. Not again.

When I got home, Kira was on the sofa watching TV. I threw my gym bag on the floor, sat down next to him, and curled up into his side with my head on his chest.

He slid his arm around me and kissed the top of my head. "You okay?"

No.

Not at all.

I miss you.

I'm sorry.

I'm dying inside.

"Yeah, babe. I'm fine."

THE NEXT TWO weeks were hard. Training and sparring at the FC with the boys was intense, but good. It was being home with Kira that was difficult.

I was always busy, doing stuff around the house, volunteering to do some yard work at his parents' house, just so I wasn't alone with him. So he couldn't corner me and make me tell him what the hell was wrong with me.

I was struggling with the deceit and the dishonesty, and he could see it. I knew he could. He was quiet and sad around me, just waiting for me to say something, to finally explain, and of course, I couldn't.

Seeing the disappointment in his eyes nearly broke my heart.

Kind of like how I'd changed, how I was trying a little too hard to act like nothing was wrong was breaking his heart.

I could feel a distance settling between us. One of silence, where we didn't talk, where the guilt of knowing it was all my fault made my heart ache.

And making myself busy eliminated time to think of the mess I'd made of everything.

When Sal and Yumi said they needed some pavers fixed on their back patio, I said I'd happily help out. It was a welcome distraction and something else for me to do to keep busy. Kira came with me, of course, and Yumi said she'd make a lunch, which would inevitably become a dinner. We always ended up there for hours.

And that was the very kind of diversion I needed. I got to spend time with Kira and his family, but because I'd be busy, it was without the pressure of admitting what a mess I'd made of everything.

"You sure you don't mind?" Yumi asked. "It's not an easy job." She inspected my face, looking at the faded bruising to my eye, and pursed her lips.

"Of course I don't mind," I told her, ducking my head so she wouldn't fuss over the almost healed cut. "It'll save you having to pay someone to do it, and I used to do a lot of the stuff around the house for my mom, so it's no big deal."

Sal had all the gear I'd need near all the old, uneven pavers, and before I could start, Kira was beside me. We'd hardly spoken that morning, so I was surprised when he put his hand on my arm. "Sure you don't want me to help?"

"You can if you want," I said, really hoping he wouldn't. "But I think your dad had you pegged for backgammon. Your mom won't play with him."

"Because he cheats!" Yumi yelled from the kitchen, obviously overhearing us.

We looked back at his blissfully unaware, deaf father, who was carrying the game board to the back table. Then Kira looked at me and tried to smile. His sadness was killing me.

"If I need your help, I'll give you a yell," I told him. "Or if you need saving, give me a sign." Kira gave me a sad nod, so I gave him a peck on the cheek. "Enjoy this time with your dad."

I spent the majority of the time on my knees as I set about pulling up the old pavers, stacking them to the side. It wasn't exactly hard work, but it was hot in the LA summer sun, and I soon had my shirt off, tucked into the back of my shorts as I listened to the sound of slapping hands as Kira and Sal argued in sign language and Yumi singing to herself in the kitchen.

It was so family.

It was everything I wanted in a family. Yumi had even put a photo of me on the mantel. Not *just* of me, but a picture of Kira and me together at Thanksgiving last year, but it was the first time I'd been included in anyone's family since I was seventeen.

It was the little things like a simple photo on a mantel, or how Yumi barked orders at me like she did to Kira, or how both Yumi and Sal signed behind my back like I was one of them that made me think I'd finally found another family.

It was the little things like that that made me realize what I was risking.

"Matt!" Yumi called out. "Lunch is almost ready. Come inside and clean up."

I looked up from my shovel, where I was spreading out some sand for underneath the newly laid pavers, to find the back table empty. I hadn't even realized Kira and Sal weren't there anymore.

I went inside to get cleaned up, and as I came back from the bathroom, I walked into the living room to find Kira and Sal mid-conversation. I didn't exactly catch Sal's hand movements to see what he said to Kira, so I couldn't be certain, but I think Sal signed the words 'talk to him.' But it was the way they both stopped signing and looked at me. I was pretty sure I was their subject of conversation.

I wanted to be angry that they were talking about me, but I could hardly blame them.

Kira's parents saw how quiet he was. They saw how strained it was between us. It was their right to be concerned for their son.

The fact I was the reason behind how miserable he was made my stomach twist.

"I'll just see if Yumi needs anything," I said quietly, leaving father and son alone, but not before seeing Kira frown before I walked out.

I smiled at Yumi when I went into the kitchen. "Need help?"

"No, all done," she said. Then she stopped and looked at me. "You okay?"

"Yeah," I lied. "Why wouldn't I be?"

"Did you two have a fight?"

"No," I said, playing ignorant. I looked down at the dishes of meat and salad. "Want me to carry these out for you?"

"Are your hands clean?" she asked.

I held up my freshly washed hands as proof.

Yumi rolled her eyes, handed me two of the plates, and nodded toward the dining room, which was just off the living room where Kira and Sal were.

"Lunch," I announced as I walked in.

And it was a little awkward as we sat around to eat. Sal looked between me and Kira, and Yumi stared pointedly at the three of us.

"Something wrong with my food?" she asked. "Normally you never shut up."

"The dumplings are dry," Sal signed, and Yumi threw a bread roll at him. I laughed, then Kira chuckled, and the normal Takeo-Franco conversations started. They talked about Kira's job, my latest fights, the cabin at Wrightwood, and Yumi's hinted again spring weddings.

Sal gave her a quick glance that told her to drop the subject, then she looked between me and Kira. Before she could ask us bluntly, as only she could, what the hell was going on, I stood up, taking an empty dish to the kitchen, declaring those pavers weren't going to lay themselves.

By mid-afternoon the pavers were done, and although Yumi offered for us to stay for dinner, Kira said we should be going.

They'd spent most of the afternoon talking, and no doubt I was the subject of some of that conversation. What was said, I didn't know. I didn't want to know.

We got home and I could tell Kira wanted to talk, like he was trying to find the words to start. I didn't want to hear it. I couldn't. I could feel everything I'd known slipping through my fingers, and I couldn't bear to have this conversation right now. So with a quick kiss to his lips, I told him I'd have a quick shower, then he could choose what we did for the night.

In the shower, I scrubbed my body, brushed my teeth, and scrubbed myself again, and after I put off going back out to the living room for as long as I could, I put on some old sweat pants and found Kira on the sofa.

"Feel better?" he asked.

"Much." I sat down beside him on the new sofa, leaning into his side under his arm, where I fit just right.

"Matt," he said, and my stomach knotted. I knew what question was coming. He was about to ask me what the hell was wrong with me, what had changed, why was it different now?

But that was not what he asked at all.

His voice was quiet. "Why won't you look at me?"

"Huh?" I asked, sitting up, looking at him. "I look at you."

He shook his head and shrugged. "Just feels like you won't make eye contact with me."

It broke my heart to see him so sad. I slid my hand along his jaw, pulling his face around to mine. "I look at you. Kira, you're all I see," I told him, and I pressed my lips to his.

He pulled back and searched my eyes. His voice was just a whisper. "Am I losing you?"

My eyes widened, and I shook my head. "No," I said, my voice breaking on just one word. I grabbed his face and kissed him, hard. I crept up his body, keeping my mouth on his, and slid my leg over his hips so I straddled him.

I needed to feel him, his warmth, his body. I needed to make him feel me. I needed to connect with him, to be with him. I needed him to have me.

I ground down on him, trying to have as much of me touching as much of him as possible. I pulled my mouth off his to tell him, "I need you."

"Matt," he murmured my name.

He was about to tell me no. He was about to tell me we needed to talk this out, not take it to bed. So I took his earlobe between my lips and breathed the words in his ear. "Make me yours. Show me, please."

There was no resistance, no telling me no. So I climbed off him and led him to bed. I undressed us both and kept my eyes on his. He wanted me to look at him, so I did. I never took my eyes off him. I never looked away.

It almost killed me.

His eyes were searching, searching for doubt, for hope, for some recognition of the man he fell in love with.

I don't know what he found.

When he was finally inside me, I tried to set the pace. I wanted him to fuck me, harder, harder. I wanted to be reminded of who I belonged to, of who owned me. I wanted him to take me from behind, so he could have his way with me. So he couldn't see the pain in my eyes, how lost I was, how my heart was breaking. But he kept me on my back, pushing deeper inside me, with his face just an inch from mine.

And he wouldn't fuck me. He wouldn't pound into me, no matter how much I begged, no matter how I pleaded. I dug my fingers into his ass, urging him to hurt me, but he leaned back off me, grabbed my wrists, and pinned them above my head.

Then he proceeded to make love to me. He kept his face above mine, kissing me, staring into my eyes. So slow, so deep, so utterly heartbreaking.

When he let go of my hands, I gripped him and held

him so tight. My arms wrapped around him, then my legs, so his weight was on me, holding me down, holding me together.

I closed my eyes and buried my face into his neck so he couldn't see me cry.

CHAPTER TWELVE

____

THINGS WERE different between Kira and me after that. Not better. Different.

Like we'd acknowledged something neither of us wanted to admit.

The two weeks leading up to my next fight were hard for both of us. There were awkward silences between us, where neither of us was sure of what to say. I could see Kira look at me like he was trying to figure out what was going on in my head, like he was trying to figure out where the man he fell in love with went.

I trained harder, longer, and he spent more time at work too. He said his boss, Chris, needed more time away, but it was an unlikely excuse. It was as though he couldn't bear to watch me self-destruct.

I didn't blame him one bit.

And things at the FC got weird for me too. I found myself dropping my guard, lowering my hands when I was training and sparring, letting myself get hit.

I knew it wasn't rational, but I liked it.

It felt real. When everything else in my life seemed to be slipping away, physical pain was real.

And by the time Friday came around, I knew my head wasn't in it. I was actually feeling pretty low, and emotionally, I was not up for a fight.

It was a closed door, in-house fight, which meant I was getting in the cage with someone from the FC. In this case, it was Jamaal.

The bell went for round one, and we bumped fists, but I just couldn't bring myself to fight.

I didn't want to hurt anyone anymore.

I wanted to *be* hurt.

I wanted to feel a physical pain that matched the war in my head and the ache in my chest. I needed a physical pain to balance the internal pain. To validate it.

I made a few half-hearted attempted strikes at him, barely touching him with any force. I deflected some of his punches and kicks but let most of them hit me. In the face, in the ribs, the thighs, I didn't care. I wanted him to hit me.

When the bell sounded, I went to my corner. Boss wiped my face down and asked, "What the hell are you doin'?" He gave me a sip of water and put ice on my face. "Don't give this guy a chance, he's got a mean right hook."

My head fell back a bit, like I was too tired to hold it up, and I looked at Boss and smiled.

In the second round, I could tell Jamaal knew I wasn't really trying. I pushed him when I should have struck or kicked him, or I'd leave myself unprotected, giving him opportunities to hit me, but it seemed he was holding back.

I was getting frustrated with it and pushed him harder, trying to make him angry. But for most of the second round, it was push and shove and mostly wrestling. I'd taken a few jabs to the eye and the ribs, but it wasn't enough.

When all I wanted was for him to fucking hit me.

Boss sat me down at the end of round two and put more ice on my face. "Don't know what you're playin' at here, Elliott. But get out of your fucking head. You're all twisted in there." He thumped the heel of his hand on my head. "The only thing that'll do is get you beat black and blue."

I took a sip of water, trying to catch my breath. I stood up, ready to fight. "Good."

Boss threw his hands up, took the little stool, and walked out of the cage, shaking his head.

Someone else I'd let down.

Excellent.

The bell went, I tapped fists with Jamaal, bounced on my feet, and didn't even put my hands up.

But he wouldn't hit me.

I pushed him, trying to piss him off so he'd throw some punches at me. The guys outside the cage were yelling at him to take the fucking shot.

"I want a fair fight," he called out to them. Then he looked at me and said, "Put your hands up."

"Hit me," I replied.

He looked at me, confused. "What?"

"I said hit me! Just fucking hit me!"

Jamaal ran at me, picked me up, and drove me into the mats. I struggled with him a little, more only to keep him angry, but when he finally threw his fist at my face, it was almost a relief.

A fucking relief.

And while he repeatedly struck my ribs and face, somewhere in my head was telling me this wasn't right. It wasn't a normal thought process to want this or to need this. Something wasn't right with me.

But it was cathartic. The more he hit me, the more I was hurt, in some strange, fucked-up headspace, the better I felt.

I wasn't resisting his punches, I wasn't even trying, and Jamaal's hits became slower and lighter until eventually he just stopped. He got off me and shook his head. "What the fuck, man?"

I couldn't even get up off the floor.

I didn't want to move.

It wasn't until Doc's face appeared in front of mine, looking concerned and pulling my eyes open. "He's okay," I heard him say, then a large pair of hands pulled me up off the floor.

I could hear Arizona mumbling to me as he all but hauled me to the dressing room and sat me down in the medic room. Doc was in my face, shining lights in my eyes, feeling my eyebrows, cheekbones—his fingers adding a sharp sting to a dull ache.

Then Boss was there, telling me it was the saddest fucking fight he'd ever seen. "What the fuck, Elliott? I don't know what that was." He waved his hand to the door. "You got some sick need to feel pain? Because that was fuckin' pathetic." Then he stopped and took a look at my face. "Jesus."

Doc nodded. "I'll have to see how that eye heals, but he'll be out for two weeks, at least, maybe longer."

"He's got a big fight in two weeks," Boss told him. "We're hosting the LMA boys and Tressler wants him to fight."

Doc mumbled something I didn't hear, then he was gone. Boss followed him, almost taking the door off its hinges in the process.

My head fell back to rest on the wall behind me, and Arizona sat down next to me.

He didn't speak for a long while. Whether he didn't know what to say, or if he understood my need for silence, I didn't have a clue. My head was pounding and my right eye stung, ached and throbbed at the same time. It was almost swollen shut already.

Finally Arizona said, "You wanna talk about it?"

I had to force myself to answer. "No."

He looked at me then, and sighed. "Where's your keys? You can't drive."

"I'll be okay," I mumbled.

Arizona stood up with a sigh and walked out, only to come back in a few minutes later with his bag and mine. He must have gotten it from my locker. "Come on. I'll take you home."

I didn't argue.

I didn't have it in me.

I gave him quiet, one-word directions to my house as he drove, and no other words were spoken until I got home.

He pulled into the driveway, behind Kira's car. "Kira home?"

"Yep."

"You be okay?"

"Yeah."

"Righto, let's get you inside," he said. Arizona took the keys from the ignition, got out of my car, and as he waited for me to get out, the front door opened.

Kira walked out onto the front porch. "Everything okay?"

"Hey," Arizona said in greeting. "He needed a driver."

I got out of the passenger side, feeling every ache in my body, and stood up. It was dark, and Kira obviously couldn't see my face until I walked to the steps and into the front porch light.

"Jesus."

"I'm okay," I lied again. I took the steps one at a time with Arizona following me up.

Kira's eyes were wide as he looked at my face. I didn't stop. I just walked straight inside and headed for the kitchen. I took the frozen peas from the freezer and put them straight on my eye. The cold was an immediate relief to the heat in my face.

I could hear Kira and Arizona talking quietly from the front room, so I walked back out there and fell onto the sofa, keeping the cold bag on my face.

"Does he have a concussion?" Kira asked him.

"Nah, Doc said he was fine."

"What happened?"

"He wouldn't defend himself," Arizona said softly. "Kept asking the guy to fucking hit him."

"He what?"

"He's right here," I interrupted them. I didn't want to hear them talking about me. My body protested as I stood up, and they watched as I slowly took my wallet and phone from my gym bag. I gave Arizona a fifty-dollar bill and passed my phone to Kira. "Could you please be so kind as to call a cab for Arizona," I said. "I need to have a shower and lie down."

Arizona half laughed. "Your ass better be at the FC come Monday mornin', ya hear? I seem to remember not too long ago when you fucked me up like you are right now, and I spent the next two weeks sparrin' with ya."

I put the bag of frozen peas back to my eye and flipped him the bird as I walked down the hall to the bathroom. I heard their muffled voices as I started the water, and almost by accident, I caught my reflection in the mirror.

Jesus. Fucking hell.

My face was a mess. My eye was swollen, bruised, and bloodied, and my lip was split.

But that wasn't what made me unrecognizable.

It was the look in my eyes.

No wonder Kira had a hard time looking at me. I looked... different. Lost.

I turned away from the mirror, got into the shower and tried to wash away the ache in my muscles, my chest.

Kira came into the bathroom and stood with his arms crossed, leaning against the bathroom counter. "Are you okay?"

"Yeah. Sore."

"Have you eaten? I can get you something—"

"Kira," I interrupted him. "I'm fine. I just want to go to bed, to be honest. I just want to lie down."

He was quiet for a moment before walking to the door. "I'll make you something and bring it in to you. Something my mom used to make for me."

I turned the water off, gingerly dried off, and limped into the bedroom. I didn't even remember being kicked in the thigh, but it was sore too. Naked, I climbed into bed and pulled the sheet over me and closed my eyes.

"Hey," Kira's quiet voice said beside me. "I brought you these."

I opened my eye, my left eye—the right one was too swollen—to find Kira holding a glass of water and some pills.

"Sit up," he said, waiting for me to do as I was told. Then he handed me the glass and tablets. He waited for me to swallow them down, then put the glass of water beside the bed. And he walked out without another word.

I lay down again, and the next thing I knew, Kira was sitting on the bed. "Hey," he said, waking me up. "I made some tea. It's Japanese peppermint," he explained while I painfully sat up. "Mom used to make it for me when I lived with them. It helps with sore muscles and bruising, apparently."

I took the teacup and put it to my lips and sipped it. It was all kinds of awful. "Thanks," I said softly.

"It was nice of Arizona to drive you home," he said.

I nodded and regretted the movement. "Yeah. He's a nice guy."

Kira frowned. "He told me he watched your fight. Said you didn't even put your hands up."

I sipped the tea again before answering. "Just wasn't in the right mindset tonight," I said weakly. I turned my face so he could see my eye. "Shows, huh?"

"Looks like it hurts," he offered sadly. "Can you tell me why?"

"Why, what?"

"Why you wanted that guy to hit you?"

I sipped the tea and gave the cup back to him. "I don't know," I mumbled, lying back down. "I'm tired," I added, pulling the sheet back up, putting an end to this conversation.

I wasn't up for it. My whole body ached enough without adding my heart to the list.

I closed my eyes and the dip in the side of the bed told me he'd gone. Somehow I fell asleep.

I woke up alone without knowing if Kira even came to bed or if I slept by myself. The sun through the window told me it was late, that Kira would have left for work already. I rolled over and was sharply reminded of my swollen eye.

I groaned into my pillow and slept until noon.

KIRA HAD LEFT a note saying he had to work till five and some pills with the instructions to take two after food. I made myself eat something, even though the whole right side of my face hurt, then, like a good boy, took my meds.

I was so tired. It was an exhaustion I could feel in my bones. For the rest of the afternoon, I lay on the lounge, staring at the television, dozing on and off, and the next thing I knew it was getting dark.

I sat up and checked the time. It was six o'clock. Shit.

Kira was late getting home. Kira was never late getting home. I gave him another ten minutes, then twenty, but by the time he was another thirty minutes late, with the cold dread of fear that something had happened to him, I called his cell. It diverted straight to voice mail. I might have been a little panicked. "I know you're probably mad at me right now and I don't blame you, but can you just let me know you're okay. Please? You're never home late, and if you're mad at me just tell me. Send me a text if you want, I just need to know you're okay."

My phone beeped thirty long, torturous seconds later. *On my way home. Won't be long.*

Fifteen minutes later he came in through the front door, walked through the lightless house to find me in the kitchen.

"Matt?" he asked cautiously. "What are you doing in the dark?"

I exhaled at the sound of his voice. "I was worried..."

He walked closer but kept a very cold four feet between us. "What were you worried about?"

"That something had happened to you," I admitted quietly. "That you were too mad at me to come home."

"Matt," he said, then let out a shaky breath. "I went and saw Mitch."

My head shot up to look at him. "You what?"

He nodded. "I asked one of the guys at work if they'd seen him at the office, and they said yes. So I called him and asked if I could see him."

I didn't know where he was going with this. "And?"

"I told him I'm worried about you," he whispered. "I told him about your fight last night, that I think something changed for you. Somewhere along the way, something changed."

My heart was hammering and it was getting harder to breathe. "I'm fine."

"No," he said quietly. Adamantly. "No, you're not."

"If this is about what Arizona said about the fight last night..."

"Partly, it is, yes. But something's gotten into you, Matt."

I shook my head and said the only thing I could think of to say. "Please don't leave me."

"What?"

"Remember when you said to me," I said, my words a rush. "Remember at the cabin when we stayed there for the week, you said if I were to leave you it was all for nothing. Remember? You said that?"

Kira nodded. "Yes." But then shook his head, confused.

"Well, if you were to leave me, this would all be for nothing." Fuck, I wasn't making any sense.

"Is that what this is about?" he asked. His voice croaked when he spoke. "Is this about what happened to me with Tomic?"

Yes.

Yes.

A thousand times yes.

"No."

Another lie.

My head started to spin. I think I swayed.

Then Kira grabbed ahold of me. His strong arms were around me. His warmth, his smell was everything I needed and everything I didn't deserve.

"Matt, you're *not* okay."

"I'm really tired," I told him.

"You've been pushing yourself too hard."

"I can handle it."

"It's pretty obvious you can't, babe," he said softly. "You need a break."

Not liking where he was going with the whole break thing, I sighed and tightened my hold on him. "What did Mitch say?"

"He said there wasn't much he could do now in any official capacity, but just that he'll keep an eye on you," Kira said. "Actually his words were 'Tell Elliott from me not to pull any shit like that again because I'll be watching.'" Kira pulled back and gently ran his fingers over my swollen eyebrow. "I think he was just trying to make me feel better."

"I'm sorry," I mumbled. "I didn't mean to scare you, or make you worry."

"Matt—"

"Nothing really changed for me," I told him, answering something he'd said just before. "I mean, leaving Mitch and the guys was harder than I thought, I'll admit that. But I'm trying to get my head around it." Even the half-truths were lies. "But I don't want to hurt you, Kira. It's the very last thing I meant to happen."

"It's okay, babe," he said, though I could see it really

wasn't. "I thought you'd be mad at me. For going to see Mitch behind your back."

I almost laughed. If he only knew the secrets I was keeping from him. "You did it because you care," I said quietly. "Thank you for telling me."

"I do care, of course I care." He pressed his lips to the top of my head.

While apologizing for things I could admit to, I said, "I'm sorry about earlier. I didn't mean to sound so panicked on your voice mail earlier. I just woke up and you weren't here and I thought you might have been too mad at me to come home."

He smiled sadly and kissed the not-sore side of my mouth. "How about I make you some dinner?"

I sighed at his endless supply of love. "You're always so good to me."

"Yes, I am. Now what do you feel like for dinner?" he asked. "I can do stir-fry, steamed fish or poached chicken. They're all quick and easy."

"Grilled cheese."

"Grilled cheese?"

I nodded. "You asked what I felt like eating, and I feel like grilled cheese."

Kira chuckled, and it was a sound I hadn't heard in far too long. He kissed the not-bruised side of my head. "Grilled cheese it is."

I sat at the kitchen counter while he made us dinner of grilled cheese on toast and talked about his day. I pretended my eye, head, and ribs didn't hurt, that I wasn't lying to him, that I didn't feel guilty, just so I could see him smile.

I WALKED into the FC on Monday morning, and the first thing I did was find Jamaal and apologize for not giving him a fair fight.

He thought my blackened, still-swollen eye was bad enough punishment.

"You've got a solid right hook," I told him, trying to lighten the situation. "Anyway, again, I'm sorry I didn't square up to you."

Jamaal snorted. "Let me guess, it's not me, it's you."

I chuckled at him. "Something like that."

"Elliott!" Boss called out from across the gym. "Here! Now!"

Then Jamaal laughed. "Good luck with that."

I walked over to Boss expecting him to give me an earful in front of everyone, but he didn't.

He grabbed my chin and turned my face so he could inspect my eye. "'S not as bad as I thought it would be."

"Kira's mom put this Japanese herbal paste on it yesterday," I told him. "Supposed to draw out bruising and heal damaged tissue, or so she said. Smelled like roadkill."

"Hmm," he huffed, letting go of my chin. "What else did she say?"

"She called me a lot of names, yelled at me for a while, told me to sit my ass down, and then she fussed over me for a good few hours."

I was hoping for a smile, but he ignored what I'd said and huffed again. "You got two weeks, Elliott. Two weeks before you get in the cage to fight again. Physically, you're good to go—except for the eye—and your conditioning and endurance is some of the best I've seen. But in here—" He reached up to tap the side of my head. "—in here is a fucking mess."

"Sorry, Boss," I said quietly.

"I don't wanna hear no sorry-assed apologies," he stated flatly and picked up his usual clipboard.

I looked over to Arizona, who was giving us a safe distance. "Thought I'd be Arizona's sparring buddy today, hold the pads for him while he works out."

Boss stuck the pen in his mouth and tried to draw back on it like it was a cigarette. When he realized it was just his pen, he pointed it at me. "Your boyfriend'll be fine," he started, then he stopped. "I mean, not your *real* boyfriend... Not what's-his-name, I meant Arizona, as in your new best friend, Arizona, will be just fine without you today."

I tried not to smile at his faux pas.

"Don't you dare fucking smile," he barked at me. "I'll tell ya whatcha gonna be doin' today, and that is you can start by jumpin' rope," he said, pointing his pen at the skipping ropes along the wall.

"Yes, Boss," I said. "For how long?"

"Until I tell ya to stop," he snapped at me. "Or until you pass out, or throw up, or drop fucking dead, that's when you'll stop. Or better yet," he said, this time thumping the side of his own head, "until you stop thinkin' about whatever the fuck it is that's scramblin' your brain."

"Got it," I said. "Start skipping. Don't stop."

Boss huffed again and walked past Arizona. "What the fuck do you think is so funny?" Boss snapped at him.

"Nothin', Boss," Arizona said, but then he looked at me and grinned.

I walked over to the skipping ropes, picked one up, and moving to the corner out of everyone's way, I started to skip rope.

"You okay, man?" Arizona asked.

"Yeah. Boss's got me on reprimand, though," I told him.

Every jump jarred the ache in my head. "Thanks again for taking me home on Friday night."

"No problem," he replied. "D'you talk to Kira?"

"A bit," I lied.

"Arizona!" Boss yelled out. "Leave him the fuck alone," he barked, ranting at him about me needing space to clear my head, but I tuned them out.

I kept skipping rope, regulated my breathing, and the only thing in my head, apart from a sickening ache, was the sound of my feet hitting the floor.

I don't know how long I jumped rope.

Boss spent some time with some other guys, running through their training programs, and he walked through the doors to the offices without so much as a backward glance at me.

I never stopped skipping rope. I did it mechanically, unthinking.

When he came back out and saw I was still going, he smiled. I had sweat running down my face, down my back and every muscle in my body was on fire.

But I wouldn't stop.

Even the other guys in the gym were looking at me, some with pity, some I'm sure were taking bets to see if I passed out or vomited first.

Boss eventually took mercy on me and stood in front of me while I still jumped rope, reading something on his clipboard. "Hmm," he said thoughtfully. "I gotta give it to ya, Elliott. You got more discipline than what's good for ya." Then he looked up from his clipboard. "For fuck's sake, stop skipping."

I dropped the rope and staggered over to the bench seat along the wall. Boss threw my water bottle to me, and I took a mouthful in between panting breaths. Then I wiped a towel over my face, forgetting about my eye. "Ow, fuck."

"How's the eye?" Boss asked.

"Sore."

"How's your head?"

"Sore."

"No doubt," he said. "Is it any clearer? Or still a fucking mess?"

I shrugged and took some deep breaths instead of answering.

"You wanna do this every day for two weeks?"

"No."

"Then I suggest you get your shit together, or tomorrow I'll have you on the ropes again."

"Yes, sir."

"And what the hell have I said about you callin' me that?"

"Sorry, Boss."

"That's better."

"What do you want me to do next?"

He stared at me like I'd sprouted a second head. "Next? Jesus, you are a glutton for punishment." He shook his head and watched me still trying to get my breath. "Did you get all up in your head, thinkin' about what it is you shouldn't be thinkin' about?" he asked. "Then you get past that, and there ain't nothin' in your head but the rhythm of your feet?"

I nodded. "Yeah."

"Good, now that's where you need to be," he said. "Get rid of the shit that's messin' up your head and leave it at the door. A fighting cage ain't no place for it."

All I could do was nod.

"Now, go shower and go home," he said, like he always did. "Because you stink."

I stood up and withheld the groan from my aching body. "Thanks, Boss."

"You got two weeks, Elliott," he reminded me. "Two weeks to get it right."

TWO WEEKS OF TRAINING, two weeks of sparring, two weeks of trying to separate the two lives I was living.

Two weeks of lying to Kira.

I told him I wasn't fighting. Well, correction, I just didn't tell him I *was* fighting. I told him I was going in to help Arizona prep for his fight but never told him I was getting back in the cage.

Which was, of course, a lie.

Another one.

What was one more when there'd been hundreds? Over six months of lies, all of them. Every day. Who I was, what I was doing.

Why I was doing it.

All lies.

He was working, so I knew there was no chance of him seeing me fight, and I had absolutely no intention of letting whoever I was fighting even land one shot. My game plan was to get into the cage, bump fists with my opponent, then knock him fucking senseless.

My eye was almost healed. The eye itself was still a little bloodshot, the bruising was a pasty yellow, but the swelling was almost completely gone.

Doc wasn't happy with me getting back into the cage, but Tressler had insisted I fight. And apparently neither

Doc nor Boss would argue with Tressler. If he wanted someone to fight, then they fought.

The fact we were scheduled to go up against the LMA Center, coupled with the fact Tressler adamantly wanted *me* to fight, told me he had a motive. A monetary motive, I'd guess. He had said there was a large pool of money on my last bout, so maybe he wanted in on it. I didn't care for the money, but if I told Tressler my eye wasn't up for another round, I risked being pulled from the next underground fight. And I wasn't about to let that happen.

We got ready in the dressing room, getting strapped up and psyched up, when Boss walked in. He ran through the roster, calling my name last. "You got the short straw, Elliott," he said. Then he mumbled, "Can't say I'm surprised."

"Who'd I get?"

Boss sighed. "You got the best fighter they got."

Of course I did.

He shook his head. "Hope you brought your game tonight, Elliott."

I watched the other boys do their thing. I stood with our team like I did every Friday fight night and cheered our team on. I watched Cody and Amil, Jamaal and Benji each fight, then Arizona.

The LMA team was watching their boys fight, except for Yuan, who spent the entire time eyeballing me. And I ignored him, which of course pissed him off.

I tried to convince myself I was up for it. I tried to convince myself I was angry enough to beat the shit out of this guy. I tried to convince myself I was doing the right thing and this was a case I was working on, and I wasn't *really* lying to Kira if it was for my job.

Boss pulled my face toward his. "Get out of your

fucking head, Elliott," he barked at me. Then he pushed me. Twice. "Get in there and show me those anger management issues."

I stepped into the cage, biting down on my mouthpiece, letting the rage fester in my belly. Because I *was* angry. I was pissed off at what I'd done, at the position I'd put myself in, at what I'd done to Kira.

I might not have been pissed off at Yuan personally, but I was *pissed* off. I was just pissed off with me.

I bumped fists with him when the ref called 'fight' and I remember giving him a kick to the ribs.

I don't remember a thing after that.

CHAPTER THIRTEEN

THE PAIN in my head was remarkable.

I wondered how it was even possible to *think* about the level of agony with an ax buried inside my skull. An ax, an ax that had been taken from a fire so the metal was white-hot, so it simply sliced through the skull, to leave a blinding pain piercing through to the center of my brain.

I didn't dare open my eyes.

I knew I was lying down, though I had no idea where I was.

I felt a sharp stabbing twinge in my ribs and it hurt to breathe, but it was preferable to the torture in my head.

Fuck.

I heard far off voices, familiar-but-couldn't-place, far-off voices, and I wanted to tell them to please take the ax out of the side of my head. Why weren't they taking it out already? What the fuck were they waiting for?

I lifted my hand to my head, searching for whatever was piercing my brain to remove it myself, but there was nothing. Just my head. Then a hand grabbed my arm and a far-off voice told me not to move.

"My head," I mumbled.

"Yeah, it's gonna hurt," a voice said, becoming clearer.

Doc. Doc said that.

Then I tried to open my eyes.

My right eye wouldn't open at all, and when my left eye finally opened, the light pierced the pain in my head. It made me nauseated, and I groaned. "Fuck."

I heard Boss mumble something, then Doc spoke again. "I won't know unless he has it x-rayed, but it looks like a broken nose, possibly a fractured cheekbone."

Me. They were talking about me.

I tried to sit up, but they held me down. "Don't get up," Doc said. Actually, I didn't want to get up, I didn't want to move. I closed my eyes instead.

Then someone took my hand, and a familiar voice whispered, "Jesus Christ."

My left eye opened, and I saw Kira. Somehow, he was there, kneeling beside me, looking over me, his eyes filled with pity and horror. He turned his face and spoke to someone I couldn't see. "Does he need to go to the hospital?"

"No," I rasped. "No hospitals." I sat up, not wanting Kira to think I was too badly hurt and immediately regretted it. My head felt heavy and off-balance, like one side of my brain was too heavy. My ears buzzed and my stomach rolled. I groaned, "Think I'm gonna be sick."

I was handed a small bowl and sat with it between my knees, and Kira kneeled in front of me. He asked, "What happened?"

"Don't know," I said, though it sounded kind of slurred to me. I didn't remember any of it. I remember getting into the cage. I remember bumping my fist to Yuan's...

Arizona answered. "He fought well in the first two

rounds. Had him beat on points. Then just before the end of the second round, Yuan took him to the floor. The bell went, but as soon as the third round started, Matt went to take him out with a kick to the head, but Yuan took his knee out. Once he had him on the floor, he just kept elbowing him in the head."

"Where the hell was the ref?" Kira asked. "What the fuck kind of unprofessional referee lets a fight go on like that?"

"One who's paid to," Doc said.

"What?" Kira said, standing up. "What do you mean 'paid to'? You mean someone was *paid* to let this happen?" I knew that tone. That was Kira's pissed-off, just-about-to-lose-his-shit tone of voice.

I put my hand up. "'M okay," I told him.

"You're not okay!" he snapped at me. Then he sucked back a breath and started again, much more restrained. I still had my head down and my eyes closed, but it sounded like he spoke through clenched teeth. "Matt, you're not okay. This whole thing is not okay. This is not *fucking* okay."

Doc's voice spoke next, defusing the anger in the room. "Kira? Is that your name?"

"Yes," came his curt reply.

"You'll be looking after him?"

"Yes."

"There are a few things I need to run through with you," the medic said. "I've reset his nose and I think he could have a fractured cheekbone, but there's nothing we can do for it. He's had a bad concussion. He'll have nausea, headaches, and dizziness for the next few days, even weeks."

"I know what concussions mean," Kira told him. "I've had a bad one myself."

"Then you'll know to wake him every few hours when he sleeps, and if his symptoms get worse, or if he doesn't improve, take him to the hospital," Doc said. "The cut above his eye should heal without stitches, as long as it stays clean and he doesn't bump it. He's to have bed rest for a day or two, then nothing strenuous at all. Then I want to see him again in a week and we'll take it from there."

"I can take him now?"

"Yes," Doc answered. "But first," he said, his voice closer to me now. I lifted my heavy head to look at him. "I'm gonna give you something for the pain, okay?" he asked me.

I felt the jab of a needle in my arm, and within seconds, could feel the numbness as it crept through my body.

I heard Kira say thank you for calling him, and I heard Arizona tell him it was no problem. They talked about something else, but I couldn't listen. The words were like they were spoken underwater and in a language I didn't know.

I closed my eyes, dropped my head, and reveled in the numbness.

I WOKE UP, surprised I was still in the car.

"Matt?" Kira said softly. "We're here. Can you walk?"

I looked out the window, but it wasn't our house. It took a few seconds for me to realize we were stopped in front of the cabin.

"What are we doing here?" I asked. My voice croaked. It hurt to move my mouth. "How long was I out?"

"About two hours," Kira answered. "We put you in the car, I drove home, collected a few things, then got the keys to the cabin from Mom and Dad's and drove straight here."

I turned my head to look at him, not sure what to say. "I'm tired."

He nodded. "Come on, let's go inside."

It was as though I had to make my body move, like every movement was a slow, conscious, deliberate act. And when I got the car door open and went to get out, my body seized up in protest. It was an anesthetized pain—a blurry ache kept tolerable by whatever injection Doc gave me. I knew the pain was real underneath it, under the chemical surface, but it was just out of reach.

I groaned as I tried to stand, then Kira was there with his arm around my shoulders. "We'll get you inside and up the stairs," he said. "You can go straight to bed."

All I could do was nod and put one mechanical foot in front of the other. I took the stairs one at a time. Hurting all over but at the same time, numb.

I didn't want to feel any of it.

The pain in my face, the blinding ache in my head, the biting sting in my left thigh.

The heartache.

The guilt.

I didn't want to feel any of it.

I pulled the covers back on the bed and lay down, not even bothering to pull them back over me, and I closed my eyes.

Sometime later, Kira woke me up. He asked me to sit up and gave me some pills, which I took without a word. He asked how I was feeling, and I shook my head as my answer. I didn't have the words.

I slept, he woke me, I slept, he woke me.

The sky went from dark to light and back to dark again. He'd ask me questions or give me pills. All I wanted to do was sleep.

I'd never been so tired.

When the sky became light on the second day, I lay in bed not wanting to move. Not wanting to get up and face Kira or to admit what I'd done.

Unfortunately, I didn't have much choice. Kira walked in and threw the covers off me. "Come on, get up."

"I'm tired," I said weakly.

"It's been two days," he said. "You need to get up. You need to eat, to shower, and these sheets need washing."

Realizing he wasn't going to let me off easily, I slowly sat up and put my feet on the floor, feeling every muscle stretch and ache. My left eye was still swollen shut, my head spun, and I felt the room spin in the opposite direction. "Whoa."

"Just sit up for a while before you try and stand," Kira said. "How's your head?"

"Sore," I admitted quietly. "Everything's sore."

Kira never said anything else, and his lack of words hung heavy in the air. I knew what his silence meant.

He was angry, and hurt, and disappointed.

I didn't blame him. I couldn't. This was my doing, my mess, my fault.

I nodded, agreeing with myself that whatever he dealt me, I would take. I deserved his anger, his disappointed eyes, and his silence.

Very slowly, I stood up, biting back a groan as pain ripped through unused, cramped-up muscles. I kept one hand on the wall for balance and moved my feet slowly as I walked to the bathroom.

The shower was hot and stung like hell, but I stood, letting the stream of water hit the back of my neck, feeling my muscles unwind. I let water run over my face but didn't touch it. I didn't dare. Brushing my teeth was painful enough with the swollen side of my face, but I did feel better afterwards. Remotely human, even.

I had to sit on the stripped bed to put some shorts on, and although I just wanted to lie back down, I thought Kira stripped the bed intentionally so I wouldn't spend another day in it.

Very slowly, one step at a time, I made my way downstairs.

Kira came out from the small laundry room, surprised to see me. I was shirtless and his eyes scanned my body. Not in a sexual way, but more of a visual inspection for any wounds. My ribs were still sore, but it was my thigh that had taken a beating. And my face... Sore didn't begin to describe my face.

I couldn't look at Kira. But I stopped when he walked over to me. He took a few breaths and asked, "Are you hungry?"

I nodded.

Without another word, he turned to the fridge and pulled out a range of foods, cutting cold meat, salad, and fruit into bite-size pieces. I'd done the same for him when we were up here after his abduction ordeal. He'd said the smaller the pieces of food, the less it hurt to eat. He must have remembered...

I took small bites until it was mostly gone, while Kira pretended not to watch. I still couldn't look at him. I didn't know what to say.

I should have said sorry. I should have told him I loved

him. That I'd never meant to hurt him. I should have told him about my job, that I was still a cop. I should have told him everything. But I couldn't.

So I shuffled slowly out to the deck that overlooked the valley and the mountains. I gingerly lowered myself onto one of the deckchairs, closed my eyes, and I slept.

Kira woke me up, sat down beside me with a glass of water in one hand and more pills in the other. I sat up in the chair, trying not to wince at the pain. "Thanks." I swallowed them down.

"You feel any better?"

"Not really. My headache's not so bad."

"Does your face hurt?"

"The whole left side."

He nodded. "Those pills the medic gave me for you should help," he said.

"Are they a sedative?" I asked.

Kira shook his head. "No. It's just Extra Strength Tylenol."

It was funny that I, undercover narcotic agent, almost wished for narcotics like Percocet or Vicodin, prescription or not. I shook my head. "I'm just really tired. Sorry you brought me up here and all I want to do is sleep."

Kira looked out over the view. "It's okay, Matt."

"You took time off work?"

He looked at me then and nodded. "Four days was all I could get on short notice. I would've liked to stay up here longer."

My head fell back against the chair and I looked at him for a long moment. Then something occurred to me. "You got the key for the cabin from your mom and dad? Did you tell them about me?"

"They saw you," he said quietly. "You were passed out in the car."

Oh, fucking hell.

"I'm sorry," I told him. "I'm really sorry."

He stared at me. "Exactly which part are you sorry for?"

"All of it," I told him quietly. "For these last few months, for this." I waved my hand at my face. "I'm sorry I didn't tell you I was fighting on Friday. I'm sorry Arizona had to call you to come get me. That must have been horrible for you, and I'm sorry. I'm sorry I've been so caught up in my head lately." I took a deep breath, and telling him about my involvement in the FC was on the tip of my tongue. But I couldn't. "I'm sorry for everything."

Kira gave me a sad smile. "You've been... not very you." It was like he was choosing his words carefully. "Matt, you have to talk to me," he pleaded. "Promise me you'll talk about things and not let them weigh you down."

I nodded. "I'll try."

"No, not *try*," he corrected. I knew he'd pick up on my choice of words. "You will. You have to, Matt. I love you, but I can't help you if you won't talk to me."

I was about to protest that I didn't need help but figured I was sick of lying to him, so I just let it go.

Kira took my hand and played with my fingers for a while, and when I didn't say anything, he spoke. "I don't know what demons you're fighting in your head, Matt. And as much as I don't like it, you don't want to tell me right now, and that's okay. As long as you tell me one day."

I nodded. "I will," I promised him. And one day I would. "I just need to get my head right." Then without giving too much away but giving him some kind of reassurance, I added, "I won't be fighting forever, maybe another couple of months." I wanted to give him a finish line so he knew this hell wouldn't last forever.

But he shook his head. "I've never understood why you wanted to do it in the first place," he said quietly. "And I know you're not telling me the whole truth." He looked back out over the view and sighed. Before I could say anything, he continued, "But it doesn't matter. Matt, I'm going to ask something of you..." He trailed off.

My stomach dropped. "What is it?"

"You know I'll support you in anything you want to do?"

I nodded, suddenly scared where this conversation was going.

"But not this. I can't watch you go through this," he whispered.

I didn't understand what he was asking. "Kira?"

"I'm asking you to not fight anymore."

"What?"

"I don't want you to cage-fight anymore," he said simply. Then he exhaled loudly. "Guess you've got about six or eight weeks to decide, given they won't let you fight with your nose the way it is. It'll need time to heal completely. And I was kind of hoping in that time you'd decide you didn't want to do it anymore."

Fuck. How could I explain that I *had* to fight again in just four weeks whether my nose was healed or not?

I didn't. I couldn't.

Which meant more lies, more guilt.

I felt suddenly nauseated.

"You okay?"

I shook my head. "No, I don't feel too great." And just then, a cold shiver ran through me.

Kira saw me shiver. "Come on, back to bed with you. Or the sofa. What would you prefer?"

While I really wanted to lie down in bed and pull the covers over me and disappear, I wanted to be near him even more. "Sofa."

When I was inside, Kira sat me down while he made me some Japanese peppermint tea.

"Mom's been calling every couple of hours," he said from the kitchen. "Mom and Dad saw your face when you were asleep in the car. She kind of freaked out."

Oh, fucking hell.

"I should call her and apologize."

Kira walked out and handed me the tea, then went back to get some of his mom's foul-smelling herbal mixture for my face. He sat beside me, gently applying the ghastly paste to the side of my nose, my cheek, and around my eye. I hadn't shaved since my fight, so I could only imagine what I looked like.

"I've told her you're okay," he said quietly. "She wanted to come up here, but I asked her not to." Then he added, "I thought we could use some time."

I hated watching him struggle to be around me. It killed me to see him so sad. His beautiful, almond-shaped eyes looked... sad. I took his hand and gave it a squeeze. "I've missed you."

He rubbed his thumb over the back of my hand. "I've missed us."

I nodded, knowing this whole mess was my fault. "I'm sorry."

"You keep saying that."

It wasn't lost on me that he never said my apology was accepted or that I was forgiven. Still holding his hand, I pushed his ring and middle fingers down to his palm and made the sign-language sign for *I love you* like he did to me the first time he told me he loved me.

He looked from his hand to my eyes, and he smiled sadly. "Do you?"

I nodded quickly. "Very much. I love you very much. More than I've ever loved anything. Kira, baby, you're it for me."

Kira took my hand then and put it to his face. He sighed into my palm and closed his eyes. "Thank you."

I rubbed the pad of my thumb over his cheek. "Can I kiss you? Please?"

His eyes shot open. "Not with that stuff on your face. It smells putrid." But then he smiled and pressed his lips to mine for a soft, sweet kiss.

And his cell phone on the kitchen counter buzzed with a message.

"If that's your mom, I'll call her," I told him.

Kira got up and collected his cell. He read the screen, and he hesitated. "Um, Mitch has been calling too."

Shit.

"He somehow knew about the fight, and he's been calling my cell every morning and night. He's been really worried about you too."

I didn't even know where my phone was. I didn't know whether to be relieved or concerned to hear he'd been calling Kira's phone and not mine. I was, however, pleased to hear he'd been worried about me. "Has he?"

"Don't sound so surprised," Kira said. "Of course he'd be worried about you. You're still his best friend." He read the message. "He just wants to know how you're doing this afternoon." He handed the phone to me. "Call him."

I thumbed Mitch's number, and he answered on the second ring. "Hey, Kira, how's the boy?"

"The boy's okay," I said, knowing he'd recognize my voice right away.

"Oh, man," Mitch said with a sigh. "Fuck, are you okay? I've been so worried."

It was good to hear his voice. "Yeah, I'm okay. Sore and sorry. And I'm sorry about what happened at the bar the other week," I added, trying to answer so Kira wouldn't suspect anything.

"Is Kira there?" Mitch asked. "Can you talk?"

I looked up at Kira. "Yeah, he's been right here the whole time," I said, knowing Mitch would understand that no, I couldn't talk.

"Matt, we were so ready to come in and pull you out of there," Mitch said. "Fuck, we had a guy planted who said you got your head smacked in and had to be carried out of the cage."

"Really?"

"Yes, really," he repeated. "I told you we were watching."

"That's good to hear. I'm glad the wedding plans are coming along," I said as a distraction for Kira who was sitting with me. I looked at him and he smiled.

"Berkman said if it happens again, we're to pull the plug. Especially after your last phone call to us," Mitch said. "It sounded very... final."

"Because it was."

"Look, Matt, this can all end right now if you want."

I faked a laugh. "I don't think so."

Mitch sighed into the phone. "We've looked into Yuan Hua. He's second-generation Vietnamese, got a bad rap sheet, Matt. He's a crazy fucker."

"I know that."

"Well, we're looking into his background with Tressler,"

Mitch said. "They're connected, Matt. They're involved in some legal business outside of the FC, so no doubt there's an illegal connection too."

"Really?"

"Yeah, so if you're scheduled to fight him again, don't. Don't get into the cage with him. Tressler wanted you to fight him. Asked for it specifically."

I leaned back on the sofa and put my hand on Kira's thigh, trying to appear relaxed. "Thought so," I said.

"Can you tell Tressler you're not well enough to fight in the next underground match?"

I faked another laugh. "Hardly. But I'll have to get you to keep an eye out for some of that for Kira."

He knew exactly what I was trying to say. "We're watching Kira, Matt," Mitch said softly. "It's you we're more worried about."

"It's been good to speak to you," I said, shutting down this conversation. "Give Anna a kiss for me."

"Matt, be careful."

"Say hi to the others for me."

"Matt..."

"Okay, bye."

I ended the call and handed the phone back to Kira. He put it on the coffee table and picked up the cup of peppermint tea and gave it to me. "Here, drink some more."

"Thanks." I took a sip.

"Mitch's been worried about you."

I smiled. "It was good to speak to him." In more ways than one.

So Yuan and Tressler were connected. It made the fact Tressler adamantly wanted me to fight him very suspicious. Was he trying to test my loyalty? Did he know I was undercover and he was trying to kill me? I didn't know, but my gut instinct leaned toward the latter.

I gave Kira the best smile I could manage. He picked up the remote control, turned on the TV, and leaned back on the sofa with me. Very carefully, very tenderly, he nestled himself into my side. I wrapped my arm around him, savoring his touch. He gently laid his head on my chest and listened to the thump of my lying heart.

CHAPTER FOURTEEN

I WOKE up in the middle of the night and couldn't get back to sleep. I guess after sleeping for three days, I was all slept out. So I lay there next to Kira, staring at the ceiling, overthinking everything, and the room was suddenly too small.

I needed air.

The weight of what I was doing, how I was lying to everyone, sat heavy on my chest, and the walls seemed like they were closing in on me, like there wasn't enough air. It had nothing to do with my concussion and everything to do with me.

Trying to not wake Kira, I walked out onto the deck. I held on to the hand railing and sucked in deep breaths, trying to breathe, trying to get my shit together. It felt like everything was vast and empty and unreachable, but crowded and claustrophobic at the same time.

All I could do was focus on my breathing. I don't know how long I was out there for, but I could finally breathe again, despite the burn in my lungs.

"Matt?" Kira's voice startled me. I hadn't heard him come out. "You okay?"

"Yeah," I lied, an automatic, knee-jerk reaction.

"What are you doing out here?" he asked, joining me on the deck. "It's two-thirty in the morning."

"Just needed some air," I told him. "And I didn't want to wake you."

I could see a little out of my left eye, though it was still swollen and still sore, but I could see Kira's uncertainty and the doubt in the way he looked at me. "Are you in any pain?" he asked. "You were breathing pretty hard."

I shook my head. "No, I'm okay. Pain's not so bad."

He nodded but was obviously concerned. "Okay, then come back to bed." He took my hand and led me inside, up the stairs, and when I stood at the bed in the darkened room, I stopped him. He wouldn't have sex with me earlier when we first got into bed. He said he didn't think it was a good idea.

But I needed it. I needed him.

"Kira," I murmured his name. "I need you," I whispered into his chest. "I need you to take me to bed." I fisted my hands in his sleep-shirt, digging into his sides. "I need to feel you. I need you to have me."

Kira took my hands from his waist. "Matt, I don't think—"

I cut him off. "Please." I knew I was begging. I knew I sounded desperate. I *was* desperate. I *needed* him. "Please, Kira," I whispered.

"Matt, no." His dark eyes swam with worry, and I couldn't bear to see him look at me that way. So I closed my eyes and nodded.

I understood.

Never mind the headaches, broken nose, and bruised thigh, it was rejection that stung the most.

I took a step back from him and sat on the bed. Pulling my legs up, I lay down and curled onto my side.

I felt the bed dip, then his voice from beside me. "Matt, it's not that I don't want you. It's that you're too banged-up, and I don't want..." He stopped talking, then said, "Matt, will you look at me, please?"

I opened my eyes, but only barely. "It's okay. I shouldn't have asked."

"Matt..."

I just spoke over him, though my voice was just a whisper. "I'm really tired." I closed my eyes, and when I woke up, I was alone.

I WALKED downstairs to find Kira cleaning up and putting things away. He wouldn't look at me. His voice was quiet. "You sleep okay?"

I nodded. "Yeah. You?"

He didn't answer my question. "We need to head back this morning," he said instead. "I have to work tonight."

"Okay. I'll just go pack my things."

"You can have some breakfast first," he said. His eyes met mine then. "Your eye looks better."

I shrugged. "I wouldn't know. I haven't seen it."

"You haven't seen it, at all?"

I shook my head. "No." I scratched my not-sore cheek through the four-day stubble. "I haven't been game enough to shave, so I haven't looked at myself..." I let my words trail off because I knew how pathetic I sounded. I suddenly wasn't very hungry. "I'll just grab a shower."

I'd no sooner walked into the bathroom when Kira was behind me. He surprised me. "What are you doing?"

He put his hands on my shoulders and turned me around in the small bathroom so I faced the mirror. "Look at yourself."

I kept my eyes down. "Kira," I started.

"Look at yourself," he said again, interrupting me. "Why won't you look at yourself?"

Because I don't like what I see.

Because I don't know the man staring back at me.

I shrugged, still unable to look at my reflection.

He stood behind me, and putting his hands on either side of my head, he forced me to look up. I saw his reflection first, his beautiful, sad, and resigned eyes, and couldn't bear to see the pain in them. It was easier to look at me.

My hair was a dirty mess, my face unshaven, and the left side of my face from my cheek to my temple was dark purple. I had a cut above my eyebrow and dark red grazing beside my eye. My nose was swollen and cut along the bridge, with dark purple bruising from my nose down under my right eye. My left eyeball was bloodshot, the whole area was still swollen, and the skin stretched tight.

I looked like fucking hell.

Kira just stood there, behind me, watching me. He didn't need to say anything. It was written all over his face.

I exhaled a shaky breath, blinking back tears. My gaze fell to him and I nodded.

I was a mess.

Kira turned me around, and I was expecting him to tell me I was a disgrace and that I'd ruined everything. But he didn't. He leaned me against the bathroom counter and turned the tap on with hot water to fill the sink. He took the shaving cream and spread it over my stubble, then with a love that almost broke my heart, he started to shave me.

Without a word, he turned my face, lifted my chin, and with such care and a gentle hand, he ran the blade over my face. He concentrated on his task at hand, studying me and taking the most gentle care with the left side of my face. There was nothing but love in his eyes, in his touch.

I fought tears the entire time.

He tapped the razor on the side of the sink one last time and pulled the plug. "All done," he said softly. "Have a shower. I'll start packing."

I nodded again, and by the time I could finally say *thank you*, he was gone.

THE DRIVE back into the city was quiet. There wasn't much said between us at all, and when we got to Kira's parents place to drop off the keys to the cabin, it was fairly obvious to them things were strained between us.

Yumi fussed over my face, but she was quieter than normal and kept eyeing her son. Normally, she was very upfront and vocal about things she thought were important to say, but she was cautious about the state of us.

And that's when it really hit me.

I'd taken for granted Kira and I would be together forever. I'd taken for granted we could withstand me going undercover, with the lies and betrayal.

I'd thought what we had was solid. I'd thought we were unbreakable.

I was very wrong.

I'd broken us.

I thanked Yumi and Sal quietly but told them I'd wait in

the car. I couldn't bear to see their disappointment, their sadness.

We went home, Kira went to work, and for the next few days, we rarely spoke. I tried, and he tried, but the things that needed saying were words I couldn't say.

He knew I was withholding something and just waited for me to talk, but I didn't. I couldn't. He couldn't know. I wouldn't allow it.

I wouldn't risk his safety. Not again.

He said his boss was having some problems and needed him back at work, but I was sure it was just a ruse to avoid me.

I didn't blame him.

And I could feel the divide between us gaining ground. There was a distance, a separation between us. And I was watching it tear us apart—the best thing that had ever happened to me—helpless to stop it.

I could have walked into HQ and said no more. I could have called Ross Berkman and given him the code word, my safe word, that would tell him I needed saving.

But I knew I wouldn't. I'd see this out to the very end, even if it meant Kira left me. And as scary as that thought was, there was a part of me, the guilty part of me, that told me he deserved someone who wouldn't hurt him.

And I deserved the pain.

ON FRIDAY, a week after my fight, I walked back into the FC. The guys all bumped fists with me, inspected my black eye and cut eyebrow, and talked about the fight.

"Man, that Yuan was fucking mad," Amil said. "When

the ref declared he'd lost on a technical foul, man was he pissed off."

"He what?" I asked. "He lost?"

"Yeah, man," Jamaal said. "Hell, where you been? It's the hottest topic in all the gyms."

"Yuan lost?" I asked again. "He KO'd me!"

"With repeated illegal shots," Cody said. "The judges made the ruling, the ref had to call it. Some people lost a lot of money, some won big."

Fuck. I'd had no idea. I shook my head. "I didn't know."

Arizona came over and clapped his hand on my shoulder. "Here he is, the man of the week."

"Hey," I greeted Arizona.

He smiled at me. "You're the only man I've met who can win a fight while you're unconscious on the floor."

"It's a talent," I joked, trying to mask this new realization. Well, if Yuan didn't want me dead before, he certainly fucking would now.

And Tressler.

Jesus.

Boss put an end to our little "handbag discussion" as he called it, telling everyone to get back to "fucking work." I smiled at him. He was rough and crude, but he was a hardworking, honorable man. "You," he barked at me. "Come with me to see the Doc. Need to know when you're in the clear."

Doc poked, prodded, and pressed along my eyebrow, my cheekbone, then felt the bridge of my nose. It fucking hurt. I pulled back from him. "Can you fight?"

The medic raised one eyebrow at me. "Think you're good enough?"

Boss laughed beside us. "No fightin' in the first-aid room."

Doc stood up straight and sighed. "Well, give it another week," he said. "How's the head? Any dizziness, memory loss, trouble concentrating...?"

"Nope," I answered. "Headache's all but gone. I'm more tired than anything. I swear I could just sleep all day."

Doc's brow furrowed. "Mmm, that's a common side effect of concussion. Nothing else?"

I shook my head. "Nah."

Doc turned to Boss and said, "Light duties only. No sparring this week, get him back in cardio, but no contact."

Then he looked at me. "You'll need more conditioning for cardio. Thirty percent of all breathing is done through the nose when you fight. Now that yours is swollen, you'll be more inclined to open your mouth to breathe." He turned my chin to see my face in different light. "Well, your nose will have a slight bend, and with a scar above your eyebrow, I think you can cross pretty-boy off your resume."

"Thanks," I said, rolling my eyes.

He smiled as he walked out. "Should be all healed just in time for you to get back in the cage in three weeks."

I nodded and exhaled. Three weeks. That was all I had to get through. That was all I needed to put Kira through, then this whole thing would be over, whether they'd busted Tressler or not.

Just three more weeks of lies.

All I had to do was keep it together for a few more weeks like there was nothing wrong, act like the man Kira fell in love with.

If I could just hold it together for that long, we'd be fine. It'd all go back to the way it was, and he'd still love me.

I should have known better than to hope.

AS THE FIGHT got closer and as Kira and I grew further apart, I could feel myself losing it. I wasn't sleeping properly; I had no appetite. Even sexual release was... unfulfilling. Not that Kira and I had been sexual. He wouldn't touch me. But even jerking off in the shower didn't give me any peace. It just left me spent and frustrated.

I tried too hard to act like nothing was wrong, and he mostly nodded, knowing damn well I was close to falling apart. He tried to talk to me, and I tried my best to ignore his concern and tell him I was fine.

But then on the Wednesday before the fight, I'd been at home for a few hours, with too much time by myself and too much time to think. I was all alone in this case, left to wonder if Mitch and the boys had this case in the bag. I wondered if they were working as hard as I was. If they were losing their fucking minds over this like I was.

I was starting to doubt their dedication. I was starting to doubt my own.

I was... agitated.

I was losing my fucking mind.

Kira was avoiding me by working overtime, and when he finally came home after nine that night, I was sitting on the new sofa. The only light in the room was from the TV. He slowly put his gym bag on the floor and sat down next to me.

He looked at me guardedly and put his hand on my knee to stop it from bouncing. I hadn't even realized I was doing it.

"Matt?" he said. "You okay?"

I nodded and tried to smile. "Yeah, I'm fine."

He bit his lip and nodded doubtfully. "Okay."

Shaking his head, Kira took his hand off my knee, stood up, and walked away. I jumped up from the sofa, followed him into our bedroom, and grabbed him, pulling us together. I tried to hold him, just to touch him. I kissed him roughly on the mouth, then on the neck. "Kira, I need you," I told him. "I need you. Please."

"Matt," he said, trying to pull away.

I slid my hand over his ass and kissed down his neck. I could have sworn right there, if he didn't take me to bed, I wouldn't survive. "I need you to fuck me. I need you to own me, make me yours." I dug my hands into his skin, holding on too tight. "Don't tell me no," I rasped. The desperation coursing through me was making my body shake.

"Matt, stop!" Kira said, taking me by the arms and shoving me off him. "Just stop. You don't want me to *fuck* you. You want me to *hurt* you, and I can't do it."

I shook my head, desperately. "No."

"Yes," he nodded, staring into my eyes. "Matt, this has to stop."

I took my arms from his hands and shook my head. "I'm doing the best I can," I told him. "I'm trying to hold onto everything I can."

Kira blinked, confused at my words. "Trying to hold onto what?"

"Everything," I said again. "You, my sanity." I almost said 'my job' but instead I said, "You. I'm trying to hold onto you."

I kind of sagged and sat down on the bed, and Kira knelt down in front of me. "Matt, please talk to me. I do love you, Matt, I really do. But this is killing us."

"I know," I whispered. "And I'm sorry."

Kira frowned, then looked at me with sad, sad eyes. "Babe, you need to see a doctor. You need to get yourself some help."

"I'll be okay," I told him. "Next week, it'll all be over, and I'll be fine."

He took his hand from my knee. "What do you mean, it'll all be over?"

I shook my head, realizing I'd just said the wrong thing.

"Matt," he said my name slowly. "What will be all over next week?"

"The fight," I whispered. "My time at the FC. All of this mess."

He was quiet for a long moment, thinking about what I'd just told him. "Why next week? Why not now?"

I had to tell him. He deserved some truth in this. "I just have one more fight."

"You what?" Kira asked. His voice was quiet and disbelieving.

"I've got another fight this weekend," I said, not able to look at him. It had been two weeks since Doc gave me the all-clear to resume training, and Kira knew I was back at the gym. I just hadn't told him exactly what I was training for. Until now.

"No, you're not," he said quietly. "Matt, you said you wouldn't."

"No, I didn't," I countered pathetically. "You said you didn't want me to fight. I never said I wouldn't."

His eyes were hard and his voice was barely a breath. "So, you know I don't want you to fight, but you're gonna do it anyway?"

He wasn't yelling. He wasn't mad.

He was resigned.

"I have to," I whispered. "I have to do this."

He shook his head and stood up, taking a step back from me. I could see his chest rise and fall with his measured breaths, but he wouldn't make eye contact with me. And he was quiet. Far too quiet.

I'd prefer it if he yelled, or threw something, or pushed me or punched me. But not silence.

I couldn't stand the silence.

"Kira, I'm sorry."

He put his hand up, palm facing me. "Don't. Don't apologize," he said. When he looked at me, he had tears in his eyes. "I can't do this, Matt. I can't stand here and watch you fall apart." He sucked back a ragged breath, and tears fell down his cheek. "I've tried," he said as he cried. "For months I've tried to support you, to go through this with you, to understand. But you won't let me in, you keep pushing me away, you can't even look at me!"

I shook my head. I knew where this was going.

He was saying goodbye.

And my mind wouldn't work. I couldn't speak, I couldn't think. I could barely fucking breathe.

He walked into the closet and I could hear him pulling clothes off hangers. He was packing his things.

And I just sat there. I couldn't move. My ribs were all too tight, and my heart hurt, a very discernible pain in my chest. I pushed on it with the heel of my hand and tried to take deeper breaths, but it didn't seem to help.

Then Kira was in front of me. All I could see were his feet. I didn't want to look up and see the pain on his face. He must have watched me trying to push against the pain in my chest for a little while.

"Matt."

I tried to speak. I tried to stand up, but all I could do was shake my head and gasp for fucking breath.

"I need a few days," he said, struggling to speak as he

cried. His words brought on a fresh wave of tears. "Do you have *anything* to say?"

I tried to speak. I opened my mouth but couldn't make a sound. No words would come. So with my hand still pressing against my chest, I closed my fist and rubbed circles over my heart. I signed to him instead.

I'm sorry.

I'm sorry.

A quiet sob escaped him, and I half expected him to come to me and tell me we'd be okay. But he didn't.

He picked up the bag at his feet and walked out the door.

And I felt it—a very distinct shift, a soft snapping pain in my chest. And as I slowly lay back onto the bed and curled up into a ball, I realized what it was.

My heart had just broken.

I DIDN'T MOVE. For hours, I just lay there. I didn't sleep, I just stared at nothing. The room became lighter, as night became day, and I just lay there.

I heard my phone ring. It rang out again and again, and still, I didn't move.

I had no reason to.

I fell between a sleeping state and an awake state, but nothing else registered.

Somewhere in my brain, I knew I was expected at the FC; it was the final few days in the lead up to the fight, so Boss had our schedule booked. But I didn't care. I didn't get off the bed. I didn't move.

The pain in my chest had become a constant ache,

searing and tight, and very real, and my body hurt from being still for too long. But mostly I was numb.

My phone rang again, but I closed my eyes to the world around me and must have fallen asleep. A knocking sound woke me, and I opened my eyes to find the light in the room had started to fade. I'd not moved the entire day.

The knocking continued. "Go away," I mumbled, my voice too low and croaky for anyone to hear. Then I heard the jingle of keys and the front door opened. The only other person who had keys was Kira. I tried to sit up, as my body screamed in protest, just as Yumi walked into the room. Realizing it wasn't Kira, I fell back onto the bed.

She frowned and her eyes welled with tears. Then she started to yell. "What the hell you think you doing to my boy?" After so much silence, her voice was far too loud. "What you hurt him for? He turn up home last night a freaking mess, Matthew."

She called me Matthew. She'd never used my full first name.

"He spend all night telling us what you been doing," she said, now pointing her finger at me. "He was crying. You know what that does to a mother? To see her boy crying?" she asked rhetorically. She certainly didn't give me time to answer. "He sleep all day and could barely go to work tonight. I thought *he* was a mess," she said, throwing her hands up. "But then I see you!"

Sal was now standing in the doorway behind her.

I couldn't look at them.

My voice croaked. "I'm sorry."

Yumi ignored me and came over to me, pulling on my arm. "Get up," she ordered. "Get off this bed. You think lying there all day will fix anything?"

I let her pull me up to a sitting position and let my feet fall to the floor with a groan. "Yumi, please…"

"Don't you 'Yumi, please' me," she said and pulled me to my feet, then the tiny woman dragged me past Sal, down the hall toward the kitchen. My body ached and stung with every step. "You need food."

Yumi led me to the dining table, where I fell into one of the seats. I scrubbed my hands over my face, wincing at the pain when I pressed against my nose. Sal sat down across from me, but I couldn't look at him.

He was the closest thing I'd ever known to having a father, and to see his disappointment, to be the cause of his disappointment, was too much. Yumi banged down a glass of juice on the table, startling me. "Drink that," she snapped, then went back into the kitchen.

I happened to look at Sal, and regretted it immediately. He looked so sad. My stomach turned at the thought of food, and I pushed the juice away. Half a minute later, Yumi came back in with some buttered toast. She sat down in the seat next to me and tapped the table with her finger. "Eat it."

"I'm not hungry," I managed to say.

She glared at me, and not wanting to upset her anymore, I picked at the slice of toast. Yumi crossed her arms. "Why do you fight?"

I shrugged and barely whispered my answer, "I want to."

"Don't lie to me," she snapped. "You can say what you want to everyone else, but you not lie to me!"

I felt like a scolded child. Like *her* scolded child. She was treating me like a mother would treat her child, chiding them because she loved them. Because Yumi loved me.

And I realized then, not only had I lost Kira, but I was

losing his parents—my only family—as well. I shook my head, fighting tears. "You're like parents to me," I whispered. "I'm sorry if I hurt you. I never meant to hurt anyone."

"It's too late for that, Matthew," Yumi said. "You broke Kira's heart. And your own, by the look of it."

I nodded. "I'm sorry."

"You love him?" Yumi asked. "You love my Kira?"

I nodded quickly and looked her in the eye. "He's everything to me."

"Then you need to fix it," she said simply.

"I will," I promised. "I'll do anything."

"Then don't go in this next fight," Yumi said.

"I have to," I whispered.

Then Sal signed something I didn't quite catch. Yumi translated for me. "Sal want to know if you punish yourself for what happened to Kira last year?"

I looked at Yumi, then at Sal, then I looked away. Was I punishing myself? Of course I was. Because feeling pain was my penance for what had happened to him, what he had gone through with Tomic. My eyes filled with tears, which slid slowly down my face. "It was my fault."

They were both quiet for a long second, then Yumi said, "You think what happened with Kira and that crazy man was your fault?"

I wiped the tears from my face with the back of my hand, and I nodded. "Of course it was."

"And you think getting beaten up and having your face broken make it better?" Yumi snapped.

I nodded and more tears fell. "I deserve it."

Yumi shook her head. "Oh, Matty, no."

I nodded. "He wouldn't have gone through that if it weren't for me. He almost died because of me."

"Not because of you," Yumi said. Her tone was softer now. "Because of that Tomic crazy man. He live because of you. You saved him."

I shook my head. I could feel this dam of emotion and anger and rage was at the breaking point. I was at the breaking point. The words were there, and for the first time since this whole mess started, I was about to let the floodgates open.

"I never saved him. He saved me," I told them. "I thought I could handle it. I thought I could get past it. But I can't. I see it play over in my head, every day, every night. I live with it, every day. Kira can deal with it okay because he's so strong," I said, shaking my head. "But I'm not... I thought I could handle this. I thought I could go into the FC and it would get better. I started out just getting angry and using that rage to fight with," I admitted. "I was so angry."

"We saw," Sal signed.

I nodded. "But then I got hit, and I liked it. I thought if I felt half the pain he felt, then it made it better," I said, knowing how fucked up it sounded. "I liked the pain, it made the guilt easier to bear. But it didn't last, and it only hurt Kira to see me banged up," I said, wiping more tears. I could barely finish. "And then it makes me feel even more guilty, and it makes everything worse."

"Oh, Matty," Yumi said. She cupped her hand to my face. "You silly boy."

"I ruined everything."

She shook her head. "He loves you. He'll listen. You just need to talk to him."

I wiped my face again and took a deep breath. "After this fight..."

Yumi's eyes widened disbelievingly. "You still want to fight?"

"I have to," I said, taking a shaky breath.

"What you mean you have to?" she cried. "You don't need to prove to him you can get beat up like he was. You need to *talk* to him."

"This fight isn't about Kira." I stood up and took my plate of untouched food to the sink.

Yumi followed me. "Matthew, you talk to me," she said. She was back to angry, back to calling me Matthew. "I can't stand to see you like this. Or Kira. You need to fix this."

"I will," I promised again. "After this fight. He won't want to talk to me if he knows I'm still fighting."

Sal was standing in the doorway, watching me. And then I heard something I'd never heard in my year and a half with Kira.

Sal's voice.

He was deaf, and I'd never heard him make any sound but laughter. Though he certainly didn't look happy now. "Are you still a cop?"

I stared at him, and his voice even surprised Yumi. It was obvious he didn't speak often. Or maybe it was his question that surprised her. She turned from him, to me, and they both waited for my answer.

I raked my hands through my hair, let out a shaky breath, and I had to look away from them. This couple who'd loved me like a son. Who wanted me to be a part of their family. My stomach twisted and fresh tears filled my eyes.

I was so fucking sick of the lies.

I didn't have to say the words out loud. My lack of response was answer enough.

"Matthew, what have you done?" Yumi asked quietly.

It was then I really started to cry.

Tears streaked down my face and I sobbed. "Everything I've done these last six months is a lie."

Yumi stood in the small kitchen with disbelief on her face and tears in her eyes as she stared at me. Slowly she shook her head. "Kira knows?"

"No," I answered. "He can't know. No one knows. You can't tell anyone."

"Oh, Matthew," she replied in a whisper. "No."

"There's a drug cartel that ships cocaine through the fight club circuit onto the streets," I blurted out, not even bothering to wipe my tears. "I was the best man for the job because I knew how to fight."

"Undercover?" Sal spoke again.

I nodded again, and this time I scrubbed at the tears on my face. "Kira can't know. I won't jeopardize his safety again. Not ever. So if lying to him keeps him safe, then that's what I'll do." I sucked back a shaky breath. "I won't put him in danger's way again. If anything else were to happen to him..."

I had to put my hands on my knees, bending over, trying to catch my breath. I felt like I was going to throw up. "I'm sorry. You have no idea how sorry I am," I told them. I stood up straight, my head fell back, and I tried to breathe. "You've both been so good to me. I've made a mess of everything."

Yumi nodded and her bottom lip trembled. "Yes, you have."

"Can you see why he's better off without me?" I asked, and my eyes welled with new tears.

"No," Sal spoke again. Then he signed the rest. "You're a good man, trying to do the right thing."

Then Yumi reached into her pocket and pulled out a crumpled Kleenex. She handed it to me. I remembered my mom doing the same thing when I was a kid. I gave her the best smile I could manage and wiped my eyes then my nose.

Yumi scowled at me. "I am *so* mad at you, Matthew." Then she huffed and threw up her hands. "But Kira loves you."

"Do you think he'll ever forgive me?"

"I don't know," Yumi said bluntly. "He was very upset."

"Yes," Sal said with a nod. Then he signed, "He loves you."

I signed back, probably getting words wrong. "I love him. I love him so much."

Yumi walked over then and touched my arm. "I know you do." Then she checked her watch. "Need to be home when Kira get there. He doesn't know we came here."

I nodded. "Thank you for coming to see me. It means a lot to me."

"Well," Yumi said. "Don't you tell Kira we came here. We said we wouldn't go see you." Then her tone softened. "But of course we would. I worry about you too, Matty." I smiled at her words, and she scowled again. "Don't think I won't play favorites, Matthew," Yumi snarked back. "You're both my boys, but Kira's my favorite."

I think I even chuckled at that. "I won't tell him I saw you."

"Good," she replied. "You keep our secret, we keep yours."

I looked at them both. "Thank you."

Sal signed something, but I didn't quite catch it. Normally Kira would translate, but Yumi did. "Sal say you need to speak to Kira. After this fight, you grow some balls and tell him everything."

Sal's mouth fell open and he looked at me. "I didn't say that," he signed and spoke at the same time.

Yumi shrugged. "I paraphrase."

"Be honest," Sal signed and spoke together again. "Speak from the heart."

I nodded, and blinked back new tears. "I promise I will. After this weekend, after this last fight, when he's not in any danger, if he'll listen, I'll tell him everything."

Yumi hugged me and told me, "Go shower. You not smell good." While she was on her motherly rant, she added, "Get some sleep. You look like hell."

I gave her a nod. "Yeah, I'm tired."

"And eat," she said as they were walking out. "Don't think I didn't see you not eat."

Sal rolled his eyes as he followed her out the door, and I gave him half a smile. I signed, "Thank you."

Sal stopped and smiled, then signed and spoke at the same time again, "You fight, yes?"

I nodded.

"Then you fight for my boy."

CHAPTER FIFTEEN

"WHERE THE FUCKING hell were you yesterday?" Boss barked at me, pointing his stubby fingers in my face. "You don't have the balls to show up, then you better have the manners to call."

"Sorry, Boss," I mumbled.

Boss looked at me and shrugged. "So, what? No explanation? Just 'Sorry, Boss'?"

"Wasn't a good day."

"I can tell," he said. "You look like shit."

"Didn't sleep much."

Boss pulled out his clipboard and sighed. "Well, no word yet, but chances are you're fightin' tonight. For your sake, I hope it's tomorrow 'cause, if you get in that cage tonight lookin' like you do now, Yuan will beat you dead."

"Is that who I'm fighting?" I asked. We all presumed I was, but nothing had been confirmed.

"Won't know till you get there," he said, going through some list on his clipboard. "But if I were a betting man..."

"I better get straight into training," I said.

"Start with the normal routine," he told me. "I'll be around to check on ya later."

I got changed, dropped my belongings into my locker, and hit the gym floor. Stretches, skipping rope, then treadmill just to warm up.

I wanted to hide, not speak to anyone, and just zone out, but it wasn't long before Arizona found me. "Hey, man," he said, eyeing me carefully. "Missed you here yesterday. Everything good?"

Saying things out loud for the first time was always the hardest. I took a deep breath. "Kira left me."

Arizona's eyes went wide. "Really? Oh man," he said. "Oh, shit, man. I'm sorry."

I never stopped running on the treadmill. "I don't want to talk about it," I told him.

"Oh, sure," he said. "Of course."

No, I didn't want to talk about it. Or I'd end up a blubbering fucking mess in front of these guys. Since I'd spoken to Yumi and Sal, all I'd done was cry. I'd cried in the shower last night. I'd cried myself to sleep. I'd woken up with a bastard of a headache, but I'd thought I was holding up okay until I saw his breakfast yogurt and muesli in the fridge.

Needless to say, I couldn't even stomach coffee after that.

So, knowing I wasn't up for conversation but not wanting to leave me alone, Arizona took the treadmill next to mine and started running.

I really liked the big guy. He was a good man. And I tried not to think about the ramifications of this next fight and where it would leave him or what he'd think of me after the truth came out.

Arizona was on a long list of people I wished wouldn't get hurt when this all went down but whom I also knew I would hurt the most. No, he wasn't involved in any drug running, but this was his only livelihood, and I was killing myself to see it shut down.

I forced these thoughts out of my head, telling myself just one more day. *Just one more day. Just one more day.*

I had to keep it together for just one more day.

This whole thing could be over as early as tonight.

I just had to survive getting in the cage one more time. I had to survive one more fight against Yuan. As my feet beat out an even rhythm on the treadmill, I tried not to think about what state I'd be in come morning.

WE STOPPED TRAINING FOR LUNCH, and as much as I didn't feel like eating, I knew my body needed some protein and carbohydrates to make it through tonight.

We had about an hour before Boss expected us back on the floor, so I spent the time in the dressing room, sitting on the bench seat, turning my phone over in my hand. I had four missed calls yesterday—two from Mitch, which told me he somehow knew Kira had left me, and two from Yumi before she'd come to visit last night.

Mitch's messages were short and his voice was sorry. "Matt, call me," and "Just need to know you're okay. Call me. Please."

How he knew about Kira leaving me, I didn't know. I didn't call him back.

But I turned the phone over and over in my hand. I wanted to call Kira. I wanted to speak to him, though I had no clue what I'd say. But he'd said he needed time, which meant he didn't want me calling him. I pressed his name on my screen, tempted to send him a text instead, when Arizona sat down beside me. "How you doin'?"

I shrugged one shoulder. "I'm okay."

"No, you're not."

"No," I agreed. "I'm not."

"Have you spoken to him?"

"He said he needed time."

Arizona sighed. "You gonna text him?"

"Thought about it. But don't want to push him further away."

"You know what?" he asked. "When my girl's mad at me and says she wants some space, what she really means is the opposite."

I snorted. "Not sure Kira does. I think he means it."

Arizona stretched out his feet and sighed. "Yeah, guess we're different than girls." Then he said, "Send him a quick message. Short and sweet, just a quick message so he knows you're not going anywhere."

"When did you become the expert?"

He laughed. "Man, I've had to say sorry more times than I can remember."

I looked at him and my smile faded. "You think I should?"

"What have you got to lose?"

Nothing.

Everything.

But he was right. I needed to let Kira know I wasn't going anywhere. When he was ready to talk to me, if he was ever ready to talk to me, he should know I'd be there.

I hit Messages on my phone and typed out a text. *Take all the time you need. I'll wait forever. I love you. I'm sorry.*

My thumb hovered over the Send button. I looked up to

Arizona, and he raised one eyebrow at me. "What the fuck you waitin' for?"

I exhaled through puffed cheeks and looked at Arizona. I said a silent prayer and hit Send.

There was no reply when I checked my phone two hours later.

And there was no reply two hours after that. I stood at my locker with my phone in my hand, checking and double-checking for messages from Kira that weren't there.

"Any reply?" Arizona asked beside me.

I shook my head and answered quietly. "No."

"Boys!" Boss called out. "Tressler's office. Now."

Fuck. I threw my phone into my locker and followed Arizona to Tressler's office. The man sneered at us as we walked in. "Fight's on tonight. You two, plus Jamaal and Cody," he said, reading off papers in front of him. Then he looked up at the both of us. "There'll be the usual merchandise pickup beforehand. They'll give you the address."

"Right," Arizona said. "Anything else?"

"You leave in five minutes," he said. "Go tell the other two."

I was hoping to leave without speaking to him, but he stopped us at the door. "Elliott?"

I turned to face him. "Yeah?"

"Hope you're bringing your anger issues with you tonight," he said smugly. "Word is you'll need it."

I smiled at the arrogant son of a bitch. "I have a score to settle," I told him. I didn't elaborate on how that score was with him.

He'd find out soon enough.

Arizona went to find Jamaal and Cody, and I went straight to the locker rooms, got changed quickly, and grabbed my phone.

Ignoring Mitch's messages about how I was coping, I typed out a quick reply. I didn't need to be cryptic. I didn't have time to be cryptic. It was going to be all over soon anyway, and I knew Mitch would read the message and know this was it. There was no going back from this.

Fight tonight. Leaving in five mins. Merchandise pickup first.

I hit Send and switched it to silent, just as Arizona walked in and opened his locker next to mine. "Any message from Kira yet?"

I threw my phone into the gym bag in my locker and shook my head. "No. Nothing."

"You ready?" he asked. "It's time to go."

"Yeah. Ready as I'll ever be." I grabbed my gym bag and shut my locker door.

"Did you leave your wallet and phone in your locker?" Arizona asked.

He saw me throw my phone into my locker but had no way of knowing the phone went into my bag. "Yeah," I lied. I looked at Jamaal and Cody. "You guys ready?"

The younger men both nodded excitedly. I envied their enthusiasm.

Going into the fight was the last place I wanted to be. My cop's intuition, the knot in my belly, told me tonight wasn't going to end well—that I was walking into a death trap. I was putting myself in a situation that chances were I wouldn't be walking away from.

AS WE DROVE from the FC to the pickup point, I rode shotgun while Arizona drove. I kept an eye on the side-view mirror to see if we were being followed. I couldn't see anyone tagging us, but I had no doubt they were.

They'd better be.

The only way Mitch could know where I was going was if they followed me. I hoped to God they were.

"You okay, man?" Arizona asked.

I turned to face him. "Yeah."

"Stop wonderin' if he'll call," he said. "You need to get your head in the game."

I nodded. "I know."

We pulled up in the back alley behind the same sporting goods warehouse as we went the last time. And just like last time, when we stood at the roller door, I pushed Cody to separate our body mass and minimize the target range. Then Cody pushed Jamaal to do the same. "Spread out, man," he said, like he was some expert. It made me smile.

The roller door went up, and just like last time, we collected a van full of gear. Mats, a variety of punch and kick pads, strapping tape, and the very important three boxing bags.

Arizona signed for the goods, and in return the two men gave us the delivery address.

The drive across the city was slow in Friday night traffic. I kept my eye on the cars behind us and although I couldn't be certain, I was pretty sure there were not one but two cars trailing us.

I rummaged through my backpack pretending to look for a bottle of water but quickly swiped my phone screen to bring up the last contact. I hit Call, pulled out the water bottle, and turned and laughed at something Cody was saying in the backseat.

I took a drink of water, then asked Arizona, "So, where

are we headed?" hoping Mitch could hear me on his phone through the backpack.

"East LA," he answered. "There's old manufacturin' warehouses off Pamona. I've fought there before." Then he eyed me. "Why?"

"Just wondering how far Yuan'll have to go to the nearest hospital."

The three men in the car laughed and started talking up their own fights. And I laughed along with them. Knowing if Mitch could hear me, I'd just given him an address. I'd done all I could do.

I had to concentrate on this fight. I knew stepping into the cage with Yuan was a dangerous, risky move. I just had to have faith in the Fab Four, that they'd get me out of there before the fight even took place, while still trying to mentally prepare for five rounds of hell.

We pulled up, just like Arizona said, at some abandoned manufacturing plant. Tressler's two men, Fridge One and Fridge Two, met us at one of the falling-down back docks. Arizona gave them the keys and we took our bags and went inside.

The main floor space was set up like last time, with different fight clubs set up along the walls and a cage in the middle. The betting audience filled the space in between.

Doc was there, and Pete the other trainer, and it wasn't long before Tressler came out to make his presence known. Dressed in his expensive suit, he stood out among the rest of us. He came over to where we were and asked Cody and Jamaal if they'd like him to put any bets on their fights on their behalf. They did, of course, but nothing more than a couple hundred apiece.

Then he turned to me and Arizona. "Now, you boys are

in for something special," he said. "It's like a two-for-one deal, but double the money."

"What's that mean?" Arizona asked.

"What that means," Tressler explained, "is that you're fighting together."

That didn't make sense. "Together?" I asked.

"Yes," he said cheerfully. "Not against one another, but together. You two will go into the cage together against two of their men."

"What?" Doc asked. He was the only one who I'd ever seen really question anything Tressler did. "What the hell kind of fight is that?"

Tressler looked directly at me. "The kind of fight that makes a lot of money." Then he turned to Doc. "The kind of fight you're paid to shut up about."

Doc turned his back on Tressler, and so the suited man looked back at us. "Lot of money on the floor tonight. And just to let you know," he said, almost conspiratorially, "Yuan is really pissed off they declared you the winner last time you fought. So I'd, um, how do I put this?" He paused for effect, like he actually had to think about what to say. "I'd watch not only your own back, but his as well," he said, nodding pointedly to Arizona.

Fuck.

Instead of showing him the fear I felt, I grinned at him instead. "Tell Yuan to fucking bring it."

Tressler threw his head back and laughed. "Now, if you're feeling so confident, how about putting your money where your mouth is?"

"Um, five hundred," Arizona said.

"Five thousand on us," I said coolly.

Arizona's eyes nearly popped out of his head, and even Tressler couldn't hide his surprise. "That's fair coin."

"It's about what I've got left from the last fight," I told him. "And I'm a double-or-nothing kind of guy."

A slow smile spread across Tressler's face. "Good luck, gentlemen."

As soon as Tressler was out of earshot, Arizona whisper-shouted, "What the hell, man? Have you lost your fucking mind?"

I didn't have time to answer. Pete was in front of us. "This is fucking bullshit," he said quickly, pulling my left hand up and starting to strap it. "He hasn't ever done this before. Now you boys both listen to me," he said, clearly concerned. "You get in that cage and you keep your backs together, and you keep them separated. They're gonna look to join forces, so you need to keep them separated. You understand what I'm saying?"

The urgency in his voice was unnerving.

Pete kept talking. "They're trained in jujitsu so they'll look for a takedown. Their strength is on the floor, so stay on your fucking feet. Use the cage if you have to. There won't be no rules in this fight. It's against regulation for two fights to run together, so this is gonna be a free-for-all."

Arizona looked at me, and I could tell he was worried, even though he tried to act like he wasn't. "We'll handle it."

Pete shook his head, not disagreeing with Arizona, but more in disbelief. "Someone's paid good money for a fight like this."

"Yuan," I said. "He wants me dead."

Pete looked at me, wide-eyed. "As in for real?"

"As in for real," I said with a smile. "But don't worry, I'm gonna kill him first."

"Glad you're on my team," Arizona mumbled.

Maybe I was talking it up, maybe I was telling the truth. I couldn't tell. I was psyched up and fucking pissed off, and my adrenaline was pumping for what I knew was going down tonight.

Everything I'd worked for in the last six months.

Everything I'd jeopardized.

Everything I'd lost.

For Kira. My everything.

I quickly looked around the crowd, looking for any signs of police activity, but there weren't any. Although I'd left a message and called his number from my cell so he could track us, as far as I knew, Mitch and the boys weren't even aware I was here. I had to carry on like I was here on my own.

Pete dropped my hand and told me I was good to go, and he started strapping Arizona's hands. I held the punch pads for Cody while he prepped for his fight, then Jamaal when it was his turn.

We watched the younger two guys fight. It helped us focus. It also gave us plenty of time to be eyeballed by Yuan and his cofighter, who, as it turned out, was the guy I'd beat at the FC a few months back.

"I've beat him before," I told Arizona.

"Is he right- or left-handed?" he asked.

"Don't know," I said. "I knocked him out in the first ten seconds of round one."

Arizona laughed, though it was nervous. "How 'bout you do it again this fight?"

I smiled at him. "That's the plan. But listen," I said. "You get in that cage and you look after yourself. Don't look at me; don't worry about what I'm doing. I'll watch my guy. You watch yours. You don't take your eyes off your opponent, okay?"

He nodded quickly.

"Arizona," I said seriously. "No matter what happens in

that cage, you look out for yourself. If you take your guy out early or if I take mine out early, then we can help each other, but listen," I said, getting right up close. "If he takes me out and they both turn on you, you don't even bother fucking tapping out, you hear me? You just get the fuck out of that cage, okay?"

He nodded quickly again, but this time he really looked worried. So I smiled at him, and held up my fists, which he habitually bumped with his own. "Now let's get in there and take these fuckers down."

I gave another quick glance around the old warehouse, at the crowd, and the other fighters. There had to be at least two hundred people in there, and I knew Berkman, if he was even out there, would need every strategic line in place. It'd have to be timed perfectly, or there'd be too big a risk of mass panic and possible loss of life.

Even though, I was guessing, the point of entry for the police wouldn't be in the main area where I was. It'd be in the back where Tressler had the punching bags of coke split and divvied for distribution to his dealers and their mules. That was where they'd go first.

But Berkman would also be looking at keeping everyone in the main arena, and the best possible time for mass containment would be at the biggest fight of the night.

Which was mine and Arizona's.

As much as I didn't really want to get in that cage with them, in a way, I was kind of glad. I wanted someone to pay for this fucking mess. For everything I'd lost and everyone I'd hurt. And if Yuan was tied up with Tressler, then he was the perfect candidate.

I wanted someone to hurt as much as I did.

When Pete came around and told us we were up next, I knew I didn't have a choice. I went through last-minute prep talks with Arizona, and before we stepped into the cage, I went up to Cody, Jamaal, Pete, and Doc and told them to leave.

"What?" Cody asked.

"You guys don't need to be here to see this," I answered.

"I wanna watch you two take these clowns down," he replied.

I turned to Pete and Doc. "Get them outta here."

Pete's eyes widened. "You're not really gonna kill someone, are you?"

I didn't answer that. I just didn't want any of these guys implicated in this mess if and when the police stormed in. "You all should go."

"I'm not leaving you two here alone," Doc said, and after I'd seen him argue with Tressler, I knew there was no reasoning with him. I turned back to Pete and spoke so only he could hear. "Believe me when I tell you, you don't want to be here tonight."

Arizona, standing near the cage, called my name. I was out of time.

"Pete, I can't explain. Get the fuck out of here. You hear me? You don't want to be here in about ten minutes. Get these kids and get out. Do you understand?"

Maybe it was my tone, or maybe he saw the seriousness in my face. Maybe I scared him. I didn't know, and I didn't care. But he was wrangling a very pissed-off Cody and Jamaal with their gear toward the exit as I walked up the steps to the cage.

It was like slow motion and fast-forward at the same time. My heart was hammering. My adrenaline was spiked. I was ready for this.

I was fucking scared.

I wanted it to be over.

The crowd was yelling and hollering, and the sound was deafening. Never before had four men stepped into the cage. I stood side by side with Arizona and we faced off with Yuan and Juarez, and the noise in the arena was so loud, I couldn't hear a word the referee said.

I guess it didn't matter.

I wasn't expecting this fight to have rules.

Then the ref called, "Fight," and Arizona and I immediately stuck together, the sides of our arms almost touching. Yuan went straight for me, trying to draw me away from my partner with direct jabs and thigh kicks. I landed some good kicks to his thigh and ribs, but he dodged my attempts at straight hooks, and somehow Arizona and I got separated.

I kept trying to get back to the center of the cage, but Yuan kept me drawn out and relentlessly kept his attack on me. He punched and kicked me, and I fucking gave it back to him. But no matter what I did, I couldn't get the advantage. I even landed a right hook to his face and he still didn't falter. He didn't even flinch.

Then out of the corner of my eye, I saw Arizona get picked up by his leg and driven into the floor. His opponent landed heavily on top of him with his knees and elbows, and instead of lunging at Yuan, I swung left and knocked Juarez off Arizona.

I turned quickly, knowing Yuan would take my back turned as an opportunity to take me down, but he was right on top of me. He slammed me into the side of the cage and pinned me, holding me with his weight while kneeing me in the thigh and the ribs and trying to head-butt me at the same time. When Yuan lifted his knee to my ribs, I took out his leg and threw him off balance, causing him to take a step back from me.

I charged at him, not giving him a chance to step onto

his front foot, and pushed him backwards, punching as I went. I landed an even kick to his face, and although it split his cheek, he never looked like he was going down.

He must have had a jaw of steel.

We danced around each other a little, confined by Arizona and Juarez doing the same. The fight space was halved, and although I tried not to worry about Arizona and keep my focus on Yuan, I was very aware of where he was.

I'd told Arizona not to worry about me and to look after himself. But that didn't mean I wouldn't look out for him too.

For the last six months, Arizona had been my partner. Like I used to have Mitch, I now had Arizona, and of course I'd look out for him.

It was what partners did.

Then I saw Arizona get taken to the floor again. He got elbowed repeatedly and I couldn't get to him. Yuan was all over me. I couldn't turn my back, not even for a second. He kept me distracted with hard kicks to the ribs and sharp jabs to my face. But I turned us around so I could see Arizona, only to find Juarez had him in the sleeper-hold. It could be fatal for the guy on the ground if the other fighter didn't let go immediately.

I saw Arizona's arm fall out against the ground and he tapped the floor. He was calling submission, telling the ref he was in trouble, to put an end to his fight.

It was then I realized the ref wasn't even in the cage.

I didn't even think about it.

I didn't have a choice.

I charged at Yuan like a footballer, pushing him away, and launched myself at Juarez knocking him off Arizona. We crashed to the floor, into the side of the cage, and as I swung off him, I kneed him in the head.

I knew it was a foolish thing to do. I knew it left my back exposed to Yuan and left me incredibly vulnerable. But I couldn't let Juarez kill Arizona. Not like that.

Not because of me.

And everything after that was like an out-of-body experience. Like I was watching it happen to someone else.

I felt the two men grab me, pulling me down and holding the side of my head to the floor. I know I fought them, but it was useless. I was outnumbered and pinned on the ground. My most vulnerable position in the cage.

I felt the punches and elbows to my body, and I felt the knees to my head, but there was no pain. It was like it was happening to someone else. All I could hear was the noise of the crowd. It was a roar.

I remember thinking it wasn't supposed to end like this.

I remember thinking of Kira and how glad I was he wasn't here to see this.

To watch me die like this would kill him.

I remember seeing blood from my head seep out and pool on the floor in front of me, and I remember thinking blood shouldn't be so dark.

Then I heard shouting, words I couldn't make out from so far away. Then I saw flashing red and blue lights from somewhere outside, and people were running in every direction. There was a buzzing in my head that sounded like a muted rumble. Then the two men weren't holding my head to the floor anymore. Instead there were police-issued boots in front of my face and someone familiar saying my name, yelling for a fucking paramedic.

I wondered why it sounded like I was underwater.

I don't remember anything after that.

CHAPTER SIXTEEN

I TRIED to get up and open my eyes, but hands were holding me down. "Don't move, Matt," a distant, familiar voice said. "We got you."

My vision was blurred and my head felt off balance.

Then the familiar voice seemed too close and too far away. "Where the fuck is the paramedic? We've got an officer down."

I tried to wonder who was injured, but my eyes closed and I fell back into darkness.

THERE WAS a mask on my face and muffled voices, far off sirens and bright lights. I reached up to pull the mask off, but a hand stopped me.

"It's okay, Detective. Just relax, take some breaths for me," a woman said. "You're in the ambulance. We'll have you at the hospital in five."

That's good, I thought. *Because I have some pain... everywhere.*

I WOKE up and tried to open my eyes, but the pain in my head was extraordinary.

"Hey, Matt," someone said. It was a familiar voice. A very faraway voice, like he was in the next room but somehow right beside me. "Don't try to move."

I thought not moving was a *great* idea. So I didn't.

I WOKE up again and knew better than to open my eyes. So instead, I tried lifting my arm, my left arm, but it was too heavy to lift off the bed. It was then I realized my entire body was on fire. Not just a pain in my head, but everywhere.

Every. Fucking. Where.

"Detective Elliott," a quiet, far off voice said. "Try and keep still."

THE NEXT TIME I woke up, I didn't dare move. I didn't try and open my eyes. I was surprised I could still breathe.

I could feel something move along my fingers. Someone was holding my hand.

"Kira?" I asked. My voice croaked and barely made any sound. It didn't sound like me.

No one answered, so I tried to open my eyes. It took a long while for me to focus, but when I did, he wasn't there.

I closed my eyes.

I WAS awake but didn't open my eyes. I didn't try to speak. I didn't try and move.

I tried to listen.

There were sounds, but they were... displaced.

I heard a voice I recognized. Mitch. "No, he has no family. We're his family," he said. "Well, he has a partner, a boyfriend, but they separated just recently." Then his voice was softer. "He was very close to his in-laws. They treated him like a son."

My heart lurched, literally hurting in my chest, and I sank back into sleep.

THE NEXT TIME I woke up, the room was quiet, and the light was dim. I was grateful.

I was thirsty as hell, and when I tried to sit up, I groaned as sharp pain stabbed from my head down my side to my legs.

A nurse was quickly beside me. Her voice sounded distant, even though she was close. "Ssh, Detective. Don't move," she said. "You're in the hospital."

"Thirsty," I rasped out.

She disappeared only to come back with a cup. "Use the straw. It'll save you trying to sit up."

Even sipping the water hurt my head. "Hurts."

"Yes," she said. "You've been through quite the ordeal."

I had another sip of water, then the nurse took it away. I groaned again. "There was another man?"

She moved around my bed and her voice wavered, like

someone was turning the volume up and down. "Who came in with you?"

"Yes," I answered. "Arizona. Abel Koczur."

"He's here," she answered.

"He okay?"

"He's in better shape than you." It sounded like she was far away or even speaking from the next room, and I figured the searing pain in my head had something to do with it. I just wanted to know Arizona was okay.

I couldn't get my bearings. I knew people had been here before, but they weren't here now. "What's the time?" I mumbled, closing my eyes.

"Five fifteen in the morning," she answered faintly. "Rest, Detective. They all said they'd be back to see you first thing."

I WOKE up again to a smell that made my stomach roll. And piece by piece my brain registered pain in my body. My left leg, my ribs on both sides, my stomach, my right shoulder, my head.

Fuck, my head.

I'd thought it had hurt last time, but that was nothing. Instead of feeling like there was an ax lodged in my skull, this felt like the right side of my head was crushed. The pain was baffling. My jaw, my nose, my cheek, my eye. My skull, my brain, my skin—it all hurt.

I felt like I wanted to vomit.

"Detective Elliot?" a voice said. "Detective? My name is Doctor Stenner. Can you open your eyes?"

I groaned, and slowly my eyes opened. Or as I found out, one eye.

"Your right eye will be swollen shut for a while," he said. "You've had some serious blows to the head."

I was looking straight at him, and his voice sounded... one-sided.

My throat was dry and it even hurt to talk. "Sound funny." I lifted my right hand slowly up to my ear. It was bandaged.

The man in the white coat nodded. "Yes, that's what I thought."

I didn't know what he meant. My brain hurt to think.

"Think you're up for some breakfast?" the doctor asked.

I groaned. "No."

"Hey," someone interrupted. I turned my head slowly to find Mitch standing in the door. He looked like hell. He walked straight up to me and took my hand. "Hey," he said again. He had tears in his eyes. "Fuck, Matt."

Then Berkman, Kurt, and Tony were there, trying not to look at me with pity.

"I'll leave you alone for a bit," the doctor said. "I'll be back."

The four men looked at me but didn't know what to say.

"Arizona?" I asked.

"He's okay," Mitch answered. "Beat up. Sore and sorry, but alive."

"Witnesses say you saved his life," Kurt said.

"Nearly cost you yours," Berkman added.

"Tressler?" I asked, my voice barely a whisper.

"We got him," Mitch said. "And Yuan. We got them all. It crossed state lines, so the DEA and FBI took over. It was much bigger than what we thought."

I closed my eye and sighed. It was really over. I should have felt relieved, but I didn't. "Hurts."

Mitch let go of my hand and replaced it with something

small, cylindrical, and cool to touch. "Here," he said. "It's your morphine feed. Press the button when you need it." His fingers moved my thumb over the button on the end.

Then I heard another familiar voice. "Oh, my goodness." I opened my not-swollen eye to see Yumi standing in the door with her hand to her mouth. Her eyes welled with tears. "My Matthew," she said, walking to the bed.

Sal followed her in, but she turned to the four policemen around the bed and pointed her finger at each of them. "Don't you speak to me," she said. "None of you. Look at what you did to my boy!" She waved her hand at me. "This is the second time." She held up two fingers at them. "First my Kira be in a hospital bed, now my Matthew."

Sal put his hand on Yumi's shoulder, so she turned to him. "They should know!"

"Mrs. Takeo Franco," Berkman started apologetically.

She spun around to him, clearly upset, and pointed her finger at him. "I said you not speak to me!"

Then Kira was there. He had his arm around his mother. "Mom," he said softly. "It's—" he started to say, then he looked at me and his words just stopped. His mouth fell open and his eyes welled with tears. "Jesus."

"Kira," I tried to say. Seeing him, finally seeing him, even upset, he was beautiful. It felt like I hadn't seen him in a hundred years. "Kira."

He shook his head and tried to speak as he stared at me. A single tear rolled down his cheek, and he sucked back a breath. "You lied to me," he said. Then he turned to Mitch, Kurt, Tony, and Berkman. "You all lied to me." He looked back at me. "Oh, Matt," he cried and scrubbed his hand over his face. He tried to say something again but turned on his heel and walked out instead.

Everyone stood silent, not knowing what to say or where to look. Berkman moved first. "I'll go talk to him," he said, following him out the door.

I gasped back a breath, like I'd broken the surface after being held underwater, and my heart squeezed to the point of pain. I instinctually curled onto my side and had to push my hand against my chest to try and keep the hurt inside. I groaned loudly at the movement.

The doctor was suddenly there, checking machines and peeling my hand from my chest so he could press a stethoscope to my heart. "Are you having chest pains?"

Sal put a hand on the doctor's arm and shook his head. The doctor looked at Sal and he signed. He put his two fists together and motioned as though he was snapping a stick.

I knew what that meant.

Broken.

My heart was broken.

I pressed the morphine button again and again and waited for oblivion to take me.

I DIDN'T WANT to wake up. I didn't want to know. I lay there, not moving, not caring. But there were people talking in the room. Voices sounded funny. I didn't know why.

But I heard Yumi first.

"He blame himself for what happened to Kira," she said softly.

Then someone squeezed my hand. I hadn't even realized someone was holding it. I didn't want to look. I wanted so much for it to be Kira, I could almost imagine it was his hand, his fingers, his warmth. I didn't want to risk looking and finding out it wasn't him.

I couldn't bear any more pain.

"Please understand," Berkman said next. "He went through a psych evaluation to go undercover. He passed with flying colors. There's no way we'd have let him go through with it if we didn't believe him capable."

"He fooled us all," someone said. Kurt. Kurt said that.

"I don't think so," Mitch said quietly. "He hasn't been himself for a long time. He kept acting like nothing was wrong, like if he pretended for long enough it'd become the truth." Then he said, "I saw it. I just didn't want to admit there was something wrong. He's my partner. He's like a brother to me."

My hand got squeezed again.

Then Yumi spoke. "He told us he wanted the pain. He wanted to get hit. That's why he did it. He said the pain was his penance for what happened to Kira. That's what he said. *Penance.*"

Then my hand got lifted to press against someone's face, muffled with a soft cry and a sniff. I opened my eyes then, to see who it was.

My hand looked pale against his warm brown skin. With his mass of spiky, black hair and closed almond-shaped eyes, he looked exhausted.

"Kira?" I croaked out, choking on tears.

His eyes shot open to look at me, and they scanned my bandaged face and swam with sadness and worry.

I needed to tell him. "I'm sorry."

He lifted his other hand and gently pushed some hair from my forehead, then he looked into my eyes. "I'm so fucking mad at you." But he gently pressed the back of my hand to his face and frowned as a tear rolled down his cheek.

"I love you," I said, my voice still hoarse.

Squeezing my hand in his, Kira nodded.

"I'm sorry," I said again.

He didn't say anything else. He never said he loved me; he never said I was forgiven. He just bowed his head.

But he never let go of my hand.

It was a start.

"OKAY," the doctor said. "We're going to take off these bandages and take a look. I need to do one more test." I had the bed elevated so I was almost sitting up, so he could unwrap the bandages easier. The doctor shined a light in my good left eye, then in my right ear. "Hmm."

It was getting late, and I'd been in the hospital for almost twenty-four hours. Not even a day.

It felt like a lifetime.

Yumi, Sal, and Kira were still there, along with Mitch and Berkman. The doctor had said there were far too many people, so Tony and Kurt opted to leave, knowing no one else would leave willingly.

Yumi cringed when she saw my unbandaged face, and Kira had to look away. I couldn't have stitches because it was too swollen, so the two cuts, one above my eye, one along my cheek, were held together with some type of surgical glue.

But apparently the most damage was on the inside.

I had six cracked ribs, a bruised kidney, an enlarged spleen, a rebroken nose, and the one the doctors were so concerned with, a fractured temporal bone.

"X-rays show a transverse fracture here," he pointed to the side of my head, between my eye and my ear. "It's common in blunt force trauma, or in your case, repeated knees to the side of the head."

I didn't dare look at Kira or Yumi. I looked at the doctor. "What else?"

The doctor carefully put a foamy plug in my left ear, and all of a sudden, my world went quiet.

There was nothing. Complete silence.

That was why everything sounded wavy and one-sided before.

I couldn't hear in my right ear.

I looked at the doctor and he pulled out the earplug. "Anything?"

"No."

He nodded. "Sensorineural hearing loss is a common side effect from head injuries of this kind. From the MRI and CT scans we can see there's no hemorrhaging or fluid build-up, but the blows to the head and ear caused nerve damage to the inner ear, and that's why you can't hear."

"What does that mean?" Mitch asked.

The doctor turned to face everyone else. "It means he's deaf in one ear." Then the doctor looked at me. "It also means you'll have balance issues that might get better over time, or might not. There's going to be headaches for a long while, along with dizziness."

"Is the deafness permanent?" I asked.

"In your right ear, yes," he answered bluntly. "Some people gain some percentage of hearing back by six to twelve months, but in your case, I'd say it's highly unlikely." The doctor flipped open my file and said, "Now, as for your work..."

"It doesn't matter," I said quietly. All eyes were on me. "I'm not going back."

"You're what?" Kira and Mitch asked in unison.

"I'm not going back," I said again, suddenly very tired. "I haven't been a cop for a long time," I whispered. "Not since... not since Tomic..."

"Matt," Kira said softly.

"'S okay," I told him, trying to stay awake. "I stopped being a cop the day it nearly took you away from me. I didn't love my job after that."

Kira took my hand. "It wasn't your fault."

I ignored that. "It doesn't matter. Narcotics detectives can't be deaf in one ear, anyway," I told him. "Kind of makes the decision for me."

I could barely keep my eyes open, and the splitting pain was trying to crack my skull once more. "Kira, babe?" I whispered.

"Yeah?"

"Can you press the meds button for me?"

"Yeah."

"Babe?"

"Yeah, Matt. I'm here."

"Press it twice."

CHAPTER SEVENTEEN

I WOKE up early on the second day feeling a bit better. My head probably felt worse and same with my ribs, but my muscles didn't seem so sore. And waking up to see Kira asleep in the chair against the far wall made me feel like a million dollars.

I knew he wouldn't forgive me easily, and I knew we'd have a long road ahead of us in talking things through and rebuilding the trust I'd killed between us, but I didn't mind.

I'd do whatever it took.

And the fact he was still here gave me hope that he wasn't ready to quit on me either.

I lay in the hospital bed, looking at the stained ceiling, thinking about my life—what I'd been through, where I was now, and where I wanted to be.

I couldn't see out my right eye, though the doctor said once the swelling went down, I should have full vision. Not so much for the hearing. I was completely deaf in my right ear, and whether I regained any hearing, only time would tell, though it was unlikely.

It was weird that I didn't mind.

The doctor said I was very lucky it wasn't worse. Apparently there were a series of nerves for vision and hearing, much like the audio and visual cables on a TV, that ran along the temporal bone, and I was lucky both weren't damaged. I was lucky I didn't have brain damage. I was lucky I hadn't been killed.

Last night before Yumi and Sal had left, the doctor had told them there were worse things than loss of hearing, and Sal signed, "Yeah, I think we'll manage."

Kira translated, and the doctor laughed, telling them he'd be back to see me in the morning. Kira's parents stayed until dinnertime, and when they asked him if he wanted a ride home, he looked at me and shook his head. "I'll stay."

It was the first time I'd felt any hope in months.

He still didn't talk much, though I knew it was coming. Knowing Kira, he'd wait until I was better, but he was going to let me have it. He was going to tell me how bad I'd fucked up, how I'd broken his trust, how I'd broken his heart.

How I'd better spend the rest of my life making it up to him.

And I would.

The weirdest realization was that I was no longer a cop. Well, I hadn't resigned formally, but in my head it was over.

I felt relieved.

And that was weird.

I wasn't relieved when they told me they'd gotten Tressler or even Yuan, but realizing I wasn't a cop anymore gave me a sense of relief. Like closure.

Berkman said he'd be back to see me today, and Mitch too. Probably to see if I'd change my mind or to see what options a half-deaf detective had, but I knew. I didn't want to be a cop anymore.

I hadn't for a long time.

If I was honest with myself, I should have stood down a year ago. I certainly shouldn't have signed up to go undercover. I shouldn't have lied to the shrinks who had analyzed me. I shouldn't have lied to Mitch or to Berkman.

I most certainly shouldn't have lied to Kira.

I should have resigned.

I should have told him everything.

"Good morning," a nurse said brightly. "Breakfast time."

"Ugh," I groaned at the thought. "No thanks."

"The doctor wants you to eat something," she said matter-of-factly.

"He never eats breakfast." I smiled at Kira as he sat up and stretched. "Just coffee."

"I ate a little dinner last night," I told her.

She flipped through the folder at the foot of my bed. "Your chart says you had two mouthfuls of soup."

"It was awful."

She huffed at me as she walked out, then returned with a full tray of food. "Eat," she ordered. "Doctor wants to get you up and about today. But you need to eat first."

I didn't like her.

She cranked up my bed so I was in more of a sitting position, making my ribs hurt and my head spin and throb. Then she swung the tray around in front of me. "Eat."

I reached for my morphine release button, but she took it and moved it out of reach. "None of that until I see you eat."

I didn't like her at all.

I looked at the food in front of me. Oatmeal, cold toast, and sliced fruit. My stomach rolled.

But then a tiny woman wheeled in a drinks tray. "Coffee? Tea?"

"Yes! Coffee, please!" I said. I looked at the little lady as she put a cup on my tray and filled it. "Now you, I like."

The nurse glared at me, but I was saved again by Kira's parents. Yumi walked into the room like she owned it, carrying a white paper bag, and Sal followed her in carrying an overnight bag and a tray of coffee.

It hurt to smile.

Yumi looked at the tray of hospital food like it had offended her personally, then looked at the nurse. "He not eat this," she said like she was stating the color of the sky. "He only have coffee for breakfast."

The nurse grunted before rolling her eyes and walking out. The little drink-cart lady held up my cup of coffee she'd just poured, and said, "You still want?"

"I still want," I told her. "Thank you."

I sat with my two coffees in front of me and listened while they sat and ate their bagels and talked. I loved watching them just be themselves.

"You okay?" Yumi asked me. "You in pain? Use your button," she said, getting up and handing me the morphine button.

"No thanks. It makes me sleepy. Figure I need to get used to this," I said, waving my hand in the direction of my face. "They want me to get up today, apparently."

"Then just rest," she said. "Close your eyes. We stay most of the day."

But before I could close my eyes, there was a quiet knock on the open door.

"Come in," Yumi said.

Arizona slowly walked into my room. He was limping and had white gauze over his eyebrow, a bruised eye and cheek, but apart from that he looked okay. The way he held his torso told me he wasn't great.

"Hey," I said. It was good to see him.

"Hey, man," he said quietly. "Jeez, you look like shit."

I huffed, and it stung my nose. "Thanks. You doin' okay?"

He looked over my bandaged head, black eyes, cut face, and broken nose. "Better than you." There was an awkward silence before he spoke again. "So, is it true? You still a cop? Is that why Tressler wanted you dead?"

"Up until yesterday I was, yes," I told him. "It was a covert operation to bring down Tressler. Yuan and Tressler ran a cocaine syndicate and distributed to the streets through both fight clubs."

He shook his head. "So you lied to me?"

"I lied to everyone," I admitted quietly. "Sorry doesn't begin..." I trailed off, knowing an apology wasn't anywhere near enough. "For what it's worth, Arizona, I consider you a friend. You were like my partner. You're a good man, and that's rare these days."

He looked at Kira, then to Yumi and Sal, who all just watched him. He swallowed thickly. "You saved my life in that cage."

"And you saved mine."

He nodded and took a deep breath. "I gotta get goin'," he said. "I ain't got no medical insurance, but a fella by the name of—" He opened a folded discharge form. "—uh, Ross Berkman, signed off on a night stay under some cop policy. Told 'em to make sure I was okay." Arizona looked at me and shrugged. "I don't know who that is."

I smiled but figured he didn't need to know who that was.

"Anyways," he said. "I gotta go. My girl'll be here soon to get me."

"Tell Lashona I'm sorry," I said, trying not to fall asleep.

"I'm sorry for everything. Arizona, it might not mean much to you, but I promise I'll find a way to make it up to you."

He nodded but walked out without a word. He was someone else I'd let down. Someone else I'd lied to. Someone else I'd put in danger.

I tried to think of a way to repay him, but fell asleep before I could.

THE PAIN WOKE ME UP. There was no other way to describe it. It just fucking hurt. "I wanna get up," I mumbled. "I'm starting to ache from lying down too long."

So the nurses sat my bed up again, and after I'd been upright for a little while, I slowly sat up on the side of the bed. They lowered the bed so my feet touched the floor and made me sit like that for a while.

Everything hurt, only now there was new pain. My head spun and pounded a whole new level of headache, and my ribs screamed at the change of position.

But I needed to do this.

Yes, I wanted to get up, I wanted to move, and I wanted to shower. But I wanted to get on with my life. I wanted to start fresh, and that involved getting out of the hospital.

It involved walking to the shower first.

They unhooked my drip and got me ready to stand. And sitting on the edge of the bed was a walk in the park compared to standing up. I had a nurse on one side, an orderly on the other, and I took baby steps to the shower.

Everything hurt. Every fucking thing.

They put me in a shower seat, unwrapped and peeled off all my bandages, and left me to rest for a few minutes.

When there was a knock on the door, I expected a nurse to walk in, but it wasn't. It was Kira.

"Hey," he said softly. "You okay?"

"Yeah." I tried to smile. "Just dizzy."

"And in a lot of pain."

"Yeah."

He stood in silence for a few seconds, then he said, "Stand up."

I looked at him, unsure.

He said it again. "Stand up."

So, taking a deep breath and resting my hands on the armrests of the chair, I slowly lifted myself up. I gritted my teeth through the pain in my ribs, and when I swayed with dizziness, Kira caught me.

He turned me slowly and faced me to the mirror beside the hand basin. I was completely naked, no bandages, no plasters. And completely riddled with dark purple blotches. Bruises. Up my legs, my hip, my abdomen, my ribs, my shoulder, my arms were covered in large, swollen bruises.

My gaze fell to the floor.

"Look at yourself," he said quietly.

"Kira..."

"Look at yourself," he said again, this time more sternly.

I did as he asked and looked at my reflection once more. This time I looked at my face. The right side of my face was cut, swollen, dented, black and blue.

Kira stared at me in the reflection. "Can you see what I see?"

I gave a small nod.

"Want to know what I see?" he asked angrily. "I see a man who was too scared to talk to me. I see a man who almost lost everything because he was fucking scared." Then his voice was softer. "I see a man who lied to me, betrayed me, because he wanted to protect me. A stupid, *stupid* fucking man." He shook his head, and his eyes welled with tears. "I see a man who wanted to get beaten as penance for his guilt, for something he was *not* responsible for."

I didn't try to hide my tears. I just let them fall. "I should have told you," I whispered.

"Yes, you should have," he said. "Why didn't you? Right from the beginning, why didn't you tell me how you felt?"

"Because after the whole Tomic thing, you seemed to cope so well," I told him. "And I didn't. I didn't want to keep reminding you."

"And why did you lie to me about fighting at the FC?"

"I wanted to protect you."

"Well, you failed," he said. "It wasn't some drug-crazed psychopath who hurt me this time, was it?"

I shook my head. "No."

"It was you, Matt."

I started to cry. "I'm so sorry."

"You should be."

I sobbed, sucking back a breath, and my ribs pulled. Kira slowly sat me in the chair and kneeled in front of me and held my hands. "Oh, Matt," he said, his tone softer, but he was still angry. "For what it's worth, I do believe you were trying to protect me, in some fucked-up, deluded way. I do believe that. But you messed up big time, and to be honest, when I found out you were fighting undercover, I swore we were through."

I looked up at him then, scared to death of what he was about to say.

"But then Mom and Dad told me they spoke to you," he said quietly. "That you were doing it to protect me, because you couldn't bear the thought of someone hurting me. Because you loved me."

"I do," I mumbled with fresh tears.

"And then you were almost killed, Matt." His eyes were full of pain. "You were almost taken from me, and I swear, I've never been so scared in my whole life."

"I'm sorry."

He shook his head. "All because you were too scared to talk to me."

"I'm so sorry."

"I know you're sorry," he said. "But if you want to be with me, then you are going to have to talk to me. We are going to talk about this. All of it. You are going to talk about everything you don't want to talk about, then you're going to talk about it some more. You are going to talk to an entire fucking team of shrinks, do you understand?"

I nodded.

"Because if we stand any chance of getting past this, you need to fucking talk."

"I know," I whispered through my tears. "I will. Whatever it takes."

"Matt, I love you, I do. But you hurt me. If you lie to me one more time—about anything—we're through. Do you understand?"

I nodded and started to cry again. I couldn't seem to stop. And an exhaustion I'd never thought possible came over me. My head lolled forward, and Kira seemed to catch me, taking my face gently in his hands. "Oh, Matt... Shower first, then you can sleep."

"'Kay," I mumbled.

The nurses were there then, and soon enough the hot shower and soap was both heaven and torture on my skin. I even managed to gently brush my teeth, though the right side of my mouth was painful, but it made me feel half human.

I was dressed in a clean gown and got into a clean bed. The nurse handed me a paper cup with pills in it, which I took without question. I settled back onto the pillows and closed my eyes and not a moment later, I felt familiar fingers wrap around my left hand and a gentle kiss to my forehead.

BY MIDAFTERNOON, I'd slept a bit more, eaten some fruit, and although the pain was still there, I was feeling remarkably better.

It had little to do with medication and a whole lot to do with Kira. What he'd said had been a very hard truth, and one I'd known was coming. He knew it wasn't going to be easy, he knew he'd chosen the hard road. I had a lot of shit to deal with to try and get my head right, and yet there he sat beside my hospital bed holding my hand.

The doctor ordered some more hearing tests and told me that failing any downturns in my condition, I could go home the next day.

"Did you want to go to the cabin?" Sal asked in sign language.

"No," I answered. Then I looked at Kira. "I just want to go home. If that's okay?"

"Of course it is," he answered.

"I miss it," I told him. "I miss being there with you. I just want to spend some time at home, just us, ya know?" Then a thought occurred to me. "Only if you want to be there," I said, unsure if he intended to move back in. "If you don't, I'll understand."

Kira smiled. "Of course, I want to be there."

Just then there was another knock on the door. Berkman stuck his head in the room. "Up for visitors?" he asked, then proceeded to walk in anyway. "How's the patient?"

"I'm okay," I answered.

"What'd the doc say?"

"I'm still deaf in one ear," I told him. "And I can go home tomorrow."

Berkman nodded. "That's good then," he said. "I mean, about the going home part, not the still deaf part." I think it was the first time I'd seen him look unsure. He looked at Kira, Sal, and Yumi, then finally back at me. "Just wondering if you've thought more about what you said yesterday?" he asked. "You don't need to make any decisions right now. You can take paid leave—"

"Ross?" I interrupted him. "I quit. Medically unfit for duty, or call it whatever. I'm out."

Berkman stared at me for a long moment, then he sighed. "You sure?"

"Yes." I was sure. "Absolutely."

He shrugged. "What will you do?"

"I don't know," I answered honestly. "I need to take some time, get my head on straight." I looked at Kira and he smiled. "I need to start making some other things a priority in my life."

Berkman nodded thoughtfully. "Fair enough." Then he said, "The medical report for this case shows you could have residual side effects for up to six months."

"Yeah, so the doctor said," I answered. "So?"

"That means you can go on full sick-pay while you get better, and the department can line up the best shrink—" He stopped short. "I mean, the best person to help you get your head straightened out, and you won't have to worry about paying for it while you're not working."

I smiled at him. "And people think you're an asshole?"

He snorted, but then he was serious. "You're one of the best detectives I've had the privilege of working with." He was quiet for a moment, then he frowned. "Anyway, think about what I said."

"I will."

"And let me know if there's anything else I can do," he said. "I mean it, Elliott, anything at all."

"Now that you mention it," I said, "there is something you can do for me."

Berkman blinked. "What is it?"

"Just how good is your professional relationship with the Chief of Police and the Mayor?"

Two weeks later

"I know you're probably wondering what I called you here for," I said to the little audience. They were the five guys I'd come to know and think of as partners, the five guys I'd hurt the most when the FC shut down.

Boss, Arizona, Cody, Amil, and Jamaal stared at me, and Kira who stood beside me, waiting for me to speak.

I looked around the empty gym, what used to be their second home. "You have every right to be pissed off at me, and I don't blame you, but I'm asking you to hear me out."

Boss folded his arms and stared hard at me. "You still a cop?"

I shook my head. "No. Not anymore."

"That's what you said last time," Cody said. "What the hell, man?"

"Just listen to what I have to say," I told them. "Then if you still want to hate me, you can." The five men were quiet, so I continued. "I know what this club meant to you guys, and I'm sorry you guys were fucked over when the bust went down. I'm sorry I lied to you. I'm sorry I lost your trust. For what it's worth, I really liked being here with you guys." I looked at each of them. "That's why I had the Chief of Police and the Mayor pull some strings to keep the FC open."

"You what?" Boss asked.

"The City of Los Angeles is prepared to take on the FC," I answered. "It was my one stipulation when I left the department. They asked if there was anything they could do for me, and I told them there was. I want to see this place re-open, and I want you guys to run it."

The five of them looked at me. None of them spoke.

So I explained. "Part of the deal for the city to take it over is to run special programs for school kids and street kids alike, teaching them the basics of boxing and fitness. To respect their bodies, to respect each other, and to respect themselves."

"And we run it?" Arizona asked.

"Yes. Boss will be in charge, Arizona head trainer, and Jamaal, Cody, and Amil to be instructors. Paid employment, benefits, medical, the usual."

"What's the catch?" Boss asked.

"No catch," I answered. "Well, you'll be answerable to some local government administration pen-pushers, there will be rules and guidelines, you might need to work on some community funding that kind of thing, and of course, everything will have to be done legally. But there will be programs for kids and adults, if there's a need for it, but this is all about teaching these kids some drug awareness and how they have options."

Arizona gave me a slow-spreading smile. "This was your

one stipulation? They offered you anything, and you wanted this? For us?"

"Yes. I needed to give back what I took," I said honestly. "Just so you know, so you don't think I'm hiding anything, the department is paying me for my doctor's appointments." I shrugged. "I didn't want you to find out I was still on the payroll and think I was lying to you. No more lies, no more anything. What you see, is what you get."

Boss nodded. "If we were to do this," he said, looking around the gym, "when do we start?"

"Today."

The five of them stared at me.

"There's a lot to do, a lot to organize." I looked at Kira and smiled, then back to the boys. "So, whaddya think?"

Cody grinned and nudged Arizona. "I've never had a paying job before."

Arizona eyed me cautiously. "And it's a real job, with a paycheck and benefits?"

I nodded. "Yeah."

"Well, shit!" he said, now smiling hugely.

I looked at Boss, who still didn't look sold on the idea. "Boss, this place will need you. These guys will need you. The people who come here respect you, and quite frankly, this place needs someone who won't take any shit."

He lifted his chin. "Will you be involved?"

"Not right away," I answered. "Doctors said I can't do anything too physical." Then I looked right at him and said, "Though I'd like to be a part of the kids' drug awareness programs from the start. Though it will be up to you. If you're the boss, then having me here is your call."

He nodded slowly and all eyes were on him. He was deciding if he would ever trust me again. He didn't have to like me, just like what I was trying to set up. Then he sighed and rolled his eyes. "Don't make me regret it, Elliott."

"No, sir," I said quickly.

"What the hell have I said about you calling me that?" he huffed at me.

I reached into my pocket, pulled out a set of keys, and threw them to Boss. "You'll need those. There will be some suits and cops coming by this afternoon to get it finalized." I looked at the five of them. "Try and be nice to them."

When we left, the five of them were grinning, excitedly talking up plans and dreams. Arizona couldn't wait to tell his girl. She was gonna be so proud of him, he said. I'd never seen him smile so big.

I told them I'd call back later, but right now we were expected somewhere else. I had one more thing to wrap up in a long list of things to set right.

GOING INTO HQ WAS WEIRD. I'd walked through those doors thousands of times. I knew every hallway, every turn, every face.

But this was different.

Kira was still with me, now my designated driver until the doctor gave me the all clear to drive again. I was dressed in civvies—cargo shorts and a shirt, and I moved a lot slower than I used to. People were surprised to see me, said hello or gave a wave as we headed for the elevator.

As we stepped into inside and I pressed the button to my old floor, Kira asked, "You okay?"

I gave him a smile. "I'm good."

The doors opened on my old floor and as Kira, and I stepped out into the main area with rows of desks. The cops all stopped what they were doing and watched. Mitch was straight out of his chair, quick to hug me.

"You look good!" he said with a heartfelt smile.

My face was still banged up. My right eye was still a little swollen, though I could see out of it just fine. I had a red line of a scar above my eyebrow and one across my cheek. My nose was now slightly dented, my left eye was still bruised at the corner near my nose, and the bruising on my right eye had gone from a sickening purple to a pasty yellow.

I knew he meant I looked better than I did the last time he saw me. "I feel better," I told him.

Kira and I were then greeted warmly by Kurt and Tony. Then Mitch's new partner Ricky came over, looking rather uncomfortable.

I held out my hand. "We've not been properly introduced," I said to him. "I'm Matt Elliott."

He shook my hand. "Ricky Collins. I've heard a lot about you."

"Don't believe what Mitch says. He talks shit."

Ricky smiled. "It's all good," he said. "I've got some pretty big shoes to fill."

"Just don't take any of their shit and you'll do just fine," I said. "Hope you like your coffee black 'cause that's all Mitch knows how to make."

Mitch pretended to be offended. "And I thought I missed you."

"You do miss me," I said, but I started to feel a little dizzy. I looked around for a chair, but leaned my ass on a table instead.

"You okay?" Tony asked.

"Just dizzy," I answered. "Happens all the time. I have vertigo, from my ear..."

Mitch nodded, but he looked worried. "Does it hurt?"

"Nah, just knocks me around," I told him. "Feels like the floor moves and the room spins at the same time." I smiled at the three of them. "Just like a normal Friday night at the bar with you guys."

Kurt turned to Kira, then to me. "What can you do for it?"

"Nothing," I told him. "Just have to put up with it until it goes away. Can't hear. Can't drive."

Mitch smiled. "Can't dance."

Tony chuckled. "Can't hold your liquor."

And the comments started.

"Can't sing."

"Can't take orders."

"Can't make coffee."

"Can't tell a joke."

"Can't shoot hoops."

"Can't count."

"Can't spell."

I rolled my eyes at them but smiled. "Yeah, fuck you all very much."

Then Kira added his own, "Can't cook. Can't do laundry. Can't iron."

"Hey!" I said, with a laugh.

Kira smiled. "Can't cook."

Mitch chuckled at him. "You said that one already."

"Did I?" Kira tapped his finger to his chin, as if thinking. "Mmm, what else is there? Um, can't cook."

They all laughed at me, and it probably should have annoyed me. But it was the opposite. This was how they always were with the guys. This was them treating me like I was still one of them.

Then Ross Berkman marched in and stared at all of us

standing around. The laughter died right then, and Ross glared at me. And without a word, he stalked into his office. I stood up from the desk, and Kira was quick to move in next to me, knowing I was sometimes unsteady when I moved too quickly.

I walked slowly to Berkman's office, Mitch followed me in, and I held the door open for Kira. I wanted him in there. I wanted him to be a part of everything I did.

I sat down across from his desk, but Mitch and Kira remained standing. Berkman looked up from a file in front of him. "Elliott," he said. "You sure about this?"

"Yes, sir."

"Can't be undone."

"I know, sir."

My soon-to-be ex-boss sighed, and turned the file around and pushed it to me. "Then sign that," he said. I saw the Surrender of Firearm form and signed at the X at the bottom, then pulled my gun from the back of my cargos and put it on the desk.

Then I gave him my badge.

He stared at it for a long moment, then nodded. "The Mayor and my boss have signed off on the FC. It's all a go."

"I know," I told him. "I spoke to Arizona and Boss today. They're there now, getting it all sorted out. Whatever strings you pulled were high up. Thank you, Ross."

"Well, it was a good idea," Berkman admitted.

"It was the least I could do for them. They're real good people, sir."

Berkman nodded and changed the subject. "Your appointments with Doctor Coulter went okay?"

Doctor Tamara Coulter was the psychologist who worked with police officers, working or retired, who

Berkman had lined me up with. "Yep, twice a week. I've only been twice so far, but she seems really good."

"Well, she's one of the best there is." Berkman looked at Kira and said, "If he misses an appointment you let me know."

Kira smiled. "I will."

Berkman hummed, then he sighed. "Well, I've officially taken your gun and your badge. You can get your civilian ass out of my office."

I chuckled at him. "Sure thing, sir." I slowly stood up and made my way to the door and said, "See you at Mitch's on Saturday for the game and maybe some poker. Depends on how I'm feeling."

Berkman grunted. "Need to bring anything?"

I smiled at the man who had been my mentor for years. "Just your money."

He opened his mouth to snark some comment back to me, but his phone rang, so he glared at me instead while he took the call.

Kira, Mitch, and I walked back out to where the others were. Kurt spoke first. "All done? Is it all over?"

"It's done," I told them. "Officially no longer a cop."

Tony frowned. "Won't you miss it?"

And right on cue, Berkman roared from his office. "Seaton! Webber! My office now!"

I laughed. "No. Won't miss that at all."

I shook their hands, and as the four of them, LA's Fab Four, walked into Berkman's office without me, I turned to Kira and smiled. "Come on, let's go home."

EPILOGUE

I STOOD at the bathroom mirror, trying to get my tie to look right. Eventually Kira walked in and kissed my cheek. He knew better than to speak to me from my right side, so he turned me to face him.

"Here, let me do it."

It was then I got to see him in his new suit. He looked... amazing.

Kira rarely wore suits, let alone neckties, so to see him in a dark charcoal, tailored suit and tie was something special.

"You look so good," I told him.

Kira fiddled with my tie, then pressed down my shirt. "Not too bad yourself." He double-checked his hair in the mirror, though he certainly didn't need to. He was beautiful.

"I'm so lucky," I said out loud.

Kira rolled his eyes and said. "Yes. Yes, you are." Then

he gave me his one-dimpled smile. "Come on, we can't be late."

The ceremony was short and sweet; the wedding itself was small. I stood beside Mitch as his best man and watched him fall in love with his bride-to-be all over again as Anna walked down the aisle.

I gave a very short speech at the reception about the word partner, loyalty, and love, and Berkman gave a speech after me about beautiful brides, and grooms who gave him gray hair.

Next, everyone watched Anna's father get choked up when he made his speech about little girl princesses, and he reflected on his little girl growing up. But I never stopped looking at Kira. He looked so happy. He was proud of Anna, one of his dearest friends, and he was so happy for her.

The speeches made me think about my life. How everything that had happened had brought me to this point. How everything Kira and I had been through had made us stronger. How it hadn't been easy, especially in the beginning. I was dealing with not only my physical problems, but my emotional ones, and he was trying to deal with the lack of trust. It wasn't easy. But we talked, like Kira had said we would, about every fucking thing. That wasn't easy either, but we got through it. We continue to get through it still.

When I first got out of the hospital and for the few weeks afterwards, there was no intimacy between us. He'd hold my hand, and hug me, and hold me, kiss me. But nothing else. All we did was talk. At first I thought it was because he didn't want to hurt me, knowing I'd had so many injuries, but it wasn't that.

It was trust.

It was fear of having his heart broken all over again.

I didn't blame him. How could I?

Funnily enough, I didn't miss the sex as much as I thought I would. I was getting gentle touches and soft kisses and communication in return. We'd fall into bed emotionally drained, and we'd fall asleep in each other's arms or holding hands.

It was like falling in love all over again.

I told Kira I would wait for him, for as long as it took for him to want to be intimate with me again. And for the weeks afterwards, I knew he wanted it, his body's reaction was proof enough, but it was still almost two months before he was ready.

That first time, oh, my God, it was... everything.

The fact alone that he took my hand and led me to bed was heady enough. It was proof he was on his way to forgiving me. And there was a tempered desperation in his touch, his kisses, and a fear and vulnerability in his eyes. I told him, with absolute certainty, I loved him and it seemed to reinforce his desire. And when he knelt between my open thighs and smeared lube over his sheathed cock, my breath caught.

His eyes shot to mine. "Are you sure?"

"Yes."

He took a calming breath and pressed inside me.

And he groaned, his eyes rolled back into his head, and he shivered as he leaned over me, pushing all the way inside me. Then he froze, holding perfectly still, and his eyes shot open. "I'm not gonna last."

I cupped his face in my hands and looked into his eyes. "I want to feel it."

That was all it took.

I'd never felt anything like it. It wasn't just a physical release, but an emotional one. Kira wrapped his arms around me and cried for the first time since I'd gotten out of the hospital. He held me so tight, so perfectly, and buried his face into my neck. I pulled his face up and wiped his tears and pushed his hair back from his face, just to look into his eyes. Neither one of us spoke, we just kissed softly, sweetly.

That was the day we really started to move forward. It wasn't the sex. It was the trust, the faith. It was the love.

I was jolted back from my memories by the sound of applause, to find Mitch and Anna taking to the dance floor for the bridal waltz.

Then I turned in search of Kira. He was looking at me with an amused, concerned look on his face. He must have been watching me as I was lost in my head, a million miles away. He smiled when he asked me in sign language, "Are you okay?"

I nodded, yes. The beauty of sign language was we could have private conversations from across the room.

He signed again, "Do you feel okay? Headaches?"

I shook my head no and gave him a smile. I replied in sign, "Just thinking."

Kira glanced around the room, at the bride and groom dancing, then back to me. He signed, "About what?"

"You."

Kira smiled, almost shyly.

I waited for his eyes to meet mine again, and I signed one more thing.

"Marry me."

His eyes popped, but then Anna's sister, the maid of honor, tapped my right arm, making me turn to face her. She was on my right side, and I hadn't heard her if she'd spoken to me. "Come on," she said, pulling me up from my seat. It was custom for the best man to dance with the maid of honor after the bride and groom, so I went with her as she led me around the bridal table to the dance floor.

But she didn't stop. She kept walking over to Kira's table and stopped in front of him. He looked up at me, still in shock, I think, and Anna's sister smiled at him. "I'm going to dance with my husband," she said cheerfully. "You dance with yours."

I went to correct her on her choice of words, but she smiled brightly at us and went over to a man I presumed to be her husband. Kira stood up and took my hand, leading me out onto the dance floor. People watched, probably not used to two men dancing at a wedding, but soon Kurt and Tony and Berkman joined us with their wives and no one paid us any mind. Well, not that I saw.

We didn't waltz or do any fancy dances, we just moved our feet a little and swayed. But I held him tight, trying to not let my nerves get the better of me.

My heart was hammering, my mouth was dry. I'd just asked Kira to marry me. And he hadn't answered. "It's okay," I said quietly. "You don't have to answer me right now. I'll ask you again tomorrow if you want, and probably every day until you agree just to shut me up.

Kira smiled but still didn't answer.

"Anyway," I continued to babble. "I think blue. Or gold. Or even silver."

"What for?"

"The invitations," I explained quickly. Then I continued to babble nervously. "Your mom's been asking again. She stopped asking for a while, but she's been dropping hints again. I think we should tell her a color. It would make her happy. She deserves some happiness."

Kira laughed. "You know it won't make her stop? In fact, it will make it worse."

"Worse?"

"It won't stop at the invitations, you know that. It won't even stop at the wedding," he said lightly. "Then it will be about houses with picket fences and two-point-four kids."

I shrugged. "We have the house. It doesn't have a picket fence, though. And I'm not sure on the point-four of a child, but I'd be happy with two."

Kira froze and stared at me. His eyes were wide and questioning, and he swallowed hard.

"Um," he whispered. "How about we start with a dog?"

I smiled. "I like dogs."

He started to dance again and was quiet. I'd obviously given him a lot to think about. But then his hold on me got just a little bit tighter and his lips were at my left ear. "Blue and silver," he breathed.

Blue and silver.

Our wedding invitations would be blue and silver.

"So is that a yes?"

He nodded, wrapped his arms around me completely, and buried his face in my neck. "That's a yes."

The End

EXCERPT FROM STARTING POINT

BOOK THREE IN THE TURNING POINT SERIES

Tamara Coulter was my psychiatrist. She reminded me a bit of Diane Keaton: middle-aged with gray-brown shoulder length hair and a kind face. She was very smart and soft spoken, but her words were carefully chosen and usually fired with perfect aim.

She was the best the LAPD had to offer, and I'd been seeing her twice a week for six months. We'd covered a lot of ground, from the death of my mother to my going undercover, how I'd lost my hearing in one ear, how I'd almost lost Kira.

We talked about actions and consequences, but most of all, we talked about guilt.

From my first appointment, Tamara had talked about guilt. How it can paralyze or catalyze one into action. How it, more often than not, led to resentment and depression. She'd told me we'd be focusing more on guilt so I'd gone home and researched all I could, that way, at my next meeting, we could discuss it properly.

I have a photographic memory—a mind for details. Years as a detective did that. I'd read all the documents on guilt and other associated emotive behaviors I'd been able to find, which probably annoyed my doctor more than was productive. Too much time and the Internet were not a good combination.

Tamara had been surprised and amused, but in my attempt to be prepared and dedicated to getting help, I'd also shown her what she'd come to suspect—I was a control freak.

Apparently.

So then we talked about that too.

Actually, there wasn't much we didn't talk about.

I had to realize the doctor didn't have the ability to take away my guilt. Only I could do that.

Tamara had said I needed to acknowledge that as part of my therapy, I had to seek absolution from whom I'd hurt. I'd argued that that seemed a little redundant to me. "So I have to make Kira feel guilty, in order to absolve my guilt?"

"How so?"

"If he doesn't forgive me, I can't get better. That's not fair on him. What if he's not ready to forgive me? What if he can't? You're saying that he has to, no exceptions, or I carry this burden forever? What kind of horrible responsibility is that?"

"Do you think he should forgive you?"

"I don't think it's right to ask if he *should* or not. That's not fair. I want him to, yes. But if he *should* forgive me? That's something only he can answer." I'd taken a breath and exhaled loudly.

Tamara had waited, the way she does, knowing I'd keep talking.

"I think he has forgiven me, yes. For the life of me I can't figure out why, or by what grace of whose god, but yes, he has."

"Have you forgiven you?" she'd asked.

"I'm working on it. Every single day. It's not something I'm going to wake up one day and be magically cured of. You know that, Tamara. You know I could spiel off some textbook answer so you can tick all the right boxes, but that's not how this works."

Tamara had smiled. "No, it's not."

"Then why make me say it?"

"Because it's better for you to say it than for me to keep saying it. I know you've studied all you can on this, Matt. I know you're capable of telling people what you want them to hear. You did, after all, exactly that to a team of department psychologists about going undercover."

"I lied to them."

"Yes, convincingly. I read their files on you. You knew exactly what they were going to ask, what they were going to look for, and how to be credible in your responses."

"Do you think I'm lying now?" I'd asked. I'd kept my emotions in check. I'd even given her a small smile.

Tamara had looked at me for a moment. "No. No, I don't. I think you're working very hard at getting better," she'd said.

But I was pretty sure she wondered every now and again if I was telling her what she wanted to hear. Sometimes she'd look at me as though she was looking for some telltale sign of my lying to her. Most of my appointments with her involved debate and banter, and I wondered what today's appointment might entail.

Today was a scheduled appointment, and I'd been looking forward to it. I had something to share. I was smiling. I hadn't stopped smiling yet.

I knocked lightly on the open door. The woman looked up from the file in front of her and smiled. "Matt, come in."

I closed the door behind me and sat in my usual seat.

"You're in a good mood today," she said brightly as I sat down.

My smile got wider. "I am." Then I told her, still getting a thrill to say it out loud, "I asked Kira to marry me."

Her eyes widened, and her grin matched mine. "I take it he said yes."

"He did."

"That's really good news, Matt," she said.

"I can't tell you how happy I am," I said, knowing I sounded like a school kid, and not really caring. "It's not a magical fix, and I still have a long way to go. I know that. I'm not pretending this is going to fix anything overnight, but it's a good thing, yes? We've not set a date or anything. We're just taking it one day at a time."

Tamara was still smiling. "It is a good thing," she said. "And it's good you're both aware that while it's a positive step, it's still good to be cautious." She tilted her head, in the way that she does. "Did you think I wouldn't agree?"

"I didn't know what you'd think," I answered honestly.

"You sounded like you were waiting for my approval or my disapproval."

"I tend to babble a bit when I'm nervous or excited," I told her. "But I didn't want you to tell me we weren't ready for this kind of commitment."

Tamara was still smiling at me. "You didn't plan it? Was it a spur of the moment thing?"

I nodded. "We were at Mitch and Anna's wedding."

"Ah," she said with a nod.

"And after the speeches, and while Mitch and Anna danced, I just looked at Kira. I couldn't take my eyes off him. He signed, asking if I was okay. I signed back saying I was fine. And then I signed the words 'Marry me' across the reception hall," I told her, knowing my grin was ridiculous. "He didn't answer me straight away. We danced first, and we joked about his mom, how it'd keep her happy if she at least had some colors to work with when she planned the wedding. Kira said he thought blue and silver would be nice. Just like that, he picked out the colors to our wedding, well, for the invitations anyway. I asked him if that meant his answer was yes, and he said yes."

Tamara was grinning with me. "Sounds very romantic."

I sighed, trying not to smile, which was futile. "We kept it quiet though. We didn't want to take anything away from Mitch and Anna."

"Did you tell Kira's parents yet?"

"Tonight," I told her. "We'll tell them tonight. They were up at the cabin this last week, so Kira called them and told them to come around for dinner tonight."

"Do you think they'll be happy?" she asked. She always asked questions, like every answer was a test. It used to bother me, but I was used to it now.

"I think so." Then I amended, "Well, I hope so. They've been very good with me in the last six months. I think I've earned back some trust with them."

Kira's parents were often a topic of conversation between Tamara and me. She knew how much I loved them, and how sorry I was that I'd hurt them.

"I'm sure you have," she said. "The fact that Yumi calls you *her Matty*, I'm fairly certain she'll approve."

I nodded and shrugged one shoulder. "I just feel sometimes, not all the time, but I wonder how long I have to feel like I failed them."

Tamara looked at me for a long, quiet moment. "That's an interesting choice of words, Matt," she said. "You said you wonder how long you have to *feel* like you failed them.

I'm sure they've forgiven you, but yet you still feel as though you owe them."

"I think I will for a long while," I told her. "And that's not a bad thing. A little remorse every now and then means I'll never take it for granted."

Tamara raised one eyebrow thoughtfully, which told me she didn't really agree with me. "Do you feel like you need to earn their trust again?" she asked. "Have they ever said that?"

"No, but I'd just feel better if there was something I could do that would tip the scales, you know? Make it better."

"Like marrying Kira?"

I shook my head. "No. Please don't reduce my love for him as some ploy to win favors with his parents, because that's not fair."

Tamara almost smiled. "That was a very good answer."

"To a poorly worded question."

Tamara smiled again. "Yes, it was. I apologize."

The corner of my mouth curled into a half-smile. This was the kind of relationship we had. We'd cross boundaries, prodding for reactions. Dr. Coulter knew I had the ability to keep my emotions in check and not react when someone else would. She'd dealt with enough detectives to know that. She was a little surprised I'd managed to fool the psych evaluations to go undercover, so she'd been wary with me from the beginning. But I swore to her, all pretenses were left at the door.

I'd explained to her, I was there to get better. I'd promised Kira I would do this, and I had every intention of keeping my word.

So our relationship was professional but brutally honest. "It's part of the guilt, yes?" I asked. "That I feel bad for what I've done. But there's no time limit, is there? No expiration date, so to speak."

"No, there's not," she answered simply. "You've apologized, and you're working hard at righting your wrongs. That's all you can do, Matt. It will take time."

I sighed. "I swore to them that I'd work on it forever, and I will. I just feel sometimes that they look at me, and they're remembering what I did, what I put them through." Then I admitted, "I just want to move forward."

"Is getting married going to do that?"

"Move forward? Yes. I want to spend my life with him," I told her adamantly. "I want him to know I'm serious, and that there will never be anyone else for me."

"Tell me, how are things going at the club?" she changed subjects like I'd predicted. "Really good. The guys are working so hard. Boss really runs a tight ship."

"How's Arizona?"

"He's doing really well," I said. "He's just moved into a nicer place. His wife's happy, so he's happy. He just wants to do right by her and his little girl."

Tamara smiled again. "He's become a good friend of yours."

"He has."

"Do you see your old police partners much?" she asked. "We haven't talked of them much lately."

"They call into the club every now and then," I replied. "And we try to catch up on weekends when they're not working. Kira sees them at his work at the gym. I talk to Mitch on the phone when I can. They work different hours, and I know what that's like."

"But you all make the effort."

"We do."

Tamara's smile faded a little and she looked at something in the file in front of her. "It's been a while since we talked about the kids at the club? How are they doing?" She titled her head. "Claude, isn't it? The child you mentioned before?"

I nodded. "They're okay. She's okay."

"You worry about her in particular."

"I do. I mean, I've always known kids live on the street. Everyone knows that, and as a cop, I saw it all the time," I explained. "But it's different now."

"Because you're seeing it from a different perspective."

"I am," I agreed. "But... I don't know... I worry about them all, but especially about Claude. She's a young girl on the streets... I know those stories don't always end well."

Tamara sighed. "Then you know what may very well happen to her."

"You can't know that," I said sharply. "You can't just presume she'll end up some drugged out whore or dead in a dumpster."

"Matt," Tamara said cautiously. "My concern is you, and I'm worried that if something were to happen to her, that you'd feel responsible."

I looked out of the window and bit my fucking tongue.

"You can't fix everyone, Matt."

"I don't want to fix *everyone*," I said, looking back to her. "Just her."

"Yes... No. I don't know. She's just a kid."

"You have enough to worry about with your own health, Matt."

I nodded but said nothing. She was right, but fucking hell, so was I. I didn't want to argue with her or deal with unresolved shit today. I was still on a high from Kira saying yes to marrying me. I had even been excited to come here and tell Tamara, but it seemed wasted. I looked at my watch, then back out of the window.

"Matt, you don't agree with me," she said. It wasn't a question.

"Not really."

"Would you like to discuss it?"

"No, not today," I said, finally looking at her. "These last few days have been some of the best I've had in a while, and I'd like to be able to appreciate that without arguing." I shook my head. "I think I'm entitled to a little bit of happiness, yes?"

"Of course you are," she said, in a tone that just pissed me off. All sweet and placating.

I stood up, cutting our appointment in half. "Look, maybe today's not the best day for this."

"Matt, we can talk about whatever you want," she said, her tone still not wavering. Always calm and calculated.

I stopped, knowing walking out wasn't going to help anyone. I bit back a sigh, but instead of sitting back down, I went and stood at the window instead. I didn't speak first, but I also didn't leave.

After a little while, Tamara said, "So, when you break the good news to Kira's parents tonight, are you telling them over dinner in a restaurant or telling them at home?"

I smiled, despite my sudden downturn in mood. She knew exactly what topic would make me stay. "Dinner at home. I was going to cook, but Kira thought it might be safer if he did."

And so we talked then about dinner and cooking and how I still sucked at it, leaving the session on a lighter note. As the meeting was wrapping up, Tamara reminded me of my next appointment. "I'll see you and Kira on Thursday."

"Yep, we'll be here."

"Matt, I'm sorry to put a dampener on your mood earlier," she said. "You were right. You deserve this happiness, and we should have focused on that today. Good luck tonight."

I gave her a genuine smile this time. "Thank you." I got to the door but stopped before I walked out. "We're going to revisit a few things I tripped up on today on Thursday, aren't we?"

She laughed quietly. "Yes, we will. But for now, go and enjoy dinner with your fiancé and soon-to-be in-laws."

I grinned at her words. *My fiancé.* "I will."

ABOUT THE AUTHOR

N.R. Walker is an Australian author, who loves her genre of gay romance.
She loves writing and spends far too much time doing it, but wouldn't have it any other way.

She is many things: a mother, a wife, a sister, a writer. She has pretty, pretty boys who live in her head, who don't let her sleep at night unless she gives them life with words.

She likes it when they do dirty, dirty things... but likes it even more when they fall in love.

She used to think having people in her head talking to her was weird, until one day she happened across other writers who told her it was normal.

She's been writing ever since...

The Spencer Cohen Series, Book Two

The Spencer Cohen Series, Book Three

The Spencer Cohen Series, Yanni's Story

Blood & Milk

The Weight Of It All

A Very Henry Christmas (The Weight of It All 1.5)

Perfect Catch

Switched

Imago

Imagines

Red Dirt Heart Imago

On Davis Row

Finders Keepers

Evolved

Galaxies and Oceans

Private Charter

Nova Praetorian

Titles in Audio:

Cronin's Key

Cronin's Key II

Cronin's Key III

Red Dirt Heart

Red Dirt Heart 2

Red Dirt Heart 3

Red Dirt Heart 4

The Weight Of It All

Switched

Point of No Return

Breaking Point

Starting Point

Spencer Cohen Book One

Spencer Cohen Book Two

Spencer Cohen Book Three

Yanni's Story

On Davis Row

Evolved

Free Reads:

Sixty Five Hours

Learning to Feel

His Grandfather's Watch (And The Story of Billy and Hale)

The Twelfth of Never (Blind Faith 3.5)

Twelve Days of Christmas (Sixty Five Hours Christmas)

Best of Both Worlds

Translated Titles:

Fiducia Cieca (Italian translation of Blind Faith)

Attraverso Questi Occhi (Italian translation of Through

These Eyes)

Preso alla Sprovvista (Italian translation of Blindside)

Il giorno del Mai (Italian translation of Blind Faith 3.5)

Cuore di Terra Rossa (Italian translation of Red Dirt Heart)

Cuore di Terra Rossa 2 (Italian translation of Red Dirt Heart 2)

Cuore di Terra Rossa 3 (Italian translation of Red Dirt Heart 3)

Cuore di Terra Rossa 4 (Italian translation of Red Dirt Heart 4)

Intervento di Retrofit (Italian translation of Elements of Retrofit)

Confiance Aveugle (French translation of Blind Faith)

A travers ces yeux: Confiance Aveugle 2 (French translation of Through These Eyes)

Aveugle: Confiance Aveugle 3 (French translation of Blindside)

À Jamais (French translation of Blind Faith 3.5)

Cronin's Key (French translation)

Cronin's Key II (French translation)

Au Coeur de Sutton Station (French translation of Red Dirt Heart)

Partir ou rester (French translation of Red Dirt Heart 2)

Faire Face (French translation of Red Dirt Heart 3)

Trouver sa Place (French translation of Red Dirt Heart 4)

Rote Erde (German translation of Red Dirt Heart)

Rote Erde 2 (German translation of Red Dirt Heart 2)

www.ingramcontent.com/pod-product-compliance
Lightning Source LLC
Chambersburg PA
CBHW032105180726

48284CB00002B/454